Kris & Ken
got for me
Christmas '2020

ISBN-13: 978-1544627984

ISBN-10: 154462798X

COACHED IN MURDER

Copyright @ 2017 by Helen Gray

All rights reserved. Except for use in any reviews, the reproduction or utilization of this work in whole or in any form by any electronic, mechanical or other means, now known or hereafter invented, including xerography, photocopying and recording, or in any information storage or retrieval system, is forbidden without the written permission of the author.

This is a work of fiction. Names, characters, places and incidents are either the product of the author's imagination or are used fictitiously, and any resemblance to actual persons, living or dead, business establishments, events or locales is entirely coincidental. Any references to historical figures, places, or events, whether fictional or actual, is a fictional representation.

Cover by Cynthia Hickey

HELEN GRAY

Coached in Murder

Be ye angry, and sin not: let not the sun go down upon your wrath.
                              Ephesians 4:26

Chapter 1

"I dreamed about the fire chief last night."

Nine-year-old Garrett's words from the back seat made Toni Donovan swivel her head toward Kyle, who was driving the van down Springfield, Missouri's Lone Pine Avenue. Their eyes locked.

The eeriest feeling, a tiny chill of premonition, wormed its way up her spine. She read a similar reaction in her husband's quick glance. Green eyed, with sandy hair that he kept cut in a short, almost military, style, he still made her heart beat faster after thirteen years of marriage.

"What fire chief?" eleven-year-old Gabe asked.

"I don't know, just a chief."

Kyle steered into the parking lot of Sequiota Park, but his somber expression told Toni that they were sharing memories of two stressful incidents of the past year and a half.

When their school superintendent back home in Clearmount disappeared, Garrett had dreamed about something big and black near Harry Rabbit, an injured rabbit he and Gabe had found, nursed, and then buried in Toni's body farm, a plot back of the high school where her forensics class put bodies of animals and observed the rates at which they skeletonized. The missing superintendent's body had been found in a shallow grave near Harry Rabbit.

The second incident had occurred after a trio of Toni's students found some human bones during a field trip the following spring. Later, after Garrett had mentioned dreaming about finding gold by the water, it turned out that the victim's name was Brock Goldman, and his remains had been found near the creek.

Memories of the uncanny connections didn't exactly frighten Toni, but they made the muscles inside her vibrate with a sensation of impending--- what? She had ended up getting personally involved in both of those incidents. Well, nothing was going to happen here. Those cases had been there in her hometown where she knew the people involved. Here she knew no one beyond her husband's family and the students in the summer class she was teaching at the community college. Nothing like that could possibly affect them here. She shook off the thoughts and breathed easier.

As soon as Kyle parked, the boys opened the back passenger doors and hopped to the ground.

"You guys have a good time, but don't wander off too far," Kyle cautioned.

"We won't," Gabe called over his shoulder as they dashed away.

Aunts, uncles, and cousins were emerging from other vehicles on the lot. If the pattern of past years held true, there would be nearly a hundred people present at Kyle's family reunion. His take-charge mother would command the troops, and he, his dad and two younger sisters would obey her orders.

An ideal place for this yearly gathering, the

thirteen-acre paradise just north of Galloway Village boasted a lagoon where ducks swam, open shelters, picnic tables and grills, restrooms, playground equipment, and it was one of the few places with public caves on the premises. There was also a three-mile walking and fitness trail that ran from Galloway to National Court Trail.

When Kyle opened the driver's door, hot air rushed into the van. It was only nine a.m., but the July fifth sun was already blazing, the air hazy. He and Toni wore khaki shorts and white tee shirts, but they were still going to roast in this heat.

A young couple bicycled past them as Kyle removed coolers from the back of the van.

When they headed toward the pavilion, Toni noted that the park was starting to come alive.

A family was feeding the ducks at the head of the lagoon, while a half dozen people hiked away from it. A group of youngsters walked across two small footbridges to the caves at the far side.

Their group assembling was small at this point, but more would be arriving soon. Kyle's mother, Barb Donovan, met them at the edge of the pavilion. "Just slide the drink coolers under the end table," she instructed Kyle. "Here, I'll take those, and you can go back for whatever else you have," she said to Toni.

Toni handed over her casserole without argument, the easiest way of dealing with her mother-in-law. Turning, she spied John Zachary's dark green Sable pulling into the parking lot. John was a colleague from back home in Clearmount where they both taught science at the local high school. He taught the physical science classes, chemistry and physics, while Toni taught the life sciences, biology, A & P, and forensics. She and Kyle were close friends with John and his wife, Jenny.

Toni headed that way, wanting to make him feel welcome.

"Good morning," he greeted her as he emerged from his car. "All I brought is a cooler of sodas." He was a big, mild mannered guy with light brown hair worn in a simple, short cut, an extreme contrast to Toni's five six, hundred and forty pound frame.

"That's plenty," she assured him. "You didn't even need to do that. There'll be enough food for an army."

"Yeah, that's always the case with these things," he agreed, popping the trunk of his car. "That's why I let you talk me into coming." He pulled out the cooler and accompanied her to the pavilion. A few feet beyond it, Kyle was putting charcoal in the barbecue pits.

"How is your class going?" Toni asked as her colleague shoved his cooler next to the others under the table. She swatted at an irksome bee.

He shrugged. "Okay, I guess. One week down, three to go. It's been interesting so far."

"How big is it?"

"There are only eleven of us enrolled, so we have some interesting discussions that sometimes get lively." His grin bordered on a smirk.

Kyle's youngest sister, Kathy Mitchell, was coming across the lawn now, carrying a basket of food. She and her husband, Ron, both taught school here in Springfield. Their two young daughters, Rhonda and Robin, were headed to the far side of the pavilion to join the younger set assembling there. Karen, Kyle's older sister and the middle sibling, rounded the table and went to meet them. A nurse at Cox Hospital, Karen was divorced with no children and lived only a few blocks from their parents.

A number of children, including Gabe and Garrett, came flocking to the pavilion, seeking cold drinks.

"There must have been over sixty thousand people at Firefall Saturday night," John commented as he doled out sodas and bottled water to the children.

Toni nodded. "It took us over an hour just to get out of the parking lot at James River after the fireworks display."

"But the fireworks were fantastic," Kyle pointed out, joining them in time to hear John's comment.

"I think Firefall is a nice tradition," Kathy said, taking a bottle of water for herself. "It's grown over the years and provides a lot of enjoyment for a huge number of people. There's music all day, featuring local groups and entertainers from Branson. Then there's the choir concert, followed by a fireworks display choreographed to live symphony music."

Always scheduled the Saturday night before the fourth, the whole event was a huge patriotic party in a lowly hay field near the Springfield-Branson Regional Airport.

"I liked the wing walker." Garrett had paused next to John rather than leaving with the mob of children.

"That was a stunt plane," Gabe pointed out, also still present. "The wing walker was good, but I still like the fireworks best."

"Yeah, they were great." Garrett swigged from his water bottle.

"Where did the man fall in the hole?" John asked.

Toni frowned. "What are you talking about?"

"It must have been over that way somewhere." Dan Donovan pointed to a spot up the path.

John chuckled. "Didn't you see yesterday's paper? There was a story about a man who fell in a hole at this park. It said he was only a few feet from the paved path, and he was in there for several hours before someone found him. When they got him out, all he had with him was a pillowcase of belongings, and he wouldn't talk."

Toni shook her head. "I missed yesterday's paper."

"Sounds like a homeless person," Kyle said. He unfolded a camp chair and positioned it near the south corner of the pavilion. His six one, broad shouldered frame filled it to capacity.

"That's what the people who found him thought. But it turned out he was a thief, and the pillowcase was full of stolen loot," John explained.

"Are there any more holes around here?" Gabe asked, tossing his drink bottle in the trash container.

"Let's go see if we can find some," Rhonda Mitchell, Kathy's oldest daughter, said.

The kids all took off, happy to have an exploration project.

Kyle's Aunt Madge, his mother's critical-to-the-point-of-obnoxious sister, arrived, placed a platter on the table, and faced the group. "Kyle, why don't you and Toni move here to Springfield so you can be near your parents and sisters? You could work from here, and Toni would have no trouble getting a teaching job in the area. After all, she's already teaching here this summer."

"We like it in Clearmount," Kyle responded. "Karen, Kathy, and I grew up there, and I like the small town life. So do Toni and the boys." After retirement, Dan's health had deteriorated, and he and Barb had moved to Springfield to be near their daughters, as well as the medical facilities and Karen's personal nursing care.

"But you would have so many more cultural things here, and there are so many more places to shop. Your boys would have bigger, better schools. And you could find more choices of beauty shops and clothes."

"Bigger is not necessarily better," Toni said. "In fact, I think our small school is better for them."

It's two hundred miles from you. And I'm happy with my simple medium length, natural brown hairstyle, thank you.

"Toni, can you help me here a minute," Barb Donovan called from the other side of the table.

While family members continued to catch up on happenings of the past year, Toni helped her mother-in-law slice tomatoes and cucumbers and put condiments and table service on the picnic tables. They covered everything with tablecloths to protect it from the insects and dust.

As they worked, Toni glanced out over the park, trying to spot her boys and not seeing them. To her right was the lagoon. Only about two or three feet deep, it spread across several hundred yards of the park area. Shaped somewhat like a music note, there was a long narrow section at the far end, and a large oval section here near them. An island down one side of it was populated with ducks and turtles to which visitors tossed bread crumbs to watch them dive.

She spotted Gabe at the far end of the lagoon by the spillway, but saw no sign of Garrett. A fresh twinge of unease ran through her.

"I think I'll go for a little walk," she told her mother-in-law.

"Run along. I've got things under control," Barb responded.

Toni headed across the lawn, moving at an unhurried pace while keeping an eye out for Garrett. The number of people populating the park had grown, and laughter and shouts of children echoed from the caves and play areas. No one but Gabe was squatted beside the water at the far end of the lagoon. When Toni got close enough for him to hear her, she called, "Where's Garrett?"

He looked up and shrugged, but remained squatted, dragging a hand through the water.

Toni glanced back and saw Kyle and John following her. She walked on down to join Gabe. "Do you know where he went?"

Gabe stood and peered around, his face scrunching up in thought. "He was here until just a little bit ago. He said he had to find the fire chief, or something like that."

Even though her shirt was sweat-dampened, the chill inside Toni deepened. A sense of urgency rose in the pit of her stomach. She looked around, trying to imagine where he could be.

John and Kyle joined them and grasped the situation. "Let's split up," Kyle said. "I'll check the woods down there." He pointed toward the far end of the lagoon.

"I'll go around and check those." John indicated the wooded area around the far side of it.

"I'll work my way around the water," Toni said. "Do you two have a funny feeling?" she asked before they took off.

The two men stared at one another.

"There's a feeling inside me that's not comfortable," John admitted.

Kyle nodded. "Me, too. Let's go."

Toni fought a growing sense of panic as she followed them, visually searching the area. She kept walking when they veered off into the woods. Staying near the edge of the water, she worked her way around to the far side of the lagoon.

She was near the point of panic when she spotted Garrett back over where the island down the middle of the lagoon had been blocking the view. He was running.

"Hey, Mom!" he yelled when he spotted her. When he reached her, he grabbed her hand. "Come quick. I found the fire chief."

"Kyle! John!" Toni yelled over her shoulder.

They both came running from the woods.

"Where have you been?" Kyle demanded of Garrett as he reached them.

"I found the fire chief," he repeated. "Come on, I'll show you."

They followed their youngest son along the

perimeter of the water to the back of the island. Staring ahead, Toni spied yellow coloring beneath the surface of the water about half a dozen yards from shore.

"Not again!" she heard Kyle gasp as they all ran to that spot and stopped.

"Someone's in there," Toni shouted, peering down into the water that was murky with a brownish discoloration. She could distinguish the form of a body at the bottom.

Kyle jerked off his shoes. "Call nine-one-one," he yelled at John as he jumped into the water. He waded out, leaned over and grabbed the body, and pulled it to the surface. Slipping on the slimy bottom, he dragged it to the shore.

Toni knelt and grabbed an arm. John joined them, his cell phone in his hand, starting to punch in the number. Seeing their struggle, he stuck it in his pocket and dropped to his knees. The three of them pulled the body up onto the dry ground and turned it over. It was a man, wearing jeans and a yellow tee shirt. On the front of the shirt was a big picture of an Indian chief.

Chapter 2

Kyle began to administer CPR, but soon stopped. "He's dead, probably has been for hours."

Suddenly John gasped and stepped back a pace. "That's Jesse!"

Toni stared up at her colleague's shocked expression. "You know him?"

John rocked back on his heels, his head bobbing. "His name is Jesse Campbell. He's in the class I'm taking."

"Did you get the nine-one-one call made?"

He started in remembrance and jerked the phone from his pocket.

Toni shifted her attention to her sons as John dialed. "You boys go back to the pavilion."

They started to protest, but read her don't-give-me-any-argument look and decided to do as ordered. They headed slowly away from the area, but Garrett stopped a few yards away and looked back. When she pointed a finger, he moved on.

People were beginning to gather around them. "Can you keep people from crowding in here?" Toni asked Kyle. "It's a crime scene, and we need to keep it from being trampled."

"I'll try to head them off. All right, everybody stay back," he ordered, moving toward the crowd that was growing fast.

Toni turned to John, who was putting his phone back in his pocket. "Did you get through?"

He nodded. "The police should be here soon. It looks like Kyle could use some help."

"While you do that, keep your eyes peeled for anything that might be evidence. I'll do the same."

John nodded and went to head off the people who were by now circling around the pond from the other direction. While they halted traffic from all directions, Toni did a quick study of the scene.

The dead man had darkly tanned skin, and she guessed his age to be in the late thirties or early forties. She recognized the logo on his tee shirt as that of Kickapoo High School.

Scanning hastily, she didn't see anything that looked like drag marks, nor any sign of a weapon. Near the edge of the lagoon, about two yards from where they had pulled the body from the water, she spotted some blood spatters and squatted to study them.

"Who is it? Is he dead?" Spectators were hurling questions at Kyle.

"I'm sorry. We need to keep the area clear until the police can get here," he repeated while blocking them from getting past him.

Toni shifted back around on her haunches and refocused on the body. Besides the school tee shirt, the man wore jeans and high dollar athletic shoes, nothing out of the ordinary. Then she noticed a narrow white strip of skin around his tanned wrist. Had his watch slipped off into the water?

She moved to the edge of the lagoon and peered down at where the body had been. The normally clear water was still slightly discolored with the man's blood, but she could see fairly well. She dropped to her stomach to get a closer look at the bottom of the water. She saw nothing that looked like a watch—or a weapon. She was just getting to her feet when the scream of police sirens sounded.

When two black and whites pulled into the parking lot a minute later, Toni saw Gabe and Garrett approach them and point back toward the lagoon. She waved her arms back and forth over the body to shoo away the flies that were already beginning to camp on it. Two officers emerged from the police cars and loped around the end of the lagoon where Kyle was having trouble blocking curious onlookers.

"Are you the person who found the body?" the first officer to arrive asked as he dropped to his haunches next to the dead man. His partner had stopped to help Kyle and John.

Toni nodded. "One of them."

"Stick around. We need to talk to you."

Both officers examined the body without touching it. The one who had spoken to her reached up and positioned the radio on his shoulder closer to his mouth. "It looks like a guy has been stabbed. We need the coroner and a detective out here."

Within minutes the place was populated with a detective and two more officers who began securing the area. An ambulance crew came pushing a gurney across the lawn and stopped a few yards away to wait for the photographer and detective to finish their work and tell them they could remove the body.

A news van careened into the parking lot and screeched to a halt. A woman emerged and came sprinting toward them, camera in hand. She began snapping pictures from the edge of the crowd and worked her way closer until an officer stopped her.

When the techs took over, the first two officers rejoined Toni, Kyle and John. This time Toni noticed the name tags on their uniforms. The tall black man with an impassive face was Officer Durbin. His younger partner was Officer Chilton.

Officer Durbin's eyes swept over the three of them. "Which one of you found the body?"

"Uh, we sort of all did," Toni said quickly.

He frowned. "How do you mean?"

"We were looking for our younger son—mine and Kyle's," she explained, stepping over beside her husband. "He wasn't with the other kids, and we were circling the lagoon looking for him."

Durbin's eyes bored into her. "You're saying that's how you came to be over here on this side of the lagoon?"

Toni was reluctant to bring Garrett into it, and this guy's unsmiling face didn't encourage her to open up to him. She just nodded.

"The body was in the water, right?"

Toni nodded again.

"The son we were looking for came running to meet us and said someone was in the water," Kyle explained.

Durbin's attention sharpened, and his eyes

narrowed. "So the boy is the one who actually found the body?"

Kyle nodded. "That's right, officer. Garrett saw the man and ran to tell us. I went into the water and pulled him out." He glanced down at the wet edges of his khaki shorts.

"I helped Kyle pull him onto land," John said.

"So did I," Toni added. "We weren't sure he was dead when we first saw him. Otherwise we wouldn't have moved him."

Durbin gave her a hard stare. "So you're aware that you disturbed a crime scene. Do any of you have any idea who the guy is?"

"I do," John said. "His name is Jesse Campbell."

Brows rose on both officers' faces. Chilton had his notebook and pen out, scribbling furiously. Toni assumed he was the duo's assigned scribe.

"How long have you known him?" Durbin asked John.

"I just met him this past Monday. I'm taking a summer class at Drury College, earning credits toward a specialist degree, and Jesse is, er… was a member of the class."

"Did you get personally acquainted with him?"

John nodded again. "We were sitting next to one another the first time the class met, and we introduced ourselves. After class we hung around and chatted awhile. Since I'm from out of town and just staying with a friend for the four weeks of the class, Jesse offered to take me to Bass Pro the next day."

"You went?"

John's face brightened. "Yes. We met Tuesday after class and spent a couple of hours there. I bought a new fishing rod. Then we went to lunch at Taco Bell."

"Was that all the time you spent with him?'"

"It's the only time we went anywhere off campus together. But we sat together in class every day, and we went to the library together after class one night."

Chilton looked up from his writing. "You said you're not from here. Where are you from?"

"We live in Clearmount," John said.

"By *we*, you mean the three of you?"

John nodded. "Clearmount's down in the southeastern part of the state."

"I know where it is," Officer Chilton said, adding to his notes.

Durbin faced Toni and Kyle. "Are you two also taking classes?"

"I'm spending the summer here in Springfield and teaching an eight-week class at OTC," Toni explained, referring to Ozark Technical College. "I'm filling in for someone who's on maternity leave. Her baby was born two weeks ago, and she plans to return to the classroom at the beginning of the fall semester."

She didn't explain that the teacher was her best friend and that she had been staying with Kara while Gabe and Garrett stayed at home in Clearmount with their grandparents. The class only met Monday through Thursday, so she went home every three-day weekend. This weekend was an exception because of the Independence Day holiday yesterday and her husband's family reunion today. She was to spend the final three weeks of the summer session with Kyle's parents.

The officer returned his attention to Kyle. "You're staying here with her?"

Kyle shook his head. "No, I'm a commercial pilot, and I just brought our boys up to spend the weekend with Toni and attend my family reunion. My parents and sisters live here." He pointed toward the pavilion where his family was gathered.

"I just started my class this past week," John explained. "It's only four weeks, the second four-week block of the summer schedule. My wife came and attended Firefall last night with me, but she's shopping with a girlfriend today."

"John and I teach together at the high school in Clearmount," Toni explained. "I invited him to come eat with us today."

Durbin nodded in a way that made her silently dub him Dubious Durbin. "Okay, that explains the personal stuff and your being here. But you said your son found the body. Do you know what he was doing over here?"

"Uh, he was just playing, being a normal nine-year-old," Toni said uneasily.

Durbin's gaze sharpened again, picking up on the hesitation. "Why were you looking for him? Did you think he was lost?"

"No, but he has a tendency to wander off on his own. I was concerned when I didn't see him with his brother."

Durbin considered that for several seconds. "I need to speak to the boy."

"I'll get him," Kyle said when Toni didn't move. He went to the end of the pond and called, "Garrett, come over here."

When Garrett appeared from around a tree and started toward them, the officers went to meet him on the lawn. Toni and John followed. Toni was thankful that Garrett wouldn't have to return to where the body was for questioning.

She gave her solemn faced youngest son a smile that was meant to be reassuring. "These officers want to ask you some questions," she said, trying to beam a mental message into his brain to not say anything about his dream.

Garrett's big, rounded eyes moved up over the two officers. "Okay."

"We understand you found the man in the water," Officer Durbin said, his voice gentling the slightest bit. "I need you to tell us about it."

Garrett stared at him. "I was walking along here, and I saw him in the water."

"What were you doing over here?"

Garrett shrugged. "Just looking around."

"Were you looking for something, or just playing?"

"I was looking…" Garrett started to speak, but then noticed Toni's frown and eye movements. "I was just hanging around."

She relaxed, but only for a moment.

"What's going on here?" Durbin demanded, catching the silent byplay. His eyes narrowed and his mouth tightened.

"Nothing's going on," Toni denied, returning his stare while her heart pumped faster.

"Then why the signals? What are you afraid he'll tell me? Does he know the victim?"

"No, I don't know him," Garrett spoke up,

clearly unhappy at hearing the policeman speak harshly to his mother. "I just saw him in the water and went to get help."

Durbin stared at Garrett, and then back at Toni. "What about you? Are you sure you never met that man?"

"I'm sure," Toni said. "I think I'd like to speak to my brother."

"Why?" he snapped. "Who's your brother?"

"He's a police officer, and I think I would feel more comfortable talking to him right now. He's working nights, so he's asleep, but he'll come if I call him."

"Who is your brother?"

"Quinton Nash."

Quint was seven years younger than Toni, five younger than Bill. She and Bill had adored their little brother when they were children, and had shielded him from their parents when they knew he was up to something that would get him in trouble, so much that it was a wonder he had turned out as well as he had. Now she felt a need for him to shield her.

Durbin's expression was impassive, but behind him Toni thought she saw Officer Chilton's mouth twitch. "Call him," Durbin ordered in gruff resignation.

Toni pulled her cell phone from her pocket. "Can you come over to Sequiota Park?" she asked as soon as Quint's sleepy voice came on the line.

"Whutsa matter?" he mumbled.

"Garrett found a body in the lagoon at Sequiota Park, and we're being questioned."

"Are there officers on the scene yet?" His tone

suddenly sounded more alert.

"Yes, but I need to talk to you."

There was a pause. "Has the kid been dreaming again?"

"Yes."

"I'm on my way." The line went silent.

"He'll be right here," Toni said to the officers as she ended the call and stuck the phone back in her pocket.

"You all wait until he gets here. We'll be back," Durbin ordered. He and Chilton returned to the body.

"Let's sit down," Kyle suggested, dropping to the ground. Toni, Garrett, and John sat beside him to wait.

Within a few minutes Toni saw Quint's navy blue pickup pull into the parking lot. When he came loping across the parking lot, they all stood.

"I'm sorry to drag you into this," Toni apologized as he reached them.

"Fill me in quick," he ordered as she hugged him.

Five ten, with brown hair and dark eyes, her youngest brother was more athletic than his medium-size frame would suggest. He had only been with the police department about a year, having joined it a few months after discharging from the army, where he had been an MP.

"As you know, we went to Firefall last night," she explained hurriedly.

Quint nodded.

"This morning Garrett said he had dreamed he found the fire chief. A little later he told Gabe he was going to go look for the fire chief and took off on his own. He found that guy in the water." She pointed back to where the body was now being placed on the gurney.

"Glad you're here," Kyle said, coming to shake Quint's hand. John did the same.

"Hi, Uncle Quint." Garrett gave him a tentative smile.

"Hi, yourself, Sport." Quint raised a palm for a high five.

"Good to see you two," Quint greeted Durbin and Chilton as the officers joined them. "May I explain something before you question these two anymore?"

"Please do," Durbin said, not looking or sounding happy.

Quint gave them a one-minute summary of Garrett's dreams in relation to the two earlier murder cases. "Toni isn't hiding anything. She's just a mother worried about her sons. She doesn't want them badgered or exposed to the media."

Durbin frowned. "Does this mean the boy found this body after having some kind of weird dream that made him go hunting for it?" His eyes were no longer cold, but his tone was more than a little skeptical.

Toni's nod was brief.

Durbin deliberated for a moment, and then he faced Garrett again. "Okay, young man, let's try this one more time. Can you just relax and tell us what happened? We'll do everything we can to protect you and keep your name confidential if you'll be totally honest with us."

Garrett smiled slightly and shifted from one foot to the other. "Last night I dreamed that the fire chief would be here today. I didn't see him, so I went looking around."

The officer studied the young boy. "The fire chief?"

Garrett shrugged. "Yeah."

Beside him, Officer Chilton cleared his throat to get his partner's attention. "Um, I may have a theory."

"Yeah, what?" Durbin barked, facing him.

The younger officer glanced back at the gurney that was being pushed toward them. "Well, the guy was wearing a shirt with a Kickapoo chief on it. My wife teaches at the Kickapoo Junior High, and I remember her telling me about a coach who was fired," he said, emphasizing the word, "five or six years ago in the middle of the school term. It caused quite a stir at the time, but there was never any official announcement explaining it."

Durbin shook his head dubiously. "Fired? A Kickapoo Chief was fired?"

"Hey, that's weird," Garrett exclaimed, a grin spreading across his face. "I was looking for a fire chief, but he was a fired chief."

"That's some theory," Durbin said, looking back at Garrett. "Did you see anyone else around here while you were looking?"

Garrett thought a moment before answering. "No, there weren't any people over on this side of the water yet."

"Did you see any objects around?"

"You mean like a knife or gun?"

"Yes."

Garrett's head moved back and forth slowly. "No, I just came out of the woods where I was looking and saw somebody in the water. I ran and told Mom and Dad."

Toni watched and listened to her son closely. He didn't seem traumatized, but would finding a body cause more dreams? "He found a body, but he didn't witness a crime," she pointed out, unable to restrain herself.

"Thank you, young man," the officer said, extending a hand to Garrett. "If we have any more questions later, we'll contact your parents. You may join your friends now."

Needing no prompting, Garrett trotted away.

As the gurney rolled past them, a stab of pain struck Toni in the midsection. Someone's life had ended. She didn't know him, or anyone connected to him other than John's brief acquaintance, but the man's life had been cut short. There had to be people who were going to be devastated when they learned of it. Her heart went out to them.

"I need your addresses and phone numbers," Durbin was saying to Kyle and John. Toni was more than happy to let them finish up with the officers.

"I think the guy was stabbed on the path and pushed into the water," she told Quint in an undertone. "There were no drag marks, and there was blood near the edge of the water not far from where he was. My guess is that whoever did it left through the woods."

"Are you playing detective again?" Quint asked, his brows lifting. "There seems to be a pattern developing with you."

Toni grimaced. "This one is away from my home turf and not anyone I know. So I'm not involved." She raised her palms in a declarative gesture. "Why don't you stick around and eat with the family? There's a mountain of food. And your sleep is already disturbed."

Quint sighed. "Good point. I might as well mooch a meal."

Chapter 3

Springfield was the third largest city in Missouri. Interstate 44 and Routes 60, 65, and 160 all passed through it. Many people contended that the town's name was derived from the great spring at the foot of the hill and the plain of the summit, Spring-Field. Others believed it was named in honor of Springfield, Tennessee, the home of Kindred Rose, one of the early settlers.

Toni wasn't sure which she believed, but she kind of liked the first choice. With a population of about a hundred fifty thousand, the city boasted five large public high schools, a number of private schools, and over a dozen colleges and universities.

On the way back to the Donovan home the boys were unusually quiet. Toni glanced over her shoulder and observed Garrett staring out the window at the traffic. Beside him, Gabe sat silent and somber. She started to ask if something was bothering him, but then thought better of it.

Gabe was more intense than Garrett, a scholar and a stickler for facts and details. He was also athletic, but even in that he was intense. His reading was extensive for an eleven-year-old. Something told Toni he was troubled, but he needed to examine and sort through whatever was on his mind without being pressured. Hopefully he would open up when he reached any conclusions.

The odd thing was that Garrett seemed so unaffected and relaxed. He was the one who had found a dead man, but he seemed to accept it as just another day at the park—literally. Toni still feared that he would experience some kind of delayed reaction. She hoped there were no more dreams.

The ride remained quiet until they pulled up in front of the middle class brick façade home of Kyle's parents. Located not far from Glendale High School, it was only a few minutes from the campus where Toni was teaching.

Kyle's sisters had declined invitations to come over for the evening. Toni wasn't thrilled at staying with Kyle's parents another three weeks, but that was the arrangement they had worked out when she was asked to do this class. The first four weeks the boys had stayed back in Clearmount with her parents, and Toni had spent the time with Kara and her newborn son. This week was a vacation for the boys to spend with Kyle's parents, as long as she and Kyle felt the arrangement would work. They would return to Clearmount Thursday afternoon after her class ended and remain with her parents for the final weeks she had to be in Springfield.

That evening they snacked on ham and potato salad left over from the day's meal. Then Kyle offered to play catch with the boys in the backyard, an activity they typically loved. Garrett ran to get his glove.

"You guys go ahead," Gabe mumbled. "I have a book almost finished." He left the room quietly, heading for the bedroom he and Garrett were sharing.

Toni exchanged glances with Kyle. "You and Garrett go on. We'll talk later."

When she and Kyle were finally alone that evening, Toni sat on the side of the bed facing him. "I'm angry."

He put down the shirt he was tucking into his suitcase, sat beside her, and pulled her into the circle of his arms. "That's understandable."

"It's bad enough that people are being killed, but why does it have to frighten our children?" she demanded into his chest.

He drew a deep breath. "I don't know, but I know being angry will affect you in a bad way if you let it."

She sagged against him. "I know. But it's hard to see the boys frightened, especially when it's for me."

Kyle gripped her shoulders and pushed her back to where he could look into her face. "So what are you going to do about it?"

She stared at him, reading a challenge in those steady green eyes. "Are you saying I should get involved in another case?"

He shrugged, his brows raised. "Can you leave it alone?"

She studied him another moment. Then she produced a weak smile, her spine stiffening. "There's very little likelihood of my being welcome anywhere near a case this far from home. But they'll have my input, whether they want it or not, if the boys are drawn into it."

He nodded. "That's my girl. But if that happens, be careful. Okay?"

"Okay," she promised, even as her concerns returned. "Gabe is troubled. Do you think he'll be all right?"

"I think so. Today's discovery was enough to upset anyone. He'll work through it if we give him time and space."

*

The next morning Toni and her family attended church with Barb and Dan Donovan, and then ate at Cracker Barrel. After the meal they took Kyle's parents home, since Dan said he didn't feel up to anything but a nap at that point. Then they changed into denim shorts and tee shirts and took the boys to a Double A minor league Cardinals baseball game at Hammons Field. Quint met them at the entrance, sporting a Cardinals shirt.

Garrett thrust out a hand. "Hi, Uncle Quint." Their handshake was vigorous. Quint was one of Garrett's favorite people.

"I like your shirts." Quint indicated the red Cardinal logo on both boys' shirts that matched his own. Toni's shirt was solid red, but Cardinal red. As was Kyle's.

Quint turned and held out a hand to Gabe.

Gabe shook it, but his manner lacked Garrett's enthusiasm.

"What do you think of the guy who's pitching today?" Quint asked the boy.

Gabe shrugged and managed a half smile. "He's pretty good, I guess."

"He's more than good," Quint insisted. "I'm predicting he'll be called up to the majors soon." He turned a questioning gaze on Toni.

She gave her brother an I-don't-know-what's-wrong shrug.

"Well, let's get in there and watch him show his stuff." Quint led the way inside the ballpark. When they were seated, Toni could see the green roofs of the OTC campus where she was teaching.

"Is anyone ready for snacks yet?" Kyle asked.

Everyone told him what they wanted—except Gabe.

"How about you?" Kyle asked him. "Want a soda?"

"Okay," Gabe said without expression.

By the seventh inning stretch, the Cardinals were ahead four to two. The young pitcher had done well. Garrett had been a noisy, cheering fan. But Gabe, an avid baseball fan who planned to play on the Clearmount Junior High team that fall, remained subdued.

Suddenly he began digging around in the pocket of his jeans, his face twisted in distress. "What's the matter, Son," Toni asked.

"I can't find my pocket knife, the one I got for Christmas." He searched the other pocket.

"Are you sure you put it in your pocket?"

He nodded, his subdued manner turning to panic. "I'm sure I did. I..." He paused, thinking and frowning. "Maybe I didn't."

"When was the last time you remember seeing it?"

He concentrated, squinting as he tried to remember. "I always put it next to the bed. But now I'm not sure I remember seeing it this morning," he finally admitted.

"Where could you have left it, or lost it?"

As his face went through a series of contortions, thoughtfulness slowly turned to horror. "Oh, no," he gasped. "The last time I really remember seeing it is when I was cutting a stick down by the lagoon at the park."

"We can go by there on our way home and look for it," Toni said.

"No!"

Quiet fell over the small group, the game forgotten.

"Don't you want to find your knife?" Kyle asked.

Gabe's head bobbed up and down, and then shook back and forth. His eyes became shiny with tears he fought to keep from shedding. "I can't," he finally managed to choke.

Toni's heart caught in her throat, unsure how to handle her child's distress. "Can you tell me why you can't?" she asked softly, reaching over and taking one of his hands in her own.

Gabe gulped. "We can't go back there. Someone is killing people there. They might hurt Garrett."

That pretty much confirmed Toni's suspicion about what was bothering him. His concern about Garrett was understandable, even justified, considering that someone had actually tried to harm Garrett the first time a dream of his had connected to a murder. "We'll all go together, and it's broad daylight," she reassured him. "We'll all keep a close lookout for anything out of the ordinary. You want to find your knife, don't you?"

Gabe nodded wordlessly.

"Okay, let's finish the game. Then we'll go."

"I'll tag along if you like," Quint offered, looking at Toni for a response. "Then, afterward, we can swing by the station for you to give your formal statements."

Toni glanced at Kyle and received a nod of agreement. "Okay."

"It'll be pretty cut and dry," Quint said. "Each of you will be asked to tell your story, and someone will write it down. I'll do everything I can to keep Garrett's…uh, extraordinary motivation confidential," he said softly to Toni.

"I'd like to ride with Uncle Quint, since he's a cop." Gabe eyed his parents for permission.

"It's all right with me," Toni said, relieved at his improved demeanor.

*

When they returned to the park an hour later, it was a quiet oasis. Toni took in the almost magical feeling of the tree and shrub laden refuge that was now so unlike the previous day. Only three or four people were on the lawn, but she heard what sounded like youngsters out of sight over around the caves.

They let Gabe lead the way to where he remembered having his knife. "I was sitting here," he said, stopping near the end of the lagoon and looking around.

"It's not here," Quint declared after they had searched the area thoroughly. "Which isn't surprising, since this is such a public place. If he lost it here, someone surely found and kept it."

Toni felt bad for Gabe. She started to say something to him when her attention was drawn to Garrett. He had gone to the very edge of the water and squatted to stare into it. She walked over next to him.

"I see it," he said, pointing at a spot two or three feet out.

Quint joined them and peerked at where Garrett was pointing. "It might have rolled in there, but I'm guessing someone came along and unknowingly kicked it." He dropped to his belly and reached out. Unable to reach the knife, he edged forward a little more, and almost toppled into the water.

Gabe darted behind him and grabbed a foot. "Get the other one," he ordered Garrett.

Quint glanced back over his shoulder and grinned. "Think you can hold me?"

"Sure," Gabe answered. "But if we can't, you get dunked," he added with a laugh.

Toni stepped over alongside Gabe and grasped Quint's right ankle. Kyle joined Garrett and grabbed the left. Together they held him while he stretched out to where the knife lay and plunged his hand down. When he did, his head and shoulders went in the water. As he tried to rise, everyone pulled, and he was yanked back onto dry ground.

Rolling over and holding up the knife, he grinned through the water streaming from his hair over his face and soaking his tee shirt.

Gabe took the knife. "Thanks, Uncle Quint. You're funny."

"Think so, huh?" Quint sat upright and wiped his eyes and face with the tail of his shirt. "Do you feel like going to the station with me now?"

Both boys nodded and broke into a run toward his pickup.

Kyle and Toni drove behind Quint and the boys across town. Toni liked the logical checkerboard layout of the city's streets. She found them easier to navigate than any city in which she had driven. The south district station was located on West Battlefield Road, between Scenic and Clifton Avenues.

Quint used his key card to get them inside. A female receptionist or dispatcher sat behind a glass window in front of them, but they didn't approach her. To the right were a metal detector and a fingerprinting room, according to the signs. Quint led them past a collection of chairs to a doorway and turned left.

"These are interrogation rooms," he explained to the boys, indicating each side of the hallway. "Think of them as conference rooms if that title bothers you. I'll put you in this one and let the detective on duty know you're here."

The boys stepped inside and surveyed the room, suddenly silent, and chose chairs side by side at the conference table. Toni chose a chair directly across from them, where she could watch their faces. Kyle sat next to her.

Quint and a suit clad man entered the room. "This is lead detective Meacham. He'll be the one asking questions. He'll want to know a lot of details, and your answers will be taped, but don't let that make you nervous. He's good at what he does."

Detective Meacham took the chair at the head of the table. "Thank you for coming," he said, arranging papers in front of him. "Let's see if I can get your names right."

He looked at Toni. "You're Quint's sister, right?"

Toni nodded. "Yes. I'm Toni. And this is my husband, Kyle."

"Glad to meet both of you." He glanced at his notes, and then focused on the boys. "Will you two tell me which is Garret and which is Gabe?"

Gabe spoke first. "I'm Gabe. He's Garrett. He's two years younger than me."

The detective grinned at Gabe's extra information.

Quint checked his watch. "I hate to leave you, but I need to go home and get into uniform so I can report for duty. Will you guys be all right?" he asked the boys.

"We're fine," Gabe assured him. "Will you come see us again before we go home Thursday?"

"I'll do that," he promised and left the room.

Toni bounced to her feet and caught up to Quint in the hall. "I want to say thanks for the extra attention you've given the boys." She gave him a quick hug.

"Aw, shucks," he drawled in a bumpkin manner. "'Tweren't nothin'." Then he turned serious. "Believe it or not, big sister, I like your kids. In fact, I almost wish I had that youngest one on the force with me."

Toni swatted at him. "Go to work."

She hurried back inside and resumed her seat. The next hour was tiring, but she was proud of the way the boys told their stories. And pleased at the way the detective drew the facts from Garrett without relying on Gabe. The worst part was when he asked Garrett why he had come to find the body and heard the story of the dream. He made notes and never indicated that he found the story unbelievable, but

Toni knew he surely had reservations.

The questions he put to her and Kyle were straightforward, and answered without hesitation. When they were finished, the detective gathered his notes into a pile, thanked them again for their time, and saw them to the door.

When they arrived back at the Donovan house, Toni was just taking her purse to the bedroom when her phone rang.

"Hello, Kara," she said, reading the caller ID.

"Toni! Tell me about the story in today's paper. You *were* at the park yesterday for a family reunion, weren't you?"

"Yes, I was." She didn't elaborate.

"My gut says you're the teacher whose family found that coach's body. I want to hear the details."

"On the phone?"

Kara paused. "It would be better if we could visit face to face. How about getting together tomorrow after class."

"I could meet you in the student union. You know your class schedule better than I do."

"I'll be at the entrance at one-thirty."

Toni grinned as Kara disconnected. She should have anticipated her friend's interest. After all, they were both scientists—and over-endowed with curiosity.

Monday morning Kyle left at five a.m., saying he would get something to eat on the way to the airport. An hour later, dressed in lightweight white slacks and an aqua blouse, Toni went downstairs.

"Good morning," Barb Donovan greeted her as she entered the kitchen. "Breakfast is ready, but the boys are sleeping late. Have a seat."

There was toast, juice, bacon and eggs on the table. Toni took a chair next to her father-in-law. "I'm not usually a big breakfast eater, but this looks good. I won't need lunch."

"What time will you be back here?" Barb asked, putting an egg on her own plate.

"I'll be in class until one, but I'm meeting Kara at the student union at one-thirty. I should be in no later than four, in plenty of time to help you with the evening meal."

"Oh, you don't need to do that. I already have things planned. We're taking the boys to the zoo today, so if we're not here when you get in, don't worry about them."

Toni wished she felt more at ease with her mother-in-law. Barb Donovan was a good woman, but she was so intense, so determined to do everything just right, that her nervousness was contagious.

Forced to take early retirement from the Corps of Engineers after suffering a stroke, her father-in-law had a number of health problems. But he seemed content with his life since making the move to Springfield a few years ago. He was more laid back than Barb, more relaxing to be around.

Toni ate quickly and left the house, knowing her boys were in good hands—even though they might feel a little stifled. Barb, the life-long stay at home mom and epitome of domesticity, would see to their every need once they were done sleeping in late.

It was almost seven-thirty, and Toni needed to set up for lab after lecture. Lectures were from eight-thirty to eleven Monday through Thursday, but on Mondays and Wednesdays they were followed by a two-hour lab.

Ozark Technical College had originally opened in 1991, at Cox Medical Center North, with about twelve hundred students. Focused on job-skill training and college transfer preparation, the school had achieved accreditation by 1996. Then it grew quickly, spreading to locations all over town and opening satellite campuses in other towns—and was still expanding.

Toni exited Chestnut Expressway into the parking lot of the main campus and parked near the technical center where the science classes were taught.

Inside her classroom were six tables, with four chairs at each, and a microscope cabinet below them. At the front of the room were a white board and a pull-down screen for projecting PowerPoint presentations. Against the walls were cabinets that contained models of human body parts. In one corner of the room stood a model of a full human skeleton that Kara had whimsically introduced to her at the beginning of the summer as Mr. Bones.

Three students entered as Toni finished arranging materials on the lab tables. They were chatting.

". . .paper didn't give the name of the person who found the body. . . just that it was the family of a teacher who was attending a get-together at the park. The police must be protecting someone."

Toni turned slightly so the speaker couldn't see her face.

"Since it just says her family, I'm betting there's

a minor involved," another student theorized.

"I don't care who found him," the third one said. "I bet there are a bunch of people who are glad he's dead."

"But he was a coach at Ozark," the first speaker objected. "Who in the world would want him dead?"

The third one snorted. "Don't you know he was fired? And it wasn't the first time."

As they moved on to the back of the room, Toni couldn't distinguish any more of the conversation. She went to the computer and pulled up her PowerPoint presentation.

Chapter 4

The mid-term exam at the end of the first four weeks had been over biochemistry and the skeletal and muscular systems. The second four weeks had begun last week with the nervous system. Today they would be studying the five senses.

The two and a half hour lecture served to take Toni's mind off her boys and the murder case. Thinking she might have trouble concentrating today, it was nice when material that was so familiar to her that she could have presented it in her sleep soon had her back in control.

Teaching wasn't always easy, but Toni genuinely enjoyed the work—and most of the students she taught. There were always a few who had problems and caused distractions, but she loved being able to make a difference in young lives. This was different, though, because she was accustomed to teaching high school students. There were seventeen enrolled in this class, most of them in their twenties or older, and they commuted from all over that part of the state.

"Let's start with the sense of touch." Toni moved with the students from their desks to the lab set-ups behind them. "If you'll look on your tables, you'll find some calipers. They have two adjustable arms, or jaws, and are usually used to measure diameter or thickness. Today we'll measure our sense of touch. I want you to press the instrument into your index finger, your back, and your neck. Start with the caliper arms close together, touch repeatedly, and keep adjusting the arms until they're far enough apart that you can tell you're being touched with two arms instead of only one. Work in pairs and take turns touching your partner."

"Oh, goody, we get to play touchy-touchy," someone quipped.

There were some snickers, but they all tackled the assignment.

They were given small, unlabeled containers of coffee, garlic powder, cinnamon and cocoa butter to smell and identify. The next containers held salt water, sugar water, lemon juice, and alum for them to taste and identify salty, sweet, sour, and bitter. Vision testing was done with a Snelling chart, and hearing was tested with tuning forks.

At the end of lab Toni dismissed the class and began to tidy her desk, but Nicole Warren lingered in a manner that indicated she wanted to speak to Toni.

There were a lot of single mothers enrolled at the school, and this class drew a high percentage of nursing students. Nicole was both. Somewhere in her twenties, with long dark hair that fell nearly to her waist, she was one of those who had gotten married right out of high school, ended up divorced, and returned to school to try to acquire a better way of supporting herself and her child. Toni knew from past conversations that Nicole had a little girl and was struggling to meet her bills.

Somewhat hesitantly Nicole approached Toni, a

folded newspaper in her hand. She paused and glanced around, as if checking to be sure they were alone.

"May I help you?"

Nicole shoved the newspaper toward Toni. It was the front-page section of yesterday's Sunday edition, with the story about the body being found at the park staring up at them. "I've been reading this," she said in a rush. "It doesn't name the people who found the body, but it says it was a teacher and her family and a friend."

Toni knew the article only stated the simple facts, that the body of an Ozark coach had been found in the Sequiota Park lagoon, a homicide victim, and an investigation was being conducted. It noted that the victim had a wife and two stepchildren living in Ozark. She met Nicole's intense gaze, debating how to answer.

Nicole pointed at the picture. "That was taken from a distance. It's of the crime scene, but that looks like you in the background at the left of the police officers."

Toni had been startled at seeing the picture the night before after returning to the Donovan home. The police had honored her request to keep their names out of the story, so the picture had been a shock. It had only caught part of her and John in profile, so she had hoped they would not be recognized. She was thankful that the boys had been far enough away that the reporter's camera had missed them.

"Is there a particular reason for your question?" she asked evasively.

Nicole nodded. "I was wondering if you know any more about who killed him than what's in the article."

There was something about the girl's manner that made Toni wonder if she knew something relevant. "It's me," she admitted quietly. "But I have no idea who killed him. Did you know him?"

Nicole raised troubled blue eyes to meet hers. She nodded. "I was in one of his classes when he was teaching at Branson six years ago."

Toni studied the girl, recalling the student comments she had heard earlier. What kind of guy had the victim been? "Was it a bad experience?" she asked carefully.

Nicole drew a deep breath. "He never touched me, if that's what you're asking. But he made me uneasy. He was kind of flirty, if you know what I mean."

Uh, oh! Educators involved in sexual misconduct cases was becoming way too much of a problem. Toni remembered reading an article recently that stated, of the approximately three million public school teachers in the United States, there had been over twenty-five hundred educators censured over a three-year period. "Were there any formal accusations from anyone?"

Nicole winced. "There were stories going around, but nothing was ever made public."

"What kind of stories?"

"Well, there was a senior girl he was supposed to be having a thing with."

Toni couldn't prevent a wince of her own. "Do you think the stories were true?"

Nicole sighed. "I'm sure they were. The girl was in my art class, and she seemed proud of what she considered her conquest. I overheard her talking to some other girls one day, and she was telling them about a hot date. They were whispering, but I'm pretty sure I heard her say Jesse."

Toni wasn't sure she wanted to hear this.

"You were there in the park. What do you think happened to him?" Nicole asked.

"I don't have any idea who might have killed the man. Do you?"

Nicole bit her lip. "No, but if he was fooling around at other schools like he did at Branson, there are probably plenty of possibilities. Listen, I'm sorry I bothered you. I'm sure you're busy, and I have to get to work."

"You didn't bother me," Toni assured her. "I'll see you tomorrow."

With a little wave, Nicole left the room.

*

As promised, Kara was waiting at the entrance of the student union when Toni arrived. Wearing a peach blouse and ivory slacks, she gripped the handle of an infant carrier in one hand, and had a diaper bag and purse dangling from the opposite shoulder. Toni reached over and took the diaper bag.

Kara Yates had been Toni's best friend since junior high school when Kara's parents moved to Clearmount. Ironically, their relationship had begun in science class when they were placed in the same small work group during a lesson on genetics and inherited traits. They had discovered that they had so many traits in common, including hair color, height and weight, that they decided they must really be sisters and their parents just didn't know it.

Finding that hilarious, they had partnered up in other classes and rapidly cemented their friendship.

After high school, they attended different colleges, but kept in touch regularly, and both majored in science. While Toni returned to Clearmount to marry Kyle and teach school there, Kara had remained in Springfield, graduated from Missouri State University, and taken a teaching position at Glendale High School. After six years with that district, she had resigned, become an adjunct science instructor at the local community college, and later gotten married. When she learned she was expecting Jimmy in June, she had talked Toni into holding down her summer class for her. Toni had stayed with her during the first four weeks to be with her through the time of having Jimmy while her husband was deployed to Afghanistan.

Kara looked her over. "You look like you've been running a race. I had to bring Jimmy, but he's taking his long afternoon nap."

"I haven't had lunch, and I'm starving," Toni said as they headed inside.

She ordered a fish sandwich and soda, but Kara, who said she had already eaten, just got a soft drink. They slid into a booth that had seen a lot of wear, facing one another, and Toni scooted the diaper bag to the inner wall next to her.

"Okay, talk," Kara ordered when she had Jimmy and his carrier settled.

"Did you know the victim we found?" Toni asked, unwrapping her sandwich.

Kara shook her head. "No, but it's an intriguing story, and I want to know if you're going to get involved."

"I don't have any such plans, and I'm too hungry to talk right now."

Kara grinned. "Eat. Then I expect a full revelation."

Toni downed her sandwich quickly and then told Kara about Saturday's events, omitting only the bit about Garrett's dream.

"I remembered about your reunion and knew it just had to be you," Kara said, her eyes sparkling with interest when Toni finished.

Toni eased back in the booth and tucked a leg comfortably beneath her. She started to make another comment, but her attention was diverted to the booth across the aisle when she heard the dead coach's name mentioned. A card game was in progress.

A young man, a big guy with dark bushy hair and a beard that made Toni think of a fur trapper in an old western movie, slapped a card down on the table. "See what you think of that, Jackie Boy," he said in a gloating tone. "I remember when he coached at Branson. He had a fantastic winning record. I don't understand what happened."

"I raise you two dollars. He was one winning dude," Jackie agreed from across the table, picking up a card from the deck between them and studying it. Sandy haired, he wore glasses that gave him a scholarly look.

"I really appreciate you holding down my job for me this summer," Kara said to Toni, and opened her mouth to say more.

Toni rolled her eyes sideways and blinked to signal her interest in the next table.

Message received, Kara went silent and picked up her drink cup. They sipped slowly and listened.

"I loved to watch his teams play," the third young man said. Also fair haired, his haircut resembled a fringed bowling ball. He slapped his cards face down on the table. "I'm out. I'll miss attending games to see the guy win," he continued without missing a beat.

"Too bad someone offed him," the first one said, studying his hand.

"Yeah, it's too bad," the spectacled Jackie said.

The fourth young man, who had been silent, suddenly looked up from staring at his hand of cards. "He's no big loss." The tone sounded snide. Broad shouldered, his hair was shorter than his companions. It stood straight up on top. The ends had been bleached a glaring golden color that bounced off Toni's eyeballs.

"What's your beef, Corey?" the first big guy snapped. "You shouldn't speak bad of the dead."

Corey flipped a card onto the discard pile. "Forget it. I didn't mean anything."

Jackie scooted out of the booth. "I have class in fifteen. See you around." He dashed away.

"Me, too," golden top said, putting his cards down.

The big guy raked up the cards and tucked them into his book bag.

Kara stared at Toni as the foursome walked out of sight. "I guess the story is the topic of the day. Should I run those guys down and tell them your role in it?"

Toni gave her a glare.

The Batman theme erupted. It took a couple of seconds for Toni to assimilate that one of her sons had changed the ring of her cell phone.

Startled from sleep, the baby's eyes shot open. His little body stiffened, and he set up a howl. Kara reached over to soothe him and lifted him from his seat.

Toni checked the caller ID and saw that it was John. "Hello."

"Toni, I need to talk to you," he said, his voice low and vibrating with suppressed emotion. "I just left the library. Where are you? Can you meet me somewhere?"

Struggling to hear him over the crying baby, Toni glanced at her watch. "I'm at the student union with Kara."

"I need to go," Kara broke in. "Talk to you later." She slid from the booth, patting Jimmy.

Toni nodded and put her hand over the phone to speak to Kara. "Give me a call later. Okay?"

"Will do." Kara grabbed the infant seat, her purse, and the diaper bag Toni handed her.

"I'm back," Toni said to John as Kara walked away. Do you want to come here, or would you rather meet me some place, like the park, or at my in-laws?"

There was a slight pause. "Do you have your laptop with you?"

"No, it's at the house."

"Then I'll meet you there. What's the address and what time will you be there?"

Toni gave him the address. "I can be there in

about fifteen minutes."

"Good." The phone went silent.

*

Puzzled, Toni stuck the phone back in her purse and wasted no time getting to the Donovan home. John's car was already parked at the curb. As soon as she pulled into the drive, he emerged and came to meet her, his laptop in his hands.

"Here," he said, pulling the flash drive from the lanyard around his neck and holding it out to her.

Toni's puzzlement grew. "What's the matter? Are you having trouble getting something off of it?"

John shook his head. "It's not *my* drive. It's Jesse Campbell's."

That nearly exploded her brain. "How in the world did you get it?"

His grin was wry. "He and I went to the lab after class Thursday to look up and copy some material for an assignment. I mean, why copy stuff at home if we can do it for free in the lab?"

Toni nodded, but she still didn't understand about the drive.

"We both used our flash drives, and when we finished, I guess we each picked up the wrong one," he explained. "We were sitting next to one another. Anyhow, with Friday being the holiday, we weren't in class that day, and I didn't use the drive over the weekend. When I went to the lab after class today and started to open my files, I discovered the switch."

Toni's mind was spinning. She wanted to see what was on that drive—even though there was probably nothing helpful there.

John's expression turned somber. "Do you think

I should turn it over to the police?"

Toni debated for about two seconds. "Yes, I do—after we copy it."

John grinned and indicated his laptop. "My thoughts exactly."

The front door opened, and Barb Donovan stepped out onto the small front porch. "Why, hello, John."

"Hello, Mrs. Donovan," he returned amiably. "I hope you don't mind if I come in and show Toni some files. I need some advice on a matter."

"Of course not. Come on inside. Dan and the boys are out shopping. You're welcome to use Dan's office."

"Thanks," Toni said to her mother-in-law, and then addressed John. "It's the room on the left at the end of the hall. Go ahead and get your computer going. I'll join you in a minute with mine."

Once they had both laptops on Russell's desk and booted, John inserted Jesse's flash drive into a USB port and opened the list of files on it. Toni pulled her chair up next to him and peered over his shoulder. The file names seemed simple enough.

"Some of these are class assignments," John mumbled, running a finger down the screen. He paused on a file name. "There's the one we both worked on Thursday and copied from my drive to his. I guess that's when we got them mixed up."

"There are some Excel files," Toni commented. "Did you use any spreadsheets in the class?"

John nodded. "We created a grade book one day, so he may have made more than one copy. This one looks like it could be that assignment." He clicked on it.

Finding what he expected, John closed the file and opened another. He peered closer. "This looks like it could be a copy of his personal banking records."

"Everything looks pretty straightforward," Toni said. "Let's copy all the files onto both our computers. Then we can look at them in more detail when we have more time."

John closed the file and copied everything to his hard drive. Then he extracted the flash and handed it to Toni.

"Now who do we give it to?" she asked when she had done the same.

John considered a moment. "We probably should take it to the police station. But I'm not crazy about going in there when we've just done this. I guess I feel a little guilty."

"I'll call Quint and see if he'll turn it in for us." She picked up her phone from where she had laid it on the desk.

"Uh, do you have time to come by before you go to work?" she asked when her brother answered. "John and I have something we need to show you."

"Are you at the Donovan house?"

"Yes."

"Is this about the body at the park?"

"Yes."

"I'll stop by on my way to work. I was just getting dressed."

Toni exhaled in relief as she disconnected.

Chapter 5

When Quint's navy pickup pulled to the curb a half hour later, Toni trotted down the driveway and crawled into the passenger seat beside her uniformed brother. John went around to the driver's door, and Quint rolled down the window. "What's up?" he asked John.

"I found something that belongs to the dead man." John handed the flash drive through the open window.

Quint took it, a questioning frown on his face, and turned it over in his hands. "How did you get this, and what's the significance of it?"

"I don't know whether it has any significance." John explained how he came to have it.

"Since it belonged to the dead man, we thought the police might want it," Toni said. "But we weren't sure who it should be given to."

Quint nodded. "I'll give it to one of the detectives. It may be a waste of time, but it should be checked. You never know what kind of personal information could help solve a case like this." He glanced at his watch.

Toni opened the door and dropped to the ground. "Thanks for coming by. See you later."

As she watched Quint drive away, Toni's mind

took a different turn. She faced John. "Where's your flash drive?"

"I don't know. I guess Jesse took it."

"Do you think his wife might have it?"

He shrugged. "She might be willing to check in his stuff and see if she can find it."

"Do you know where she lives?"

"No-o-o," he said on a long drawl. "But she's somewhere in Ozark, and it's not a real big town."

Toni thought a moment. "I'll call Kara. Maybe she can help."

Within minutes Toni had Kara on the line and gave her an abbreviated explanation of the mix-up. "Do you have any idea how I can locate the coach's widow?" she asked, hearing the baby crying in the background.

"No," Kara said. "Hang on just a second. Okay," she continued moments later. "Jimmy is fighting naptime. He may go to sleep if I hold him, but he isn't about to be quiet so I can chat. He's been fussy all day."

Toni waited for the explanations to run down.

"Okay, you're looking for Jesse Campbell's widow," Kara said, a note of frustration in her voice as the baby continued to cry, the uneven sounds indicating she was bouncing him in her arms. "I didn't know the Campbell couple, but I have a good friend who lives in Ozark. I'll call her and get right back to you."

"I'd appreciate that." Toni disconnected and relayed Kara's response to John. "Let's go back inside and have a cold soda while we wait for her to call back."

He nodded. "That, and the air conditioning, sound good."

They were seated at the kitchen table with their drinks and cookies that Barb had insisted they try when Toni's phone rang.

"I talked to my friend Sally," Kara said without preamble. "She says Jesse and Sheila Campbell lived in the Excelsior Gardens apartment complex. She doesn't have an apartment number, just a phone number from her staff emergency call list."

"Give it to me." Toni indicated to John with a hand motion that she needed writing materials. He bounced up and trotted back to the office. When he returned and handed her only a pen, Toni wrote the number Kara quoted on a napkin. After thanking Kara and disconnecting, she went to her computer and looked up directions to the apartments.

"I'll drive and bring you back," John volunteered when she finished making notes.

Toni went to tell Barb they were leaving and would probably be gone a couple of hours, and then she followed John to his car.

Ozark was only about ten miles from Springfield. As they traveled south on Route 65, Toni found herself wondering about Jesse Campbell. Up until now he had only been a murder victim, but in her mind he was beginning to take vague form as a human being.

Steep hills towered on each side of the highway, the mid-afternoon sun giving the horizon a shimmering glow. It only took a few minutes to reach Highway F. John swung left and was soon cruising past a sparkling swimming pool, a playground, and a courtyard with patio tables and BBQ grills. He pulled in at the office building of the complex and parked next to a late model gray van.

A huge pot of flowers stood next to the doorway, and the lawn was neatly mowed and trimmed. Toni pointed toward a cluster of mailboxes at the end of the walkway. "Let's check those before trying to talk a clerk into giving us an apartment number."

"Works for me."

"You start at one end. I'll take the other," Toni said when they reached them. She began running her eyes over the surnames on the individual boxes.

"Here's a Campbell," John announced. "It's number three-twenty-eight."

They found the apartment quickly. In simultaneous moves Toni rang the doorbell and John knocked on the door. "We'll scare her to death," Toni said in a near giggle.

It was a few moments before the door opened a couple of inches. Round dark eyes peered out over the burglar chain.

"Mrs. Campbell?" John asked politely. "I'm John Zachary, and this is my colleague, Toni Donovan. I met your husband in a class last week at Drury, and I'm shocked at his death. May we come in and talk to you?"

The woman continued to stare at them, whether doubting their identity or just reluctant to talk to them, it was hard to tell.

"I assure you we're legitimate," Toni said. "We're not media or anything like that."

After another long moment the woman slid the chain from its latch and opened the door. Her honey blonde hair was pulled back behind her ears and fell haphazardly to her shoulders, her gaze cool and questioning. Thin, with dark circles shadowing her eyes, she wore jeans, a faded green tee shirt, and worn tennis shoes. Her smoothly sculpted cheekbones, coupled with a small nose and rounded chin, made her attractive, although not a raving beauty.

Toni scanned the room. The carpeting was a neutral shade of tan. The couch and chairs were upholstered in a green and blue stripe, with throw pillows of solid blue and green. The rest of the furnishings were nice enough, but not expensive designer stuff. Photographs of two young children, framed in gold, occupied a place of honor on top of the entertainment center.

"My name is Sheila," the woman finally said. "Have a seat." She perched on the edge of the sofa and picked up the cigarette from an ashtray on the coffee table. She took a deep drag, inhaled, and then tapped the ash off with a long finger and put it back. "Now, what can I do for you?"

"Jesse and I sat together in class," John repeated. "We went to Bass Pro together Tuesday."

"Yes, I remember him mentioning taking someone," she responded, interest finally beginning to enter her eyes. "So what's the problem?"

"Well, we went to the library together after class Thursday to work on an assignment. Today I discovered that I had his flash drive. Apparently we got our drives mixed up when we each copied a file we had worked on together."

Sheila blinked. "Are you saying you're looking

for your flash drive?"

"That's right. Do you have any idea where Jesse might have put it?"

She stared past him in thought. "I guess I can look in his briefcase and check his desk and computer. I'll be right back." She stood and left the room.

While they waited for her return, Toni tried to analyze the woman. Probably in her thirties, she seemed edgy, but that was to be expected from a woman whose husband had just been killed. She was being cooperative rather than displaying antagonism over their intrusion. It also seemed to Toni that the woman didn't seem overcome with bereavement. But she might be the kind of person who could hide her emotions.

Her eyes returned to the pictures on the entertainment center, a girl and boy who looked to be about six and ten. They were attractive children, sandy haired and smiling. But as she surveyed the room, she saw no evidence of children living there.

Toni was staring at the pictures again when Sheila Campbell returned to the room. "Those are my son and daughter," she said, noting Toni's attention on the pictures. "They live with their father. He got custody when we divorced."

Toni's senses sharpened, and she pasted on her 'dumb' face. "You must miss them."

Sheila nodded. "I do. Jesse and I have...had only been married a few weeks. My former husband has custody of Cassie and Craig." She pushed back a strand of blonde hair and resumed her seat on the sofa. She bit down on her lower lip for a moment, and then regained her momentarily lost composure. "I couldn't find your flash drive," she told John. "I went through his briefcase and desk, and it's not anywhere around the computer."

"Do you have any idea where he might have used it, or what he might have done with it?"

Her brow furrowed, and then slowly smoothed out. "There is one small possibility. He kept some financial records on it, and he always took it with him when he went to see his accountant."

His accountant? A teacher needed to see an accountant on a regular basis? That seemed unusual to Toni. Teachers weren't at the bottom of the local pay scale, but they weren't exactly known for high finance, investments, and the like.

"Can you give us the name of the accountant?" she asked.

Sheila thought for a moment and then shook her head slowly. "No...I'm sure I've heard it, but I can't remember."

It looked like they were at a dead end. Toni sighed. "May we leave our names and phone numbers with you, in case you remember it?"

"That would be okay." She scooted over and picked up a pen and pad from the small table at the end of the sofa. Then she wrote down the information as they repeated their names and cell numbers in turn.

"Do you have a funeral scheduled yet?" John asked. "I'd like to attend if I can."

Sheila's head bobbed slowly. "They haven't released his body yet, but if they release it by tomorrow, as they've said they should, the service will be Friday afternoon at the local mortuary. If they don't, it may not be until next week."

Toni stood. "Thank you for your help. Please accept our condolences."

As they moved to the door, a phone began ringing in the next room.

"Go ahead and get it. We'll see ourselves out," Toni told the woman.

When they were in the car, Toni aimed a pointed look across the seat at John as he poked the key in the ignition. "They were newlyweds. She lost her kids in a divorce. Something tells me there's a story behind it all. I'm curious."

"Maybe Kara can help you research it." He started the engine and backed out of the drive.

A couple minutes later he asked, "Do you mind if we swing by Best Buy so I can buy a new flash drive? I need it before tomorrow's class."

"That lanyard does look lonely." She nodded at the cord dangling around his neck with nothing attached to the end of it. She had left her own back at the house with her laptop.

When Toni crawled into bed that night, she placed her cell phone on the table next to her. Kyle called almost every night just to touch base and chat, and she hadn't heard from him yet. She snuggled down and was just dozing off when it rang, dragging her from semi-consciousness.

She grabbed it and mumbled, "Hullo."

"Uh oh. Sounds like you were already asleep," Kyle said.

Toni ran a hand over her face in the dark, trying to clear her head. "I just dropped off."

"How was your day?"

She pushed herself up against the head of the bed. "Interesting," she said, coming awake.

"Oh?"

She gave him a brief recap of her talk with Nicole, John's missing flash drive, and the visit to Jesse Campbell's widow.

"Toni, I hope you're not getting involved in something that could prove dangerous."

"All I'm doing is teaching Kara's class and helping John look for…"

"Just so you look out for your safety," he interrupted her explanation. "How are the boys? Do they seem to be affected by the weekend find, or have they put it behind them?"

"They asked this evening if the police have caught the killer yet, but they don't seem to be troubled other than disappointed that no one has been nabbed."

Kyle chuckled at the emphasis on the last word. "They think it should happen like they see on television."

"How about you? Have you run into any problems or developments of interest?"

There was a slight pause. "Well, there was something, but…oh, it's nothing. I'm in Jamaica right now," he said, changing the subject. "I delivered a load of medical supplies to Kingston."

They talked a couple more minutes. When Toni snuggled back down in the bed, she felt uneasy. Something about the way Kyle had sounded troubled her. She sensed that something was bothering him. She would try to sound him out more the next time they talked.

*

Tuesday morning Toni dressed in a denim wrap-around skirt and a loose fitting white blouse, looped her lanyard over her head, and attached her flash drive to it. Breakfast was a quick bowl of cereal with the Donovans. The boys were still asleep when she left.

As she was pulling out of the driveway, her cell phone rang. She stopped at the side of the street and answered it.

"What time do you get out of class today?" John asked.

"I don't have lab, so I'll be done at eleven."

"I don't finish class until twelve. How about meeting for lunch?"

"After class I have to do some lab prep for tomorrow. That should take about forty-five minutes. It's perfect timing. Where do you want to meet?"

"I packed two sandwiches. I'll share them if you'll meet me at Jordan Valley Park at twelve-fifteen."

"I'll bring sodas. What kind do you want?"

"A Dr. Pepper sounds good."

"Okay, see you at the fountains."

Class was routine. The two and a half hour lecture covered chapter sixteen on the endocrine system and was accompanied by diagrams on the overhead. The students seemed fascinated by the problems that too much or too little of any hormone could cause to the body, especially the students who were in nursing.

Nicole, who was sitting at the front table, raised her hand. "Does that mean we can blame our grumpy moods on this system?"

Toni grinned. "I'd say you need to be sure it's not just the kids or spouse getting to you before making that charge." She glanced up at the clock, glad for the occasional levity and high interest level this class continued to show. The interaction pleased her.

"Okay, that's it. Tomorrow we'll cover chapter seventeen and do an endocrine and blood lab. You're dismissed."

As soon as the students were gone, Toni set up for the next day and left the room. On the way out of the building she stopped by a soda machine, bought two cold sodas, and tucked them down into the side pockets of her book satchel.

Once outside, she debated whether to bother with her car or just walk. It was a pretty day, and she needed some exercise. Decision made, she walked to the intersection, crossed Chestnut Expressway, and then hiked three blocks south to the park.

Although public, Jordan Valley was not a playground park. Several small children in bathing suits were running and splashing in the small fountains where geysers of water shot up through holes in the concrete apron. It would shoot high in the air, then lower, and gradually quit. The children would then stomp on the silent holes with their bare feet, and squeal in delight when the water started shooting up again. The sight stirred memories of trips to parks when Toni and her brothers were children.

Smiling, she sat on one of the stone slab benches on the hillside overlooking the fountains, not far from where mothers occupied square stone seats while keeping an eye on their children. Water spilled down wide concrete steps to the flat fountain area from a lagoon of still water at the top of the hill. A glance at her watch told her it was ten after twelve.

She settled her bags next to her and glanced around to see if John was in sight yet. There was no sign of him. The Hammon Center towered overhead, and Hammon Field was across the highway. The sun was high in the sky and beginning to sizzle. She tugged at her blouse that was clinging to her skin.

Fifteen minutes later she was definitely uncomfortable. It wasn't like John to be late. She pulled her Coke from her satchel and popped the tab. It was already warm, but she drank from it anyhow.

When another ten minutes had passed and her Coke was gone, Toni stood and stretched her muscles. Needing to move around, she wandered across the lawn to where K-man, a huge silver tin man with moving parts, stood next to a huge rock. Resembling a giant robot standing sentinel over the park, he was mounted on a glass and metal box that had a wheel on the bottom of it that turned to make his feet move. A plaque stated that K-man was dedicated to Ozark children by the Rotary Club of Springfield southeast district.

It was now twelve-forty, and Toni was growing uneasy about John. She wandered past a monster sized rock in the middle of a big circle rimmed by flat rocks and filled with a blue and black shaded layer of ground-up material she knew to be recycled tires.

Definitely worried by now, Toni checked her watch again. It was almost twelve-forty-five. Something wasn't right. Her gut tightened. She knew

John's class wouldn't have gone overtime, and his classroom at Drury was only two blocks from hers at OTC. He was the one who had suggested they meet, so she was sure he had not forgotten. So why hadn't he called? She couldn't wait around any longer. She had to go check on him.

She walked to the top of the hill and picked up her pace. When she got back across Chestnut Expressway, she cut west to Drury Lane and headed to the building where John's class met.

As she hiked up the block, puffing from hurrying in the heat and lugging her bags, Toni spotted a cluster of people at the edge of a parking lot. Two police cars and an ambulance were there. A sense of dread rose in her throat, making her tremble so badly that her satchel slid off her shoulder. She shoved it back up and forced her feet to propel her forward.

When she reached the perimeter of the gathering of spectators, she saw a team of paramedics kneeling on the paved surface, working on someone. Certain somehow that it was John, she edged closer.

A uniformed police officer was dealing with the growing crowd. "Get back, people. Give them room to work."

The policeman near the ambulance was making notes in a small notebook. When he looked up, Toni recognized him as the younger officer who had been at Sequiota Park Saturday. It took a couple of moments to recall his name. Chilton.

"Officer," she called across the cordoned area. "May I speak with you?"

He looked up, frowning. Then he recognized her and started toward her.

"I'm looking for my friend, John Zachary," she said anxiously as he reached her. "The guy who was with my family Saturday when..."

"I know who you mean," the officer cut off her explanation.

"Is he here? He was supposed to meet me for lunch at twelve-fifteen, and he never showed up. Has something happened? I'm worried about him." She ran out of breath.

"He's here. The ambulance just arrived. He's alive," the officer assured her, reading the fear in her face. "But he's hurt. They're getting ready to transport him to the hospital."

Chapter 6

"What happened?" Toni asked in bewilderment. "May I see him?"

The officer hesitated a moment before speaking. "He was jumped and beaten."

Toni's fear escalated to outrage. "You mean he was robbed?"

Officer Chilton shrugged. "We're not exactly sure what happened. He was knocked unconscious. A young couple driving by saw what was happening and called nine-one-one. They stopped and backed up, but by the time they got back to the scene, the perpetrator had fled. They stayed with your friend until help arrived."

Toni was speechless.

He eyed her closely. "Your name is Donovan, right?"

"That's right. I need to see John."

"Come with me."

They crossed the parking lot to where her colleague was being strapped to a gurney. John looked terrible, but he was conscious—barely. One side of his face was badly scraped and swollen and already turning dark. The medics were immobilizing his left arm, strapping it to his chest as if it were broken.

Toni took a deep steadying breath. "Hello, buddy. I came looking for my sandwich."

The slits of John's eyes opened a bit wider as he recognized her voice. "Was coming," he croaked.

"Can you tell us what happened?" she asked, knowing that Officer Chilton was listening at her shoulder.

John moved his mouth carefully. "Someone jumped me from behind." His speech slurred.

"They robbed you?" the officer asked, notebook in hand.

John started to shake his head, but winced and stopped. "Grabbed my arm and started jerking at my lanyard."

Chilton glanced at Toni in puzzlement.

"We carry our flash drives on them," Toni explained, holding hers up to demonstrate.

The officer nodded in understanding.

"I fought," John continued weakly. "We fell. He kept . . .hitting me in the ribs . . .and jerking on my lanyard." He paused before continuing. "Then he . . .slammed my head on the pavement. That's all I remember."

"Do you know if your wallet was taken?" Chilton asked.

John concentrated and shifted his body a little. "I can feel it in my hip pocket."

His unbound right hand moved back and forth across his chest, and then he gasped. "My flash drive's gone!"

"Is that the only thing missing?" Chilton asked.

John reached up and rubbed his forehead. "That's all I had with me, except for the sandwiches. They were in a little brown bag."

"We were meeting for lunch at Jordan Valley Park," Toni explained. "I was bringing the sodas."

Chilton nodded. "Did you see the guy?" he asked John. "Can you give me any kind of description?"

John grimaced. "He was smaller than me, about my height, but thin and strong. I didn't see his face."

"He took you off guard," Toni said, knowing John felt he should have defended himself better.

"Okay, we're ready to go," one of the paramedics announced. He and his partner rolled the gurney to the back of the ambulance.

Toni followed, pulling her cell phone from her purse.

"You calling your brother?" Officer Chilton asked.

Toni turned to meet his gaze and found a tiny smile lurking at the corners of his mouth.

"It's nothing against you," she said. "I just feel like talking things over with Quint. He trusts me. I also intend to call John's wife."

"No offense taken," the young officer responded. He paused a moment. "I like Quint. We chatted over the weekend, and he told me about your involvement in a couple of cases in your hometown. Durbin's off today. He had to get some dental work done. As soon as I'm back at the station, I'll talk to the chief about having Quint help with the case—cases. This makes two incidents where you're involved."

"Thanks," she said, thinking that might make it possible for her to get information, maybe even have some input.

They watched the paramedics close the door of the ambulance and roll away. Most of the spectators had dispersed by now. "Do you think this is in any way connected to Saturday's body discovery?" Chilton asked.

"I don't know," Toni said, shaking her head.

"I understand that your friend discovered a switch of flash drives with the victim. Now his is stolen."

That very thought had been whirling through Toni's mind. "We gave Mr. Campbell's drive to Quint to turn in to the police department." She didn't mention making copies of it.

"What was the one John was wearing?"

"We went to Best Buy, and he bought a new one," she explained. "We …uh, we had been to see Mr. Campbell's widow to ask if she could find John's drive in her husband's things."

The officer frowned and made a quick note. "Did she find it?"

"No, that's why we went shopping for a new one."

"So the thief got a brand new drive with very little, if anything, on it."

"That's right. I need to call John's wife and tell her about this."

"Go ahead. I have to get going." Chilton headed for his cruiser.

Toni decided that calling Jenny, who was back in Clearmount, was more important than talking to Quint.

"John's all right," were the first words out of her mouth when Jenny answered. "There's been an incident, and he's in the hospital, but he's okay." She went over everything she knew about the mugging.

"I'll be on my way in ten minutes," Jenny said. "I should be there by six. Which hospital?"

"They said they were taking him to St. John's."

As soon as they disconnected, Toni hitched her bags onto her shoulder and started back to the OTC campus for her van. She dialed Quint as she walked.

"I'll be heading to work in a little over an hour," he said after she repeated her story for him. "I'll see what I can learn and get back with you later."

"That young Officer Chilton, the one we met Saturday, was at the scene," she added. "He said he's going to talk to your chief about including you on the case."

There was a moment of silence. "That's all right. But don't get it in your head that if—and that's if—I end up on the case, that it gives you detective rights."

"Nor does it deprive me of my rights as a private citizen," she pointed out, slowing and shoving at the bags that were slipping off her shoulder. She veered into the parking lot where her van was parked.

When she arrived at the hospital, Toni went to the desk and asked about John. When told that he was just being admitted to a room and given a number, she rode the elevator up to the next floor. When she found the room, she peeked inside to see a nurse walking away from the bed. John was asleep.

"Is he all right?" she asked the nurse in a whisper.

The buxom, gray haired woman nodded and stepped out into the hallway. "He's fine. Are you a relative?"

"A close friend. I've called his wife, and she's on her way."

"Good. Seeing her will make him feel better."

"What are his injuries?" Toni asked.

"Besides the broken arm, he has some bruised ribs and a knot on the back of his head. He needs sleep more than anything right now."

Toni exhaled in relief. "Then I'll go home and check on my boys. I'll come back about the time his wife should arrive."

When she arrived at the Donovan house, the boys were in the driveway shooting baskets at the hoop Dan Donovan had attached above the garage door for them. She parked at the curb rather than interfere with their play.

Both boys raced to meet her. "Hey, Mom, tryouts for the basketball team are August sixth and seventh. Jimmy Hayes called and told me it's gonna be announced in the paper next week," Gabe told her breathlessly. Jimmy Hayes was a classmate and friend whose parents both taught at the Clearmount School, and his dad was the assistant junior high basketball coach. Gabe and Jimmy were excited about entering junior high and playing on the team.

"Well, I'm glad to see you're practicing," she told her grinning eldest.

She looked to Garrett. "Are you starting to like the game?"

"Yeah, some," he said. "But I still think I might decide to play golf instead."

"You have plenty of time to think about it."

"Grandpa said he'll take us to eat at the Pasta House tonight," Garrett added, eyes shining.

Toni grinned. Dan was a pushover where his grandsons were concerned. He loved Kathy's girls, but he saw them a lot more—and they didn't care about sports.

"You're pretty late," Gabe observed.

"There's a good reason," she said. "John was hurt and taken to the hospital."

His face expressed shock. "What happened?"

She gave them a brief explanation. "Would you mind if I don't go to supper with you and your grandparents? I'd like to go to the hospital and visit John when Jenny gets there."

"No problem," Gabe assured her. "You need to see about John."

"Why did somebody hurt him?" Garrett wanted to know.

"I think they tried to rob him," she said evasively.

"Did they?"

"The only thing taken was his flash drive," she admitted. Her youngest son was way too intuitive for his age.

Garrett frowned. "That's weird."

"You're right. Listen, these bags are getting heavy. Why don't you two shoot some more baskets, and I'll go talk to your grandparents."

*

Toni found her mother-in-law in the kitchen. "The boys said you're eating out tonight, so why are you working in here?" she chided from the doorway.

Barb grinned. "I'm just whipping up a chocolate cake for later."

"I need to talk to you as soon as I get rid of this

stuff." Toni indicated her bags. "I'll be right back."

When she returned to the kitchen and explained about John and wanting to go visit him, Barb was sympathetic. "We'll be glad to look after the boys. But don't you want to eat before going to the hospital?"

Toni shook her head. "His wife is on her way from Clearmount. Since she's alone and worried about her husband, I thought she might let me treat her to a meal."

Barb nodded. "I think that's a nice idea. Dan's at the golf course, but he should be home soon. I hope he can get the garage painted next week."

As usual, Barb's thoughts were reverting quickly to her self-absorbed domestic world. Toni escaped before her mother-in-law could get off on some zany topic that she didn't have the patience to listen to right then.

"I have to grade some papers. If you need help with anything, just call me," she said as she headed back to the guest bedroom she had been given.

Once inside, she booted her laptop and pulled up Jesse's files she had copied in a folder. This time she worked through each file one at a time, studying them in careful detail. There were four files named CLASS, with a date next to the title. She took time to open each one and examine it. They were just what the names implied, assignments for each day of the class.

When she finished checking all the text files, Toni saw that the next four files were Excel spreadsheets. The file names were just two letters. The second one, JC, was the one she and John had randomly opened before. The file name struck her as nothing more complicated than Jesse Campbell's personal initials. She knew it contained a list of receipts and expenses. She tackled the others alphabetically. When she opened BP, she saw a table of names, addresses and amounts. There were only three or four names on the list, but they repeated multiple times down the page. She clicked the print button.

Next she opened KC. It was a similar list. She printed it. Then she did the same with OT. The remaining half dozen files were articles Jesse Campbell had saved from the Internet that looked like research for class assignments.

Finished, Toni flexed her shoulders and shut down the computer. She called Jenny again, and wasn't surprised when she got no answer. There would be no cell service through a good part of the terrain between Clearmount and Springfield. She would try again soon.

After visiting with Barb Donovan for a few minutes, she called again and reached Jenny. "Where are you?"

"I'm just passing through Mountain View," Jenny said.

"You should make it to the hospital in about an hour and a half. I'll meet you there."

Traffic was sparse, so Toni made good time. When she entered the building at six o'clock and saw no sign of Jenny, she went directly to John's room—and found her sitting in a chair next to John's bed. She rose and greeted Toni with a hug. Only four eleven, she barely came to Toni's chin. "Thanks for calling me."

John was propped up against the raised head of his bed. His face looked worse than before, dark bruises and deep scratches standing out against his pale skin. His left arm was in a cast. "Hi, Toni," he said weakly.

Jenny poured iced water from the plastic pitcher on the bedside table into a glass and stuck a straw in it. "You sound parched," she said, holding the glass near his lips and bending the straw toward him.

John sipped. "That's good. Want to sign it?" he asked Toni, nodding at his cast. His voice was slurred, and the grin he attempted came off kind of crooked. Toni guessed he was on some strong medication.

"Sure." She reached into her purse for a pen and scrawled her name on it with a flourish. Giving it a gentle pat, she stepped back.

"Now, tell me how you're doing—and be honest," she ordered.

"I've felt better," he said, enunciating slowly and licking his lips. "But I'm okay. The doctor said he's keeping me overnight for observation, but I should be dismissed in the morning. I told him I need to be out by eight so I can make it to class."

Toni frowned. "Don't push. I'm sure your instructor will understand."

John's mouth twisted. "I'll be okay, but I can't afford to get behind. It's a tough class."

Toni took a deep breath. "Do you feel like looking at something?"

He shifted further up on his pillow, and Jenny hustled to rearrange the pillows behind him. "What do you have?" he mumbled.

Toni pulled the printed sheets from her purse and handed them to him. "I printed these files from Campbell's flash drive. What do they look like to you? I didn't print the one we looked at earlier."

John studied the top sheet. He frowned and flipped to the next one, and then the next. "They look like lists of payments to people," he said, speaking slowly and carefully. "But I see no evidence of what they're for."

"The file names don't indicate what they're for either. They're just two letters that make me think they're initials of some kind."

"I don't know what they are," John said tiredly, letting his head loll back against the pillow. "But I don't have a good feeling about them. I'm too tired to think."

"You mean they seem secretive?"

He nodded and closed his eyes.

Toni took the papers as they slipped from his fingers.

Jenny stood watching as her husband slept. "Just what he needs," she said, raising a hand to rub his brow. She withdrew it and returned to her seat.

Quint stepped inside the room. In full uniform, he did a cop-like visual of the room, taking in John's sleeping form and Jenny's presence next to him. "Hi, Jenny. I'm sorry about all this." He had known them for years.

Jenny's smile was tight. "Thanks, Quint. I hope you guys catch whoever did this."

"We're working on it," he assured her. "As a matter of fact, I'm here in an official capacity." He turned to Toni. "How about we go someplace else to talk and let John sleep without us disturbing him."

"You guys go ahead. I'll keep an eye on John," Jenny said.

They went to the waiting room down the hall. "Do you think this incident is connected to the Sequiota Park death?" he asked when they were seated on a short sofa.

Toni hesitated. "Are you assigned to the case now?"

He nodded. "The chief talked to me when I reported for my shift today. He said Brad Chilton indicated he would welcome any extra input I might be able to contribute. I agreed because it'll make it easier for me to keep an eye on you."

Toni started to tell him she didn't need a watch dog, but he raised a palm for silence.

"I know you're pretty good at digging out facts and piecing them together. You've proven that back home. But I don't want you playing detective and putting yourself in danger."

Toni gave him an open mouthed look. "You know I can't stay out of this. You don't think John got mugged for a school research paper. Neither do I."

"You have no business nosing around," he insisted firmly.

"But it's personal for me," she argued. "My son found the body, and now my friend has been attacked."

Quint studied her. "So you *do* think the two incidents are connected."

"My gut says they are."

"What else tells you that?"

"The fact that someone was after that flash drive. Someone thought it was Jesse Campbell's."

"I was afraid of that," Quint admitted with a long heave of breath. "I haven't had an opportunity to see what's on the one I took to the department for John."

Toni hoped her face didn't give her away. She didn't think having a copy of it should get her in trouble, but she didn't want to test the issue. She decided to go on the offense. "Okay, you've questioned me. What information do you have that you can share with me?"

"Not much. I haven't seen an autopsy report yet. The only thing I can really tell you at this point is that they found Campbell's car. The techs are still going over it."

"Where was it found?"

"Right there at the park. When it cleared out in the evening, a late model black Suburban was still sitting at the north end of the parking lot. The plates checked. Do you have any ideas?"

Toni shook her head. "I have more questions than ideas. I tend to think of the killer as a man, but I know that women can be formidable enemies, and there are some pretty strong ones around. Strength probably isn't as important as timing, catching him off guard. I'm guessing it was an act of rage, and it could have been anyone."

He grinned. "You're no help."

"Who benefits from his death?" Toni asked, needing to air some of the questions plaguing her. "Who are his survivors? What was he mixed up in? Who were his friends?" She didn't mention that she had already met his widow.

"I need to find out those things. I also need to get moving," Quint said. "I just wanted to touch base with you and check on John." He got to his feet and headed down the hall.

When Toni returned to the room, John was still sleeping. Jenny looked like she was about to fall off her chair from exhaustion. "You've had a long day, and John's fine. Why don't you let me take you to get something to eat? I'm hungry," she added in persuasion.

Jenny sighed and gathered her purse. "I am hungry."

"You're also tired. You've got to take care of yourself. Why don't you spend the night with me after we eat? My in-laws have plenty of room, and they would welcome you."

"No." Jenny shook her head in refusal. "I'm sure the friends John is staying with would take me in as well, but I want to stay here with John. I'll sleep on a sofa in the waiting room."

Jenny was small, but she was as stubborn as any redhead of Toni's acquaintance. She didn't argue with her any more.

It was dusky when they walked out of the hospital. The air was getting a damp feel that made Toni think rain might come during the night. They got into her van and headed for Appleby's. As she navigated the streets, Toni put Jesse Campbell from her mind and concentrated on Jenny.

"John's tough, both physically and mentally. He's going to be stiff and sore for a few days, but he'll be fine," she said, hoping to reassure her friend.

Jenny faced Toni, her expression troubled. "Do

you think this is related to that murder at the park?"

Toni didn't want to lie, but she didn't want Jenny to worry. So she hedged. "I doubt there's a connection, but I'll keep in touch with Quint and make sure the police keep John safe if it turns out there is."

After a meal accompanied by very little conversation, Toni drove around by the Donovan house and picked up a pillow and comforter for Jenny to take to the hospital with her.

Chapter 7

When she returned to the house about nine o'clock, Toni stepped out of her shoes at the door and wiggled her toes to get the kinks out of them. Resisting the temptation to go straight to the computer, she stopped in the den to chat briefly with Dan and Barb. Then she went to the bedroom where the boys were playing a video game. She sat on one of the twin beds and tucked her feet up under her.

"Is that a new game?" she asked.

"Uh huh. Grandpa got it for us," Gabe said, not taking his eyes from the screen.

"Are you guys having a good time this week?"

"It's fun, but it's better at home with our own stuff," Garrett said, also focused on the game.

"I'll take you home Thursday afternoon, but I hope you'll be polite to your grandparents and let them enjoy this time with you until then."

"Okay," Gabe said nonchalantly.

Garrett just nodded.

"Well, it looks like you don't need me. I guess I'll go on and leave you alone."

They paused the game and turned to face her. "We know you're busy, and we're not babies. We can take care of ourselves," Gabe said in his most serious manner.

Toni's head tilted, and her mouth curved in a half frown. "Well, it's nice to know that you can take care of yourselves, but it's not so nice to find out that I'm not needed."

Both boys grinned, got up from the floor, and gave her a hug.

"Now I feel better," she said, grinning. "Okay, finish your game. Then you probably should take your baths and go to bed. If you keep staying up late at night and sleeping in mornings, it's going to kill you when school starts."

They just laughed.

"I hope you catch that man's killer before you finish your class and go home for good," Garrett said, his small face creased with concern.

"I'm not supposed to be the one figuring that out," Toni reminded him.

He shrugged. "But you *can*, so you *should*."

His childlike logic and faith in her was touching. "You really think so, huh?"

His head bobbed.

"Okay, I guess I'll go look at some stuff on the computer." She uncurled her legs and eased off the bed. "Come tell me good night when you're ready for bed."

A couple of minutes later, while the computer booted, Toni sat studying what she had printed from Campbell's files. One of the lists of addresses struck her as being Springfield streets. She didn't live here, but she had spent quite a bit of time navigating those streets and knew her way around pretty well. One of the addresses was on Glenstone, clearly a Springfield thoroughfare.

She put that list aside and studied the other two. Neither of them had anything familiar. Since Campbell had lived in Ozark, she got out the Ozark street map she had printed when checking how to find Mrs. Campbell. It didn't take long for one of the lists to correlate. All of the streets were there.

She stared at the third list, thinking. Suddenly she remembered Nicole saying she had been in Campbell's class in Branson. She went to the computer and located a street map of Branson. Each street name on the list was there. She labeled each list and printed the Branson map.

*

Wednesday morning Toni crawled out of bed and called Jenny first thing. When she got no answer, she figured Jenny was still at the hospital where she couldn't use her cell phone. She called the hospital and asked to be connected to John's room. She was about to hang up on the sixth ring when he answered. "Zachary here." He sounded short of breath.

"Toni here," she echoed his breathless manner. "How are you feeling?"

"About how you would expect," he said, speaking clearer now. "I'm getting dressed, and having an arm in a cast isn't helping. I'm being dismissed, and Jenny's going to chauffeur me to class."

"Do you need me to pick you up afterward?" Toni assumed Jenny needed to get back to Clearmount. As for herself, she had lab until one o'clock today, and John finished class at noon. Maybe Barb or Dan could get him for her.

"No," he interrupted her thoughts. "Jenny is going to stay here until I finish class tomorrow and drive us home for the weekend in her car. That means I'll need to hitch a ride back up here with you Sunday afternoon. By then I should be able to drive with this cast."

"Your company would be welcome. You know that," she assured him.

When they disconnected, Toni felt better. By seven-thirty she had dressed, eaten a bowl of cereal with her in-laws, packed herself a sandwich, and headed for class. The hoped-for rain had not materialized, and the day was another hot, dry one.

"Forty-five percent of the blood in females is red," she lectured the class, speaking of packed red blood cells. "In males, fifty-five percent is red."

Nicole Warren's hand shot up. "So is a midget's blood only about twenty percent?" she asked when Toni acknowledged her.

The room went silent, and then someone snickered.

"Oh, duh!" Nicole groaned, covering her eyes with a hand. "I can't believe I asked that."

Toni couldn't either. Nicole was a good student. "We all get ahead of our brains once in a while," she said with a grin, struggling to not laugh. "Now we know you're human."

By one o'clock Toni was tired and hungry. She bought a soda from the vending machine and ate her sandwich while putting the classroom in order for the next day.

When she left the building, she called Gabe and told him she needed to run some errands and wasn't sure what time she would be home.

"Go look for the bad guy," he said matter-of-factly, knowing her so well it was scary. "We'll ask Grandpa to set up the sprinkler so we can play outside in the water." He disconnected.

Toni laughed and muttered, "Sounds like they have plans and won't miss me."

When she was in the van Toni pulled out her list and street map for Ozark. Noting that two of the addresses were only a few blocks apart, she decided to start with them.

She exited the highway at the Ozark turnoff and drove into the residential area where she thought she needed to be. The streets were lined with trees, the homes large, modern, and immaculately landscaped and maintained. She found the street she was looking for, and then the house number. A high wooden fence across the backyard made her think there was probably a pool back there. She parked on the street, made her way up the walk to the wide porch that ran across the front of the house, and rang the bell.

The woman who came to the door was polished and somewhat haughty looking—definitely a high maintenance lady. She wore an expensive designer dress and shoes, her hair was carefully highlighted, and her makeup professionally applied.

"May I speak to Mr. Vince Harcourt?" Toni asked, wondering if the woman's husband was as intimidating as her.

The woman directed a visual inspection that approached disdain over Toni. "What do you want with him?"

"I want to talk to him about. . ."

Just then a young man came striding through the doorway behind the woman. "Is that for me, Mother?"

"It's some woman asking for you." She continued to stand in the doorway, like a barricade between her son and a potential threat.

The young man, who appeared to be no more than seventeen or eighteen, took his mother's arm and edged his way between her and the doorway. He wore a monogrammed polo shirt, pristine Dockers, and shiny loafers. His dark brown hair was fashionably long, and he had wide shoulders and a tall lean body. Toni's instant impression was one of affluence and a young man who knew just how good-looking he was.

Scowling, his eyes raked over her. "Hello," he said cautiously. "What do you want?"

"Uh, I'm a recruiter for Missouri State University," she improvised hurriedly. A kid was the last thing she had been expecting. "I have a list of names Coach Campbell was recommending for scholarships, and I'm checking around to see if his recommended players are still interested or have made other plans." It was lame, but she was deducing that the athletic looking young man was involved in school sports.

His faint smile held a touch of arrogance. He took a swig from the plastic bottle of water he carried. "MSU was one of the schools Coach thought I should consider."

"So I can still consider you a candidate," Toni said in a manner she hoped fit her assumed role.

"I guess so," he allowed. "But with Coach gone, I have to see how this season goes."

"Well, I hope you'll keep us in your radar," she said, anxious to get away from there before she dug a deeper hole for herself.

"Too bad he's dead," the young man said, not sounding overly grieved. His attitude struck her more as one of being personally inconvenienced.

"I'll keep your name on the list," she said. "Thank you for your time."

As she walked away, Toni felt two pairs of eyes boring into her back. She didn't waste any time scrambling into her van and driving away. She now suspected that all the names on that list—and maybe all the lists—were teenage students. But she wanted to be certain. She drove around until she found the next address. The house was older than where she had just been, but it still spoke of affluence.

This time she was not surprised when a middle-aged woman answered the doorbell. She was tall and thin, almost to the point of gauntness. Her sallow skin and lank brown hair spoke of illness. "Yes? May I help you?"

"I'm looking for Mr. Tim Rutherford," she said politely.

The woman shook her head. "He's out with a friend right now. I have no idea where they are, or when he'll be home."

"That's all right. I'll get back to him later."

"May I tell him who's looking for him?"

"Tell him the recruiter from SMU," she said briefly. "Thank you for your time." She turned and hurried back to her van.

Toni was satisfied that Tim was another teen, but she decided to make one more stop. She pulled to the curb a few blocks up the street and studied her map. It looked like someone by the name of Dean Patrick lived only a few blocks from there. She put the van back into motion.

At this address she had her story ready for another mother, but a boy answered the doorbell. He looked even younger than the first young man. About five foot nine, he had a stocky build. His eyes were dark, his hair a little too long and stringy. The crotch of his pants hung nearly to his knees, and his long tailed tee shirt hung outside the pants. He sported a sparse goatee on his chin. Behind him, a television blared rock music.

"Whatcha want?" the kid asked flippantly.

"I'm looking for Mr. Dean Patrick," she said.

"Who's that, Dean?" a woman called from the next room.

"It's for me, Mom," he called back.

"Okay," she answered.

The young man stepped out onto the porch, as if he didn't want his mother to overhear.

Toni repeated her recruiter spiel, and then asked, "What year of school are you in now?" She wanted to ask him why his name was on a list of kids who appeared to be getting money from their coach, but she didn't think she would get a straight answer. And it might alert him if there was something crooked going on.

"I'm just a sophomore," he said. "So I'm surprised to hear I'm already on your list. Guess I'm better than I thought if you're already looking at me."

Toni took a deep breath. "Your coach must have thought a lot of you. How many years have you played for him?"

"Just this past year," he said. "We moved here last summer just before school started. I was nervous about trying out for the team, but I'm glad I did. I was a guard and got quite a bit of playing time. I also made first string catcher for the baseball team."

"Your teams had a good year, right?"

He grinned, slapping his right fist into his open left palm. "We sure did. Our basketball team won our district, and I won the conference gold glove in baseball."

"How long was Coach Campbell with the district?"

His eyes narrowed. "I think this was his third season here. Why?"

"I was just thinking he must have been a pretty good coach," she evaded. She had hoped to get the boy to say something that would give her a clue as to why Campbell was keeping track of payments to a bunch of kids. "Were you close to your coach?"

"Both my coaches," he clarified. "I played baseball for Coach Jolson and basketball for Coach Campbell."

"Did you ever wash his car or do odd jobs for Coach Campbell?"

He gave her a look of suspicion. "Naw, I'm too lazy to do stuff like that," he laughed it off.

He wasn't going to clear up anything for her. "Well, thanks for talking to me. I'll keep your name on the list."

Once in the van, Toni looked back at the house and saw Dean still standing on the porch, watching her. She drove away, more positive than ever that something was wrong about all this. Those boys were being paid money. But for what? The possibilities made her blood boil.

She glanced at her watch. It was only two-thirty. She had time to talk to Mrs. Campbell again. She drove to the Excelsior Gardens apartments and parked in front of the Campbell unit. Young children frolicked on the playground equipment nearby, their mothers sitting on a bench keeping watch over them. Toni marched to the door and rang the bell.

When the door opened a crack, Sheila Campbell's wan face stared across the chain at her. "You're back?" The tone wasn't outright hostile, but it wasn't welcoming.

"I was in the area and thought I'd drop by and see if you've had any luck finding my friend's flash drive," Toni said, trying to strike a tone that would gain the woman's confidence.

Sheila seemed to wrestle with herself for a moment. Then she slid the chain from its latch and opened the door. But she didn't invite her inside. "I didn't find it," she said flatly.

"I'm hoping you can help me figure out something."

A flicker of interest crossed her face. "How?"

"Well, you're the only person who knew that John and I were looking for his flash drive. But yesterday John was attacked and his new drive taken."

Sheila stared at her, and then she blinked. Her eyes traveled over Toni as she absorbed the statement. Her head shook back and forth. "I can't believe this."

"Do you have any idea who else might have wanted that flash?"

Sheila bit down on her lower lip. "Well," she said at last, "someone else came here looking for it. But I never dreamed he would hurt anyone."

"Can you tell me the name of the person?"

The woman just stood there, as if her brain had quit functioning.

"I need to know who it was," Toni repeated urgently. "John is in the hospital, and I don't want him attacked again."

Sheila gulped and firmed her shoulder. "It was Jesse's bookkeeper."

Toni's heart sank. He was the guy whose name Sheila couldn't remember before. "Have you remembered his name?"

She nodded. "When he stopped by and I saw him, I remembered. It's Barry Kuzman. Jesse called him his scorekeeper."

"Thank you. I appreciate your help."

"I'm sorry. He said Jesse was supposed to give him some important information, but it wasn't on the flash drive he gave him. His story was sort of like yours. You both said you had the wrong drive, so I thought you would want to get them swapped back. I gave him your names. I'm sorry," she repeated.

Toni's gut said the woman was innocent of harmful intent. Her husband may have been involved in something fishy, but she hadn't known about it. "If the man returns, I hope you won't mention this visit," she said gently.

"I won't," Sheila promised quickly.

*

As Toni approached her in-laws' home, she recognized Quint's navy pickup at the curb. When she pulled into the drive, he hopped from the truck, loped to her van, and slid into the seat beside her. He was dressed for work.

"Where have you been?" he demanded. "I've been trying to call you."

Surprised, Toni pulled her cell phone from her purse and checked it. It was turned off. "I guess I accidentally turned it off. Sorry. What's so important?"

He heaved a sigh. "I know you too well. What have you been up to?"

"I checked on John. He was dismissed from the hospital this morning. Jenny picked him up and drove him to class. He's really sore from the bruised ribs, and he's fighting headaches from having his head nearly cracked open. The cast on his arm makes driving tough, if not impossible."

"Toni!" Quint slapped the dash with a palm. "Stop rambling and answer me. Have you been out playing detective?"

She froze, startled by his sudden outburst. She couldn't keep guilt from showing on her face. Feeling suddenly trapped, she jabbed the button to lower her window. Hastily gathering her wits, she faced her brother. "I went back to see the victim's widow again."

"Again? Give me the whole story."

"Monday afternoon John and I looked her up. We explained how John and Jesse's flash drives got mixed up and asked if she would look for John's drive in Jesse's things."

Quint's eyes pierced her. "Did she?"

"Yes, but she couldn't find it. We gave her our names and phone numbers and asked her to call one of us if she found it."

He thought that over for a moment. "Okay, that was Monday. Then John was mugged yesterday. When you realized that, since the only thing taken from John was his new flash drive, and the widow was the only person who knew about the accidental switch, you thought she might have talked to someone about it. You went back to ask her. How am I doing?"

Toni gave him a wry grimace. "Pretty good."

He sighed. "Okay, I admit it was good thinking. What did you learn?"

"Jesse's accountant had been to see her. Jesse must have seen him, probably after he and John left the lab Thursday, and given him a flash drive. But it didn't have whatever was supposed to be on it. He wanted her to find the right drive in Jesse's things and give it to him."

"She told him she had already looked for it for someone else and couldn't find it. What else did she tell you?"

"She gave the guy our names."

Silence reigned for several long moments. "So John was attacked specifically for that drive and whatever was on it."

Toni nodded. "That's what I think."

"I hope she gave you that accountant's name."

Now she grinned, relaxing a bit. "She did. She couldn't remember it when I asked her Monday, but when she saw the guy face to face, it came to her. She said Jesse called him his scorekeeper, and his name is Barry Kuzman."

Quint yanked out his notebook and jotted a note. "I'll check him out when I get to the station. Now tell me where else you went. Who else did you dig up?"

Toni took a deep breath, tense again. "I looked up some other addresses."

"What addresses? Where did you get them?"

She felt his radar intensify. "From some lists," she said vaguely.

"What lists?"

"Campbell was recording payments to some people. I wanted to see if I could find out what the coach was paying them for."

Quint shook his head, his eyes closing for a moment. "You made a copy of that drive before you gave it to me, didn't you? I should have known. I saw those lists last night and was planning to work on them tonight."

"What I found was kind of weird," she said, not denying the charge.

He sighed in resignation. "You're obviously one step ahead of us. What was weird?"

"One of the lists seemed to be Ozark addresses. The two places where I found someone home, the names proved to be kids."

His brow furrowed. "Kids? You mean high school kids?"

She nodded. "The two I found were teenage boys."

He made another note. "You better give me their names. There's no use duplicating what you've done."

She told him who she had seen and her impressions.

"You're just not going to leave this alone, are you?" he said when she finished. "Well, be sure you keep me in the loop. I've told my chief about your involvement in those cases back home and your friendship with the chief of police there. But I don't know what he's going to say when I pass along this information and he learns that you got the jump on us."

Toni squared her shoulders and met his gaze. "Okay, you've grilled me. Now you give me something. What do you know that's helpful?"

He grinned. "I only have one thing. I had to work overtime, didn't get off until six a.m. this morning. An autopsy report came in, and I got a look at it just before I left."

She was instantly intrigued.

"Our victim was thirty-five years old. The coroner's notes say that variables such as water temperature and rigor indicate he had been in the water eight to twelve hours. That means he must have been killed sometime between ten p.m. and two a.m."

"Did he die from the stabbing, or from drowning?"

"There was a little water in his lungs, but the stabbing would have been fatal in any case. There was one puncture wound on the left chest that caught the heart. That was the fatal one. There was another smaller puncture in the right chest and one between the fourth and fifth ribs that collapsed his lungs."

"Any idea about the weapon used?"

"The report says the depth, shape and size of the

wounds indicate that the knife used was single edged with a blade six or seven inches long."

"That sounds like an average hunting knife."

"Probably," he agreed. "The coroner noted that the angle of the wounds could indicate a killer near the same height as the victim, but that's just a guess. It could be affected by the position of the victim and killer, such as if one of them was crouching."

He reached for the door latch. "One more thing. Durbin's report confirms your crime scene theory. They believe he was stabbed on the path and pushed into the water. There was no evidence of a big struggle, so he was taken by surprise and wasn't afraid of his killer."

"That means he knew him. Yes, I know it could have been a woman. But I tend to think of the killer as a man. It's just the picture my mind insists on forming."

He shrugged. "That's a good guess. Durbin and Chilton think the killer probably left through the woods. I've got to go or I'll be late for work."

"Will you let me know what you find out about the bookkeeper name I gave you?" she asked as he slid out of the van.

"Yeah, I'll do that," he agreed. "I'm also going to do my best to get my hands on Campbell's computer." He pushed the door shut and headed back to his pickup.

Toni gathered her things and entered the house. She took her bags to her room and dumped them on the bed. As she was returning to the living room, a strident shriek sounded from the backyard. It was her mother-in-law.

Chapter 8

Toni rushed to the door and out onto the deck. The sight that met her eyes was one that only a mother could handle.

One boy—it had to be Gabe, since it was the taller—took off in a run and made a headlong dive into the small trench that ran along the front edge of Dan's garden. The second, shorter boy followed. The abandoned garden hose on the lawn told her they had used it to fill the trench with water and create a mudslide.

"Oh! Oh!" Barb Donovan repeated over and over, wringing her hands. "You boys are a mess. Your mother will have a fit."

Toni wasn't sure what kind of fit to have. When they stood, clad only in shorts, they resembled chocolate coated gingerbread boys.

At that moment both boys noted her presence on the deck. They stood immobile, their eyes gleaming from behind muddy faces. Toni stared back at them, not sure whether to scream or laugh. Her eyes caught the sight of her father-in-law sitting in a lawn chair next to the house. One eye winked ever so slightly, telling her he had okayed—or been a conspirator to—

their muddy adventure.

Toni didn't say a word. Instead, she walked over and picked up the nozzle of the water hose. Before the boys figured out what was happening, she turned on the water and advanced on them.

"Don't you move," she ordered, aiming a stream directly onto Gabe's chest. She pressed a thumb over one side of the nozzle, making the water spray. "If you're going to act like pigs, you'll be treated like pigs."

"Oink! Oink!" Gabe snorted, backing away.

"I said don't move," she repeated loudly. "That means both of you," she added as Garrett mimicked his brother.

Against their protests she aimed the hose at their heads, knowing she would never get all the mud out of their hair. "You're not going inside until you're clean enough to not make a mess of the house."

Barb Donovan swept her hands upward in disgust and went to the house. With a final *humph* she slammed the door.

Both boys yelped and complained as Toni hosed them, until they realized it was more fun than the sprinkler and turned it into a game. By the time they were reasonably clean, Toni's hair and clothes were drenched.

"I think you guys should entertain yourselves without shocking the life out of your grandmother," she admonished as she twisted the knob to shut off the water.

"She'll get over it," Dan said, taking the hose. "A little dirt is healthy. It means they're normal boys." His grin was lopsided.

He looped the hose onto its mount on the side of the garage, and then returned to the yard. "You boys better go shower while I convince your grandma that a little mud won't stunt your growth or offend our neighbors. Be sure you get squeaky clean so she'll feed us."

A man of few words, her father-in-law's comments amused Toni. In retirement he was getting more laid back all the time.

The boys laughed and scampered around to the garage door so they could enter the house through the utility room.

*

After everyone was in bed that evening, Toni propped herself up against the headboard and called Kyle. "When do you plan to be home for the weekend?" she asked when he answered.

"I should be there between six and seven Friday evening. What about you and the boys?"

"I have to set up for Monday's lab after tomorrow's exam. It may be two or three o'clock by the time I can head for Clearmount."

As they went over their plans for the weekend Toni basked in the sound of her husband's deep voice. He still made her feel warm and safe. They didn't always agree on everything, but they could agree to disagree and had learned to compromise.

She brought him up to date on the murder case and Quint's assignment to it. He laughed when she told him about the boys and their mudslide.

"How has your week been?" she asked after being assured that she shouldn't let his mother's persnickety-ness bother her.

"It was fine," he said, seeming to measure his words. "The company is having some problems. I'm not sure how serious they are, but they seem to be making a number of changes, shifting personnel and flights."

"If you learn anything more, you can tell me about it when you get home Friday."

Toni slept well that night, and the next morning's exam was routine. She put the papers in her satchel to grade over the weekend and focused on setting up for Monday's lab. She was almost finished at twelve-thirty when her cell phone rang.

"Hi, Quizzy," Quint greeted her with the childhood nickname he and Bill had given her after hearing their parents refer to their boys as dynamos and their daughter as inquisitive.

"Yeah, what's up?" She placed a microscope on a table with one hand while holding the phone with the other. "Got any news or progress?"

"You're in luck. I do have an item of interest. I checked around about the dead coach's scorekeeper. Barry Kuzman is a bookkeeper all right. He's a bookie."

Light bulbs started flashing in Toni's brain. "Do you think Campbell was betting on things he shouldn't have been?"

"That's a real possibility," Quint said, his tone sounding grim. "I'm worried that he was a heavy gambler. Being a coach puts all kinds of significance into that."

"You think he was getting inside information?"

"There's always that possibility. Coaches also do some officiating."

Toni had heard and read stories of point shaving and paying officials to make calls that would affect point spreads or game outcomes.

"I know you're headed out of town, and I just wanted to touch base before you leave," he said, interrupting her reflections. "See you next week."

It was two-thirty by the time Toni and the boys were on their way home. Conversation was minimal, and the drive began to melt away. It felt good when they reached the outskirts of Clearmount. Toni had grown up here, gone away to college, and then returned home to teach. She enjoyed visiting in Springfield and other cities, but she had never found any place she would rather live than in her hometown. She realized that many people would laugh at, or hate, small town life, but she was a small town girl at heart. She belonged here.

As she drove past the school just beyond the city limits, Toni's cell phone rang.

"Hey, where are you?" her brother, Bill, asked. "I've been trying to get you. I miss the sluggers." His chuckle implied that she wasn't missed.

"I think I'll hang up on you."

"Don't do that," he shot back. Then his tone gentled. "If you're just getting in, I figure you're tired and haven't eaten. If you want to meet me at the Zinger, I'll buy."

She wasn't about to turn down such an offer. "You're a life saver. See you in five minutes."

She shoved the phone back in her purse. "Bill's taking us to eat," she told the boys.

Bill was waiting for them in front of the restaurant when they arrived. He lived there in

Clearmount, and their mother liked to refer to him as her streetwalker, which was quite literally what he did as a mailman.

Over dinner Toni and Bill caught up on events of the past week. While she related the story about finding the coach's body, Bill's expression turned pensive. "Since then you've been snooping, haven't you?"

"She has to, Uncle Bill," Gabe said. "You know she has to find the truth about what happened." His eyes were round with sincerity, his speech matter-of-fact.

"It's my fault," Garret said more quietly. "I found the man, so she wants to be sure I'm safe."

Both boys understood her too well. Toni didn't want Garrett to feel any guilt or responsibility, but she couldn't refute wanting to know he was safe.

"I understand," Bill said. "We all want you safe, but we want her safe, too."

"She will be," Gabe insisted. "She's careful."

Bill's gaze speared her. "You *will* be careful, won't you? You're the only sister I have."

"I'll be very careful," she promised. At least he wasn't demanding that she close her eyes to the case or ignore her need to know the truth. Her little brothers had always known how to get her goat—like hiding her belongings or listening in on her phone calls—and delighted in doing so. But there had never been any question of their love for her.

"You said John was jumped and hurt. Was that connected to your murder case?"

Toni nodded. "We have a name that Quint's looking into as a possible suspect."

When they finished eating, Bill paid their bill, and they parted company.

It was now eight-thirty, and Toni was beat. "You guys get your showers and toss your clothes in the laundry," she ordered when they arrived home. "I've got to get a load going."

Surprisingly there was no argument. When she had the washer running, Toni curled up on the sofa with the phone and dialed her principal at his home. "This is Toni Donovan," she said when he answered. "I need a favor."

"I believe I owe you one." Ken Douglas referred to her support when he was considered the prime suspect after their superintendent, with whom he had experienced conflict, was murdered. "What's your problem?"

"I've run into a situation in Springfield, and I need some information." Once again she related the events of the past week, including the assault on John.

"I remember hearing a brief account of that on the news, but I had no idea you were the teacher involved," Ken said. "What kind of information do you need?"

She gave him the victim's identity and the little bit she knew about him. "I'd like to know more details about the man's background."

There was a pause. "I know the principal at Ozark. I met him at a meeting three or four years ago, and we became friends. I'll call him and see what I can learn."

When they disconnected, Toni called her mother and chatted for a while. "You're still planning to leave the boys here when you go back to Springfield, aren't you?" Faye asked before they ended the call.

"If you're still sure you're not tired of them."

"We're enjoying the extra time with them this summer," she assured Toni.

When they disconnected, Toni took a shower and crawled into bed. She fell asleep almost as soon as her head hit the pillow.

The next morning she tackled some housework and put in another load of laundry. When the boys crawled out of bed at nine o'clock, she fed them French toast and bacon. Then they headed for the outdoors and their bikes.

Toni put a roast in the oven and was settled on the sofa grading exams when the phone rang. "Can you come by the school this afternoon?" her principal asked. "I have some information, and I think I'd rather share it in person."

"What time?"

"Can you make it in a couple of hours? I have a meeting in five minutes, but I'll be free by then. Say eleven o'clock?"

When she disconnected, Toni went outside where Gabe and Garrett were shooting baskets in the driveway. "I have to go to the school for a meeting after awhile. Do you boys want to go with me and shoot baskets in the gym?"

Gabe paused, poised for a shot. "The gym sounds good."

Garrett frowned, not so certain. "Oh, all right." He had yet to catch his older brother's fever for basketball.

"We'll leave at a quarter till eleven. Don't disappear on me." She went back inside.

It was convenient living only two miles from the school. Located just outside town, it sat in front of a rolling hillside. Just before eleven Toni pulled into the large parking lot. There were only a few cars on it. Summer school was over, so administrative, office, and custodial staffs were the only ones working.

When they entered the building, the boys went left to the gym while Toni veered right to the high school office. The secretary's desk was unoccupied when she entered the front office. Paula was probably running an errand—or taking a break. If so, Toni couldn't blame her for enjoying the relaxing summer work pace. She would make up for it when school started.

"Come on back," Ken called from the office directly to the rear.

Toni found him at his desk, his laptop open before him.

"Be right with you," he said, typing something. He picked up his mouse, clicked it, and put it back down. Then he pushed the computer aside and smiled across the desk at her.

Toni dropped into the chair facing him. "Thanks in advance for whatever you've spent time ferreting out for me."

Her principal was only three years older than her own thirty-six, dark haired and medium built. His speech tended to be rapid and his mannerisms somewhat nervous, but those had improved since the death of their superintendent who had put so much pressure on him and attempted to fire him over the objections of the school board.

Ken clasped his hands together before him. "I

called Grant Volner. It turns out that he and your victim grew up together in Sedalia."

"That means he knows all about the guy." Toni practically bounced in her seat. "Does he have any idea who killed his friend?"

Ken ran an index finger over his chin. "They were friends for many years, but that relationship ended this past year."

"You mean they had a big fight?"

"I'm not sure what all occurred, but there were some real hard feelings. Jesse Campbell had an affair with Grant's wife, and there was a divorce. Jesse married Grant's ex the week after school was out."

Toni was stunned. "I met Sheila Campbell. She mentioned being married only a few weeks, and she indicated that she didn't get custody of her children in a divorce."

She froze as another thought struck her. "Are you afraid your friend killed Campbell?"

Ken heaved a sigh. "I don't know what to think. I just know how quickly I was considered a suspect when Marsha Carter was killed."

Toni's mind was spinning. "How in the world did all that come about? Oh, never mind. That was a dumb question." She made a dismissive wave with her hand.

"I think that's what Grant is asking himself." Ken leaned forward on his elbows. "All I can tell you is the story he told me, which is probably not the version you'll get anywhere else. When he and Jesse graduated from Smith Cotton High School in Sedalia, they went to MSU in Springfield and roomed together. After completing their undergraduate degrees, Grant in math and Jesse in physical education, they went different directions. Grant took a teaching position in Kansas City, and Jesse became an assistant coach at Glendale there in Springfield, where he had done his student teaching.

"Glendale people must have been impressed with him."

"They were. Grant says everybody thought the guy was talented and headed for greatness as a coach. But it didn't turn out that way."

Ken glanced down at some notes on his desk. "Jesse got married during his first year of teaching, and he and his wife had a baby during the second year. Then he changed jobs, which came as a total surprise to Grant. He thinks there was trouble."

"What kind of trouble?"

"Grant thought his buddy was happy with his job and gave every indication that he meant to spend his career there. Then the next thing he knew, Jesse had resigned. Grant said he asked Jesse about it one day, and Jesse confided to him that some girl had started coming onto him, and, when he rebuffed her, she threatened to publicly accuse him of having an affair with her. He said he explained to the school board what was happening. Grant wasn't sure what else happened, but Jesse left the school at the end of the year. There was never any public story, and Jesse's reputation remained untarnished. He landed a head coaching position at Branson and was there for five years. Then there was a charge of improper conduct with a senior girl, his contract wasn't renewed, and his wife left him—but only for a few days. She had just had another baby, and Grant said he supposes she thought she needed Jesse's help—or he convinced her she did. Anyhow, they went back together."

"It sounds like a pattern of philandering was starting to develop."

"Grant says when Jesse was at Kickapoo…"

"The Chiefs," Toni blurted, interrupting as she remembered the tee shirt Jesse had been wearing when they found him in the lagoon.

Ken nodded. "He spent a full year there, but was terminated in the middle of his second one. This time he failed to find another coaching job."

"But he was teaching this past year," Toni pointed out. "How did he manage that? Oh, I get it. The buddy."

Ken nodded again. "Jesse was out of teaching for two and a half years. Grant said the combination of their friendship and a sad circumstance got him a job. A coach at Grant's school died in a car wreck at the end of September, which put the school in a bind. Grant knew Jesse's history, but he went out on a limb for his old friend. The school had a talented group of boys with great expectations, and they wanted a really good coach for them. Jesse had the reputation of being a guy who could rack up wins, so Grant told his superintendent about him. Because of full disclosure laws the superintendent had to tell the board about Jesse's history as well as his coaching talent, so they knew there could be some risk. But the board was feeling pressure from the community and district to win. They hired him in late October, just before the beginning of basketball season."

Toni grinned, familiar with the ways of human beings and their sports. "Did they win?"

Ken's grin was sardonic. "They did. Jesse Campbell went right to work with them and had a winning year. The next year was also successful. This past year was in full swing when Grant got the shock of his life by discovering that Jesse and his wife were having an affair."

"How did he handle it?"

"He and his wife started divorce proceedings, and he discussed his situation with his superintendent. They met with the board, and it was decided that they would not fire Jesse immediately. They thought he was their best chance at winning and wanted to keep him through the season. Grant went along and kept the story quiet, but he proceeded with the divorce and won custody of his kids. The board let Jesse resign. Grant's wife, who also worked for the district, resigned as well. She got another job in one of the Springfield districts, but Jesse still hadn't found a new job when he was killed. The class he was taking suggests he was planning to apply for an administrative position. Or maybe he just needed something to do during the summer and wanted to be around a school environment. I can't imagine anyone hiring him as a principal with the history he had." He shook his head in confusion.

Toni felt just as confused. "From that story it sounds like your friend isn't the only person who had a score to settle with Jesse Campbell."

"You're right." Ken made a subtle glance at his watch.

Toni excused herself. "I appreciate you taking time to check this for me. I'll go pry my boys out of the gym now."

Chapter 9

When Kyle arrived home that evening, Toni was taking a meat loaf from the oven. She looked up as he came through the door, noting lines of fatigue in his face. She put the dish on the stove top and went to wrap her arms around him. "You look tired."

He gave her a squeeze and a hello kiss. "I had a delay in Chicago, missed lunch, and got caught in St. Louis traffic. How are things going for you?"

"Why don't I save it for after we eat? Go say hi to the boys and take a shower. By that time I'll have everything on the table."

During the meal they talked baseball, local politics, and about the boys' week with Kyle's parents. After Gabe and Garrett went to their room that evening, Toni and Kyle settled in front of the television.

Ignoring the ball game, Toni studied her husband. His participation in dinner conversation had seemed forced. Now he sat staring at the television as if lost in outer space.

"What's the matter?" she asked softly.

He gave his head a little shake and swung around to face her, his expression troubled. "Do you have any idea how expensive our bills will be over the rest of this year?"

It wasn't like him to worry about money. They both had good jobs, and they were good managers of their finances. She considered his question. "Well, the miles on my van are getting too high, and it's not getting the greatest gas mileage. We might need to replace it, but it won't bankrupt us. Remember, I'm picking up some nice extra change from this summer class."

He stared at her a long moment, and then a small grin emerged. "Okay, wise woman, no worrying tonight. We'll deal with it when we have to."

"We're both tired. Let's go to bed early," she suggested. "The boys will crawl in when they're ready."

He stood, pulling her up with him. "It's good to be home."

Saturday passed pleasantly. Toni still sensed that Kyle was troubled, but she didn't press. He was so uncharacteristically quiet and introspective that she found herself wondering if she had done something to upset him.

That evening after the boys had gone outdoors, Kyle settled in the recliner before the television like the night before. But when Toni finished clearing up the kitchen and joined him, he hit the off button on the remote and faced her.

"My job may be in jeopardy," he said bluntly. "All week there have been rumors floating around about cutbacks and job reassignments. A friend in human resources tipped me that I might end up on long haul duty and have to move to the coast."

Toni turned to face him more directly, unsure how to respond. She didn't want to move and have to give up her job there in Clearmount. But she didn't want Kyle to feel even more pressured by having his wife refuse to go with him if he faced a definite choice. They were a team, and they had to decide—together—what was right for them.

"I'll be honest and say I hope that doesn't happen," she said at last. "But if it does, we'll work it out together."

Relief was visible in the relaxation of his muscles. "I thought that's how you would react, but it's a relief to hear it."

*

Sunday after church, Toni changed into comfortable slacks and a cotton blouse, packed her bags, and had lunch at the restaurant with her parents. Shortly after she, Kyle, and the boys returned to the house, she told them good-bye and drove out to Misty Valley Estates to pick up John.

Her anger about the murder case was now joined by worry about Kyle's job. She was confident she could find a teaching job elsewhere. There might be hurdles, like meeting extra certification requirements in a different state, but she could do it if necessary. What she wasn't so sure about was immediate concerns. The boys were back at home, surely out of harm's way, but she and John still had to return to Springfield where a killer could possibly be targeting them.

Words from that morning's sermon came to mind. The scripture passage had been from the twelfth chapter of Luke, where Jesus had told his disciples to not worry about their lives, that worrying accomplished nothing. The pastor had summarized it all by saying, "Pray more and worry less."

Toni breathed deep. That was good advice. She should follow it, not worry about what-ifs, and be willing to place their safety in God's hands.

When she pulled into the Zachary drive, Jenny and John emerged, each carrying a bag. Toni rounded the van and opened the back door. When the bags were inside, John gave Jenny a quick good-bye kiss, and he and Toni got into the van. As they drove away, Toni could see Jenny standing on the porch waving, her red hair standing on end as a gust of wind blew through it.

"Only two more weeks of class," Toni said, reading the forlorn expression on John's face. *And co-existing with my mother-in-law*, she added silently.

His expression lightened a bit. "I hate being away from Jenny, but I need this class on my transcript. So I'll live. How about your boys? Were they upset about you leaving again?"

"No. Kyle is still home with them. He'll drop them off at my parents' as he leaves for work in the morning." She forced thoughts of his job uncertainty to the back of her mind again.

John shifted in the seat, getting more comfortable.

"I talked to Ken Douglas," she said as she drove out of town. "He's good friends with the principal at Ozark."

John listened with interest as she related what she had learned. "I thought I had gotten acquainted with Jesse in class, but now I'm getting a whole new picture of him," he said when she finished. "He's still a victim, but no longer such an innocent one."

"I have to admit that, the more I learn, the more curious I get," Toni admitted. "We may not need to find out who killed the guy, but I'd like to know there will be no more attacks on you—or anyone."

John cradled his left arm with his right, rubbing over the cast, and then his sore ribs. "Same here."

"Oh," Toni said sharply when she remembered something else. "Quint said the guy who jumped you is a bookie."

John frowned. "Do you think he's the killer?"

Toni shook her head. "A bookie? I doubt it. Why bump off someone who's your bread and butter? I think he was just looking for Jesse's flash drive and thought you had it."

"They could have gotten into a fight. Maybe he already knew he had the wrong drive and thought Jesse was dodging him."

"But he still wouldn't have killed him," Toni argued. "If Jesse owed him money, he wanted him alive so he could pay."

"Good point," John conceded.

"Let's consider another point. Who benefits from his death? I mean in a financial sense? Who gets his money? If he has any," she added, steering onto the main highway. "I know he left a widow, and an ex-wife and two children from his first marriage. But now that we're seeing gambling in his life, I'm wondering if he was a wealthy gambler, or a broke gambler. I'll ask Quint if the police have found out anything new."

"There are just too many possibilities cropping up," John continued to muse. "He was a womanizer and a gambler, either of which could have led to dangerous associations. I wonder who wanted him out of the way."

"We need to look into the details of his past, talk to more of his friends and associates—and those names on those lists."

"I hope this amateur sleuthing doesn't get you into trouble." John leaned back in the seat, yawning. He soon dozed off.

As she drove in silence, Toni mulled over their conversation. Then she thought back over the files in Jesse's flash drive. What did those initials in the file names mean? She couldn't remember all of them, but the one containing the names of the teens she had located in Ozark floated into her mind. Suddenly a light went on. O for Ozark, of course. But what did the T represent? Suddenly a possibility struck her.

John stirred and opened his eyes. "Where are we?"

"A few miles from Mt. View. Are you ready for a pit stop and something cold to drink?"

"You bet." He moved his mouth in a way that indicated it was dry.

At the red light Toni turned right into the McDonald's parking lot. She parked and reached into the back seat for her book satchel. "I want to take another look at these lists," she said, pulling them out and sticking them in her purse.

They went inside, visited the facilities, and met back out front to get their drinks.

"Look at these again," she said when they were back in the car, pulling out the lists and handing them to John. "See if you draw any conclusions that match a theory that's forming in my mind."

He glanced at them while she placed her cup in a drink holder and backed out of their parking spot.

"What am I looking for?"

"Look at the file names I've written at the top, and then at the addresses below. Check each list and see if you can see what the file names might mean. Start with the one on top. It contains the names of the teens I found in Ozark."

John concentrated, studying the page. "The names apparently are Ozark residents, and the file name starts with an O. So what does the T mean?"

"That's what I want you to tell me. I have a thought, but I'm not sure of the facts. Do you have any idea what the school mascot is at Ozark?"

John's face creased in thought. He moved his mouth silently, reciting possibilities. "Are they Tigers?" he asked uncertainly, turning to focus his eyes on her.

"That's what I'm guessing," she said. "Look at the other lists. I checked some street maps and think the addresses on one of them are in Branson. The other looks like Springfield."

John flipped to the next sheet. "This one is named BP. It's the one you've labeled Branson. So the first initial fits. Now, what is their mascot?"

"I'm not sure, but could they be something like the Pirates? That seems familiar."

He brightened. "I think that's right." He flipped to the third list.

"What's the file name of that one?"

"It's KC, and it's the one you have labeled Springfield. That must be Kickapoo Chiefs," he said almost instantly, getting excited. "It has to be. Jesse was wearing a tee shirt with a chief on it, and we know he had taught at Kickapoo."

"So," Toni said slowly, thinking. "He had a batch of kids at each school where he had worked that he kept in touch with, and at least some of them were being paid money. What was going on? Something tells me it wasn't just keeping in touch for old times' sake."

Neither had answers.

*

When they reached Springfield, Toni dropped John at the home of his friend and headed for her in-laws. When she pulled into their driveway, she didn't get out immediately, but took her cell phone from her purse and called Quint.

"Hi, Quizzy. What's on your mind?"

Toni laughed. "Do you have time to talk to me?"

"I'm on duty now, but I'll be taking a meal break about ten. Is that too late for a day worker?"

"I can manage. Where should I meet you?"

"Make it Backyard Burgers at ten." The line went dead.

Toni managed to get her two bags, book satchel and purse all onto her shoulders and was just starting to the house when Dan Donovan walked through the doorway. "Here, let me take those," he said, taking the bags. "Are you hungry? We just finished eating, but there's plenty left."

Toni shook her head, following him up onto the porch. "I just talked to Quint, and we're meeting for burgers at ten. I don't know what time I'll be in, so don't wait up for me."

"Okay, but don't stay out so late that you're tardy

for school in the morning," Dan said, his tone wry and his eyes twinkling.

Toni laughed. "I'll watch the clock."

When she arrived at Backyard Burgers, Quint emerged from his cruiser and came to meet her. After greetings, they went inside, placed their orders, and slid into a booth across from one another. "I'm ready for an update," she announced immediately.

"Of course you are," Quint said with a grin. Then he turned serious. "We haven't been able to catch up with Barry Kuzman yet. We know he's a graduate student at MSU, and I'm sure he knows we're looking for him. He knows his way around, but he can't dodge us forever."

Their order number was called, and Quint went to get it.

"Have you talked to Jesse Campbell's principal at Ozark?" Toni asked when he returned, taking her order from the tray when he placed it on the table.

"Yes, we have. We've also checked on his history with the victim. Frankly, Mr. Volner is looking good for the murder. He and Jesse Campbell were long time friends who ended up enemies."

He paused, his eyes narrowing. "You're not asking questions. Does that mean you already know their background?"

"I know about the affair and divorce. I talked to my principal over the weekend. He's a friend of Mr. Volner's, and his feeling is that the man is a victim."

Quint shook his head. "I should have known that your inquisitiveness would have already had you sniffing out that history. After talking to Mr. Volner, we went back to talk to Mrs. Campbell again, but she hasn't been home for days. I'm afraid she may have cut and run."

Toni considered that. "Was she able to have the funeral Friday?"

Quint nodded. "It was held in Sedalia."

"In that case, I'm afraid you might be right. Of course, I can't really say I blame her. If I were in her position—her mess—I would want to get away from everything and everyone."

"You would also expect that the police would want to talk to you when you got back from the funeral," he said. "But we'll find her."

"I have something else I'd like to run past you."

"I'm listening." He bit into his burger.

"I think the letters in the file names of those lists are initials for the schools and mascots where the victim taught." She went on to explain in detail.

"You think we need to talk to every kid on those lists, don't you?" Quint eyed her over his soda cup as he drank.

"You bet I do," she returned instantly. "You need to put enough pressure on them to get someone to spill whatever it is that's been going on between them and their coach."

"Hey, calm down," he said between bites. "I agree."

"There are more things I want to know," Toni went on.

He raised his hands in mock horror. "No kidding. Now why doesn't that surprise me?"

Toni ignored his theatrics. "I'm wondering about the guy's finances. Was he accumulating a fat nest egg, or was he hurting for money? Did he have a will? If so, who was his beneficiary? And what about his car? Have the technicians found anything of interest in it?"

Quint shook his head. "Too many questions at once."

"Answer in any order."

His manner led Toni to believe he had at least some information, however small, but he was enjoying making her beg. He had served his country in combat and returned to take on the responsibility of law enforcement, but he was still baby brother tormenting his big sister.

Quint took his time downing another bite of burger and following it with a long slow swig of Coke. Then he turned serious. "The car hasn't yielded anything unusual. There were the normal papers and odds and ends in the glove compartment, an umbrella in the back seat, and debris in the floor and under the mats. As for his finances, the detectives are still checking around on that. That's one of the things they wanted to ask his widow about. As for a will, it's the same answer. He had a small checking account in a local bank, and there's a lockbox, but we need Mrs. Campbell to open it. That's all I can tell you at this point."

Accepting that there was no more to be gained, Toni turned her attention to her burger. A few minutes later they walked back out onto the parking lot.

"I have to get going," Quint said, pausing next to her van and giving her a penetrating look. "I understand that you're curious, and a scientist, and that both those parts of your nature want answers. But will you please be careful?"

"Of course," she agreed casually.

He gave her a wry grin. "I also understand that it's more fun to go sleuthing than to just spend every afternoon after school hanging out with your in-laws."

He started to walk away and halted abruptly. He pulled a folded paper from his shirt pocket and handed it to her. "Here's a little present I meant to give you."

Toni unfolded it and found that it was a copy of Jesse Campbell's resume.

"Grant Volner gave us that, and I made this copy for you later," he said before she could ask questions.

She grinned. "Thanks."

As he started walking away again, she had another thought. "Did anyone ever find the guy's watch?"

Quint stopped and turned, frowning. "Huh?"

"There was a white line around his wrist, a tan line. But he wasn't wearing a watch. Did it slip off in the water?"

"I'll check on it."

*

Before going to sleep that night, Toni curled up against the head of the bed with Jesse's resume. As she read back through the man's work history, she noted the time lengths. Two years at Glendale. Five years at Branson. One and a half at Kickapoo. Two and a half in a construction job. Almost three years at Ozark. Aware of what was behind the job hopping, she noted that the construction company he had worked for was located in Nixa. Since she seemed to be working backward through his checkered career, that was the next logical place to try to fill in some more blanks. It was too far from Springfield to make a quick run after school, but the school just preceding it in the timeline was right here in town. That was where she would visit tomorrow. But she didn't know anyone at Kickapoo and wasn't sure if she could get anyone to talk to her.

She mulled the matter a bit and had an idea. She had not met Ken's friend at Ozark. She would attempt two things at once—meet Grant Volner and form a personal impression of him, and see if he would point her to someone at Kickapoo who could be helpful.

Chapter 10

Monday morning began badly. After Toni was dressed for school, she spilled coffee on her white skirt and had to change. She grabbed a cotton dress from the closet, but when she went to put on a pair of hose, she snagged them and caused a big run. Aggravated, she pitched them and shoved her feet into a pair of white sandals.

As she rushed through the utility room doorway into the garage, she caught the side of her sandaled foot on the edge of the door and smashed her little toe. Gritting her teeth to keep from screaming, Toni hit the button to raise the garage door and hobbled across the floor past Dan and Barb's vehicles to her van in the driveway. She crawled inside and dumped her bags in the passenger seat, and then sat there massaging the injured toe. It throbbed so badly she feared it could be broken.

Toni moaned in pain, wondering how she was going to drive. At least it was on her left foot. She couldn't just sit there, so she gritted her teeth and lowered the foot. The drive was painful, but she made it across town without mishap.

By the time class started, she was able to walk without limping—if she was slow and careful. But it took real effort to concentrate. She was able to conduct the lecture on the digestive system from her desk, but the two-hour lab was more difficult because she had to circulate the room to assist students with their work. She perched on the edge of the desk any time she wasn't needed at a table.

After lab ended at one o'clock, Toni begand to tidy the room.

"Let me clean up for you today," Nicole Warren said, having hung back as the other students left. "You're limping, and I have time to help before going to work."

"I wouldn't mind a little help today," she said gratefully. As Nicole tidied the room, Toni explained how she had hurt her foot.

Nicole snickered. "I guess we both have some weird times."

"At least you're funny. I'm just a klutz. I hope you didn't think we were making fun of you Thursday. We were just enjoying a brain lapse question from the top student in the class."

Nicole's self-deprecating laugh was pleasant, but then it faded away. "Do you know if the police are making any progress on finding out who killed my former coach?"

"They're working on it, and I'm sure they're making headway, but I'm not sure if they're near an arrest," Toni said, not about to share too much with a student.

She steered the conversation to class matters, and Nicole soon had the room finished. When they parted outside the building, the heat was stifling. It was mid-July, and the days were long and dry. They needed rain, and the forecast didn't predict any in the near future.

Her toe was feeling sore and stiff, but she had been off of it long enough that it no longer throbbed constantly. Toni debated whether she should just go to the house and lie down. She was not obligated to play detective. She also knew that, even if she did go to bed, she would just lie there and think about the murder. She needed action. She climbed into her van and headed for Ozark.

When she reached the high school, Toni limped inside the building. A custodian came down the hall, pushing an industrial mop bucket. "How do I find the high school principal's office?" she asked him.

The gangly man's grin showed a gap where there should have been a right bicuspid. "Last door on the left down there." He pointed to where he meant.

She thanked him and limped in that direction. When she reached the indicated door, Toni pushed it open and peeked inside. A secretary occupied a desk in the front office. The older, somewhat plump woman looked up from her computer screen. "May I help you?"

"I'd like to speak to Mr. Grant Volner," she was saying when the door at the rear opened and a man emerged. He looked up from the papers in his hands as he noticed her.

"May I tell him who's asking for him?" The secretary hadn't noticed the man's presence.

"My name is Toni Donovan. I'm from Clearmount, and my principal is a friend of Mr. Volner's."

The man's expression changed, his eyes

brightening a little. "I'm Grant Volner," he said, rounding the desk with a hand outstretched. "Ken said he thought you might stop by. I was just going to get a cold drink. Would you care for one?"

When they were seated in the man's office a few minutes later, he set his Pepsi on his desk blotter and leaned back with a sigh. "Ken told me a little about you and said it was your son who found Jesse's body. Do you honestly think you can figure out who killed him? I assure you it wasn't me," he added quickly.

"Ken doesn't think you did."

Grant nodded, his face drawn. "As angry as I was—am—I couldn't do that. I hope you believe me."

Toni studied him. Sandy haired with deep set dark eyes, the man struck her as a sincere sort. "I want to believe you," she said gently. "I don't know you, but I like to think my principal is a good judge of character."

"That's fair enough," he allowed, rubbing a hand over his forehead. "Does your being here mean you're trying to find out who killed Jesse?"

"It means I'm too nosy for my own good," she quipped, and then turned serious. "I don't want to make you uncomfortable with personal questions, but I'd like to hear your story first hand. I understand you have young children."

His mouth tightened. "I do. And I have to admit that, if it had been anyone but Jesse, they might still have two parents together. I would have handled things differently."

"Like trying to patch things up instead of divorcing?"

He nodded. "The biggest mistake of my life was going to bat for Jesse when I knew he wanted another coaching job and couldn't get one. I knew he could produce wins, so when we lost our coach in a tragedy…" He shrugged and spread his palms. "Well, you know the story."

"I'd still like to hear it firsthand." She felt an affinity for the man. He had lost the mother of his children and his best friend. Somehow she thought he was a too tightly controlled person to have killed a man, even a friend who had betrayed him.

"Jesse and I grew up together in Sedalia," he began and went on to relate his and Jesse's history pretty much as Ken had told it.

"When did you find out your friend was having an affair with your wife?" she asked when he wound down.

He winced. "My wife was the Parents as Teachers coordinator, so she saw Jesse around the school. I don't know exactly when things turned personal between them."

She nodded and waited for him to continue.

He made a self-deprecating shrug. "As usual, the husband is the last to know. I didn't figure it out until I actually walked in on them in an…uh, clinch in her office one night after a basketball game."

"Do you have any idea who killed him?"

"I'm not even sure I want to know," he admitted, reaching for his Pepsi, as if he needed something to do with his hands. "Maybe it was a parent who was enraged because a kid wasn't getting enough playing time," he added with a touch of bitter wryness.

Toni couldn't see the point in pursuing that line

of questioning, so she shifted gears. "Can you give me the name of someone at Kickapoo who will talk to me about Jesse's time there?"

He deliberated a moment. "You mean someone who can give you a picture of the inner workings, right?"

She grinned. "Right."

"Of course I know the administrators, but I think my sister-in-law, my brother's wife, might be a more interesting contact for your purpose. She teaches art at the high school."

Toni's mouth twitched. "Her perspective might be a little different."

He reached for a pen and paper. "Her name is Michelle Carringer, and she lives in Springfield. Are you planning to try to catch her today?"

"If I can."

He finished writing and extended the piece of paper. "Here's her address. If you'll wait a minute I'll call and see if she's home."

"Fine." She sipped from her Coke while he dialed and got an answer.

"I have a lady here who would like to drop by to talk to you," he said. A pause. "She's a teacher, and she's looking into Jesse Campbell's death. It was her son who found the body."

He covered the phone with a hand and spoke to Toni. "She says she'll only be home for a couple more hours, but she'll see you if you can come right now."

"Tell her I'm on my way." She grabbed her soda can, stood, and forced herself to walk out the door without limping as he relayed the message.

*

The neighborhood where Mrs. Carringer lived was located in the south side of Springfield, so Toni found it within minutes. She checked the street addresses and turned onto South Roanoke. At the house number Grant Volner had given her, she pulled to the curb.

As she made her way up the driveway, a woman walked around the side of the house. She was statuesque and looked to be in her late thirties. She wore a smock that showed only bare legs below it and thick-soled sandals with no socks. If that didn't look funny enough, she had a streak of bright red hair down the side of her dishwater blonde, shoulder length tresses, like some strange breed of skunk.

"I was just putting some stuff in the storage shed," she said, advancing toward Toni. "Are you Mrs. Donovan?"

Toni nodded. "Yes."

A hand shot out. "I'm Michelle Carringer. Call me Mickey. Everyone does."

Toni shook the woman's hand. "Thank you for seeing me."

"Let's sit down," Mickey said, going to the top of the steps. Instead of going inside the house, she plopped on the edge of the porch, her feet on the top step. Toni made her way gingerly up the steps and sat beside her, tucking the skirt of her dress around her legs.

"Whew! It's hot." Mickey fanned her hands before her face. Then she reached down and grasped the tail of her smock. She pulled it over her head, revealing khaki shorts and a white tank top, and laid it beside her. She nodded at Toni's foot. "What's the problem?"

Toni grimaced. "I started the day by walking into a doorway. The damage isn't major, but it sure is sore."

Mickey Carringer gave a husky laugh. "It's good to know I'm not the only one who has days like that."

Toni looked up at the bright sun, wondering why they didn't go inside where it was air conditioned.

"I love the outdoors," Mickey went on. "I've been watering my little garden. I'm not ready for school to start. I'm having too much fun. Too bad I can't just retire and do whatever I want year round." Her grin showed large white teeth.

Toni perceived Mickey as a bit of a free spirit, with a perky personality, but she seemed exceptionally intelligent.

"My young son found Jesse Campbell's body at the park," she said, opting to be totally frank in hopes that the woman would reciprocate. "I'm trying to learn more about him, and you never know what little piece of information will be helpful in an investigation."

Mickey's expression changed to puzzlement. "I thought Grant said you're a teacher, not a detective."

Toni nodded. "I'm a science teacher at the high school in my hometown of Clearmount, but I'm doing a summer class at OTC for a friend who had a baby last month. The fact that a man was killed rouses my curiosity, but having my son find the body makes it more personal."

"I suppose I can understand that," Mickey allowed.

"I know Jesse worked at Kickapoo, where your brother-in-law says you teach. Did you know the man personally?"

"Oh, sure. We were on staff together, and there's a certain amount of contact—and a grapevine—in every school. Isn't there?" she added with a meaningful roll of her eyes.

Toni grinned. "I know what you mean. What can you tell me about him?"

"I assume since Grant sent you that he wants me to give you the real dirt. Jesse was a cheat."

The blunt statement took Toni off guard. She had counted on having to dig for facts, and it looked like facts might be digging at her. "What do you mean?"

Mickey heaved a sigh. "I mean he was a double cheat. He cheated with women—and at sports. He got caught with the women, but he was slicker in sports."

Toni frowned. "I need that explained."

Mickey ran her hand around the back of her neck, massaging it and tucking her hair behind her ears. The red streak seemed to have a flyaway tendency all its own. "Let me back up a little. I'm not sure how he got hired in the first place. I didn't know it at the time—so maybe the administration didn't come completely clean with the board the way they should have—but he had been cut loose from his previous school."

"Which was?"

"Branson. I still don't know the true details about that, but the scuttlebutt is he got involved with a female student. But he had a winning record that I guess the school here just couldn't resist. My guess is he had an inside track, knew someone personally who would pull for him. Too bad they didn't do more research."

"What kind of research?"

Mickey inhaled and blew the breath out in a long puff. "Call me jaundiced, but I tend to believe the talk. The guy won lots of games, yes. But there were rumors of recruiting and eligibility violations. He apparently did a lot of scouting at other schools in the area and knew the top players. He got a couple to enroll with us while living in another district. I understand he did even better than that before coming here, that he moved students into his district and rented a house for them and paid for their food and clothes."

"Was it ever proven?"

Mickey shook her head. "No, it was just talk. But there was so much talk that I side with the old cliché that says where there's smoke, there's fire. There was just too much smoke."

Toni had another thought. "How could a high school coach afford to pay that kind of expenses for players? Teachers can live on what they make, but they're not known for being rich."

The woman shrugged. "I don't know. I guess that's another reason nothing was ever proven. Payments could never be tied directly to him. The kids paid their own bills—in cash."

While Toni was mulling that over, Mickey continued. "My junior high son says he heard that Coach Campbell hosted secret beer bashes for his players."

This was getting worse. "How long was he on staff at your school?"

"One full year, during which he had an astonishing win record. He was fired in the middle of his second year. The assistant coach was put in charge for the rest of the basketball season, and the school did everything they could to keep the story quiet." She reeled off the information in a brisk manner.

"If he was fired for cheating, did the school have to accept any penalties, like forfeiting wins or being put on probation?"

Mickey's head moved back and forth. "Like I said, he never got convicted of cheating in sports. But he did with women. The word got around that he was having an affair with one of our school secretaries. Yeah, I know," she said, waving a hand dismissively. "That kind of thing doesn't always get a guy fired anymore. But along with the talk of the sports cheating, the board decided to get rid of him while they had the means. I figure they were afraid of the consequences you just mentioned if the stories were ever proven. His wife had had enough. This time she left him."

"Is the secretary still employed at the school?"

"She's still there, and she works summers, but if you're thinking of going right to the school to see her, I doubt you'll catch her. She gets off at three, so she'll have already gone home." She grinned. "I assume you want to know her address."

Toni grinned back. "I may as well. I'm intrigued with the case, and I have some free time."

"Her name is Joyce Franklin, and she lives in the University Park apartments. I don't know the number. If you'll wait just a minute I'll get it for you. It should be on our emergency call list." She bounced up and went inside the house.

A minute later she returned and handed Toni a piece of paper. "Here's the complete address and her phone number, just in case you should need it. She's a single parent. Her son, Corey, is in college now, but he was in high school when Jesse was here. In fact, the kid played on his team."

Toni pushed to her feet. "I appreciate you taking time to talk to me."

"I enjoyed meeting you, and I hope you figure it out. I don't know what more I could possibly tell you, but if you think of anything else you want to ask, call me. I'd like to help Grant if I can."

*

It was four o'clock by the time Toni found Joyce Franklin's apartment and rang the doorbell. The woman who opened the door was petite, about five-two, around a hundred ten pounds. Her hair was bleached a white blonde and pulled to the back of her neck with a pink scarf. Her eyes were light brown, with dark shadows around them. They regarded Toni warily.

"Hello, I'm Toni Donovan. I'm looking into the death of Jesse Campbell. May I come in and talk to you?"

The woman's eyes narrowed. "Why should I talk to you?"

"Why not? I'm just trying to figure out who killed him. Wouldn't you like to know?"

She gave Toni another once over, then sighed and backed up. "Come in," she said with less than graciousness, opening the door wider.

The apartment was utilitarian and fairly neat, but

it was by no means luxurious. It appeared to be a haven created by a single working woman. The furniture was simple but clean, with few frills or ornamentation. The white walls had a few pictures on them, but they were landscapes, not family photos. There was, however, a framed picture of a dark haired young man above the television. He looked familiar.

Toni walked to the sofa, being careful of her toe, and sat. "When was the last time you saw Jesse?" she asked as Joyce took a chair facing her.

"Who says I ever saw him?" she retorted sharply, her eyes bleak.

"The word is that you had an affair with him while he was employed at Kickapoo."

Joyce's face registered surprise that Toni knew such a thing, but it quickly turned to anger. "So what if I did. It's no one's business but mine."

"And Jesse's," Toni added. "And he's dead."

The woman's face crumpled, and tears welled in her eyes. Her lips trembled. "Why are you here asking me these questions?"

Toni took a deep breath, knowing that only honesty was going to get her anywhere. "It was my family who found his body. Maybe it's crazy, but that makes me feel some sort of responsibility to find out what happened. Wouldn't you like to know who killed him?"

A hand went over her mouth as the tears spilled over. Unable to speak, she just bobbed her head in affirmation.

"Had you seen him recently?"

The direction of her head movement changed. "I hadn't seen him in several months," she finally managed to say.

But you wanted to, Toni heard in her voice and manner. *He dumped you, and you're still heartbroken*. She reined in her emotions and spoke more compassionately. "You were in love with him, weren't you?"

Her shoulders shook, and she grabbed for a tissue from the box on the coffee table. "Why would anyone kill him?" she sobbed.

"That's what I want to find out."

Joyce wiped her eyes and composed herself. "He was the first person I had felt anything for since my husband was killed in a motorcycle wreck when my son was two."

"You were lonely, and he was friendly to you. One thing led to another. Right?"

She nodded miserably. "I never intended to get involved with him. But he was funny and flattering, and I fell for him."

"You knew he was married?"

"And felt awful about it," she said, nodding and swiping at her eyes.

Toni found herself feeling a little sorry for the woman. Widowed young, she had been lonely and vulnerable. It didn't excuse anything, but it provided insight. "Do you know if he was involved in anything questionable?"

Joyce looked up from wiping her eyes. "What do you mean?"

"I'm not quite sure. I guess what I mean is, was all his time spent at the school and home—and with you? Or did he have involvements and friends away from school and coaching? What were his leisure activities?"

"Women," she said bitterly.

Chapter 11

Toni studied Joyce's desolate expression. "You know you weren't the first affair then?"

"Or the last." She squared her shoulders. "But you want to know the worst? It didn't really matter. He was smooth, and he made me feel good."

"Do you think his ex-wife could have killed him?"

Her brow furrowed. "I can understand how his messing around could have made her that mad, but she didn't seem hot tempered or mean. She taught in the elementary school and went home after classes rather than sticking around after school every day like Jesse did. I mean he always had practices and games and stuff going on."

Stuff like cozying up to the secretary. Or to students.

"What about the principal at Ozark? He and Jesse were close friends until…"

"Until Jesse took up with his wife," she interrupted in a flat tone.

"Had he promised to leave his wife for you?"

Joyce shook her head. "He said he had to stay with her to look after his young children."

Toni took that to mean he never intended to leave

his wife for anyone. He had just been enjoying a self-absorbed lifestyle that included home and hearth—and women on the side.

"Do you think his wife knew about the relationship between you and Jesse?"

Joyce hesitated. "I'm not sure. She never called me or looked me up. We worked in separate buildings, so we never ran into one another."

"But she left Jesse after he lost his job at Kickapoo. That sounds like she probably knew."

Joyce's lower lip trembled, and she raked a hand through her whitened hair. "She probably did. She also knew he would have trouble finding another job."

Toni couldn't help thinking that the wife had done exactly what she would have done. It was bad enough to know he had cheated on her again, even after she had nearly left him before and warned him what would happen. The shame, as well as the financial situation, would have been enough to warrant kicking him out—or worse.

"Do you think she could have killed him?"

The idea seemed to jolt Joyce's lethargy. Her eyes rounded. Then, after a few moments of thought, she shook her head. "I doubt it. If she was going to do it, why wait so long? And why stab him at the park? She could have done it much quicker and easier."

Good points. "What about the principal at Ozark? This time Jesse broke up the marriage of an old friend."

"I don't know the guy."

This wasn't getting her anywhere. Joyce was obviously not a deep thinker, and she didn't seem all that interested in identifying a killer. She was cocooned in her own pain. Toni stood. "I should be going. Thank you for your time."

As she started for the door, footsteps approached from another room, and a young man sauntered through a doorway. He was good looking in a sulky kind of way. He wore low slung jeans and a black tee shirt with lettering on the front that said 'And your point is...' About five-ten, muscular and tanned, he had an angular face and a few light freckles. But it was the spiky dark hair with the bleached tips that sparked a memory. Thinking fast, Toni recognized him as one of the card playing young men she had seen in the student union the day before. Then she remembered hearing that Joyce's son was a student at OTC. She glanced again at the picture on the wall over the television. It was a younger image of him, with no highlighting in his dark hair.

"Hey, Mom, where are my new swim trunks?" His voice sounded younger than his age, which she guessed to be in the early twenties.

Pausing just inside the room, he plucked a couple of pieces from an M & M bag and popped them into his mouth. His gaze swept over Toni with no sign of recognition.

"They're in the bottom drawer of your dresser, along with the rest of your swim wear." Joyce gave him a look of parental exasperation. "If you would ever put things away, you might be able to find them."

She turned back to Toni. "This is my son, Corey. He's a student at OTC." She looked back at Corey. "This is Mrs....uh..."

"Donovan," Toni supplied.

Corey popped another M & M in his mouth and stepped toward her. "Nice to meet you," he said, giving her a cursory handshake and a half smile.

He turned back to his mother. "I'm due at work in thirty minutes and my gas tank's almost empty. I don't get paid until tomorrow. Can you help me out?"

Joyce's mouth tightened a bit, but she went to her purse on the coffee table and dug out her wallet. She took a ten from it and handed it to him. "I expect it back tomorrow night." Her tone implied she didn't always get it back.

"Sure," he said easily, stuffing the bill in his pocket. "Have to go make some tuition now," he said as he headed for the door. But when he got there he paused, ran back up the hall, and returned with a pair of swim trunks.

"You're going to work, not swimming," Joyce objected.

"Pool party afterward," he called, going out the door.

Joyce sighed as the door closed behind him. "He's a good boy, but it's hard to be firm with him."

"Did he attend Kickapoo while Jesse was coaching there?" Toni asked, knowing he had, but wanting to keep the conversation going.

Joyce nodded. "He was a junior when Jesse took over, a senior when he…left."

"I'm sure it hasn't been easy raising a boy alone. Did he play sports?"

"Oh, yes. I always encouraged him because I felt that sports teach kids teamwork and sportsmanship. And Jesse was very good with him." Her demeanor underwent a quick return to sadness at the mention of Jesse.

Toni changed her mind about furthering the conversation. It was a waste of time.

*

That evening, after helping her mother-in-law clean up from their meal, Toni took a shower. She was just belting her robe over her nightgown when her cell phone began to ring in the bedroom. She started to it and put too much weight on her foot. She gritted her teeth and hobbled on. "Hello."

"Toni! Do you have the television on?" Kara Yates practically yelled into her ear.

"No, I've been in the shower."

"Quick. Turn it on KY3. Call me back when it's over." She disconnected.

There was a small set on top of the chest of drawers in her bedroom. Toni switched it on and perched on the side of the bed, nursing her throbbing toe in her lap.

"Sheila Campbell, wife of murdered coach Jesse Campbell, has confessed to killing her husband," the broadcaster was announcing.

"Mrs. Campbell stated to police that she stabbed him in an act of rage during an argument. Authorities are still questioning the suspect and declined to provide any more details. An investigation is ongoing."

When the broadcast moved on to another story, Toni just sat there, stunned. What was going on here? She had detected nothing in Sheila Campbell's story or demeanor that made her believe the woman had killed her husband. As she mentally went back over that meeting, her gut tightened.

The woman had blown her marriage and lost custody of her kids. Now she was admitting to murder, with no motive beyond an argument. A sense of knowledge crept through Toni, the sure understanding that the woman had not done it. But why confess?

The ringing of her cell phone, which was still in her hand, startled her. She answered in a near whisper.

"Did you hear it? You didn't call me back."

Toni shook her head to collect her thoughts. "I heard it. I was thinking. I would have called you."

"What do you think?"

"That it's confusing," she said slowly.

"From everything I've heard, she couldn't have done it," Kara declared in dismay. "My friend who teaches at Ozark is friends with Sheila. She was totally shocked when Sheila got involved with Jesse, and even worse shocked when she divorced Grant and married Jesse. She says it was totally out of character for the person she knew. What do you think?"

"My impression when I talked to her was that she was grieving and troubled, and kind of naïve," Toni added carefully. "Maybe I just don't like this because it's too easy. But I'm afraid the woman is messed up right now, in a warped mental frame."

"I agree," Kara said. "But what can we do?"

"Hope the police don't accept it at face value just to close a case quickly."

*

Toni didn't sleep well that night. The next morning she woke feeling tired and dull witted. Her toe was still sore, but she could walk on it without limping if she was careful. She stood balanced on one foot in front of the closet, unable to decide what to wear. She had such a variety from which to choose—exactly three—the remainder of what she had brought from home to see her through the week. She grabbed the sage green pantsuit that was a longtime favorite.

When she got to school she stopped by a soda machine for a Coke, needing an extra caffeine jolt and something to wash down a couple of pain pills for her headache. She took the pills and guzzled the rest of the soda while getting ready for a lecture on the respiratory system, thankful she didn't have to do a lab that day.

By the time class was over, Toni's headache was gone and her bruised toe felt better. But she wasn't ready to give up her open toe sandals. A regular shoe would cramp it and soon have it throbbing again.

When she went to the door to see the class out at eleven, she was surprised to find Quint leaning against the wall in the hallway. "What are you doing here?"

He pushed upright. "I'm off tonight, so I decided to get up early and take you to lunch."

Considering that he often didn't get to bed until three or four in the morning, and usually slept until noon, Toni figured he had something on his mind.

"As soon as I tidy up, I'm free for the rest of the day."

*

When they were seated and had their orders placed at the Pasta House, Toni eyed Quint across the table. "Okay, tell me what's on your mind. Or is this a lecture session?"

He gave her a stern look. "It's a checkup. I can't believe you haven't been sleuthing. I want to know everything you've been doing and what you've learned."

Toni wrinkled her face at him. "I've mostly been talking to people who knew Jesse Campbell or worked with him. I've learned a little, but not much of importance."

"Then we may as well compare notes," he said in dry resignation.

"You go first."

He stared at her a moment before speaking. "I'm worried about the Campbell woman's confession. It doesn't feel right to me. What's your take on it?" He eyed her while sipping from his iced tea.

Toni knew her baby brother had dealt with some pretty gruesome situations in combat duty, but he seemed to have matured through it all. This was the first murder case he had worked on since joining the police force, and she was pleased that he was willing to talk with her about it. He was still her bratty baby brother and always would be, but their relationship was developing into something more mature and satisfying.

Their food arrived before she could comment, so Quint waited until the waitress was gone to continue. Then he glanced around the room, as if assuring himself that their conversation was private. "I listened in on some questioning of Sheila Campbell, and I don't think her story holds together. You're bound to have an opinion, so let me hear it."

Toni paused in the act of shoving a forkful of

lasagna into her mouth. She made a hand motion to convey that she wanted to comment, but went ahead and filled her mouth. Shrugging, Quint also began to eat.

"I'm glad to hear you say that," Toni said when her mouth was empty. "I feel the same way. Both times I met Mrs. Campbell, she struck me as too passive for the rage indicated in this crime. Her story sounds contrived, and I just can't envision her fighting with her new husband, stabbing him to death, and then pushing him into the lagoon and leaving."

Quint nodded. "I went and talked to Mr. Volner, her former husband, at his home last night. He still swears he didn't do it, but he says he knows Sheila better than anyone, and that she could not have done it. He figures Jesse, who knew all the tricks, came onto her and seduced her. From listening to him, I think he still loves the woman. I know he's sick about the whole mess. I found myself feeling sorry for the guy. It wouldn't surprise me if he doesn't offer to pay her bail if it's granted, and even see to it that she has a lawyer."

"Well, I hate the whole thing, but I'm glad to hear you confirm my doubts," Toni said. "Kara has a friend who worked with Sheila, and she says Sheila is too reserved to have done it."

"So who did? Have you formed any theories yet?"

"No," she said with a shake of her head. "What I *am* forming is a picture of Jesse Campbell. His life, that was a total blank at first, has started taking on a strange light. He affected a lot of people, and the more of his history I learn, the more suspects and motives I find. There are just too many people who had reason to resent or hate him. He was a womanizer…"

"Which brings us back to husbands of the married women he fooled around with," Quint interjected.

"You mean Volner."

He nodded. "He still seems the most logical, but I'm hearing your thoughts. You think there are more of them out there—angry husbands, I mean."

"My gut says he's not the only one. I think we need to find out for sure. That means checking back through his entire career. I've only talked to people from Ozark and Kickapoo. He worked at two other schools before them. I hope the police won't charge Volner without checking to see if Jesse angered anyone in either of those places."

"I'm sure you'll take care of that," Quint said with a trace of sarcasm.

"You're right," she shot back. "I can't quit now. If Volner actually did it, he should face the consequences. But I need to be sure in my own mind. There are just too many possibilities."

"There's not enough evidence to charge him."

"Good."

By unspoken agreement the conversation paused, and they focused on their food. Quint had always loved pasta. As a kid he had eaten macaroni and cheese as often as he could talk their mother into fixing it.

"Will you split a piece of cheesecake with me?" he asked when his plate was clean.

She nodded. "I shouldn't, but I will."

He signaled for the waitress and ordered it.

"What else can you tell me?" she asked between bites.

He swallowed. "We haven't been able to catch up with John's friend Barry Kuzman. He's dodging us and skipping classes. He hasn't even been to his apartment this week. So there's no question he knows we're looking for him."

"What about Jesse Campbell's finances? Have you checked into that yet?"

Quint pushed his empty plate back and took a sip of coffee. "He was surprisingly solvent for a teacher. He had a healthy checking account and a savings account with about a hundred grand in it. He must have been picking up some extra at officiating—or something."

Or something, Toni thought, a suspicion forming in her mind.

"It looks like he was doing well," Quint continued. "He also had expensive tastes. He owned two high dollar vehicles, a nice boat, an ATV, and some pricey duds."

"Did he have a will?"

"Not that anyone can find. But that's not surprising. He was young. He wasn't thinking about dying. Like any guy that age, he thought he would live forever. But he had some life insurance at school. He had lost his job, but his paychecks and insurance were good through August. His kids were named as beneficiaries. The ex wasn't on it, nor the new wife. Maybe he meant to name her when he found another job, but he obviously meant to keep his kids on it."

Toni liked the idea that the guy cared about his

kids. "He was only married to Sheila for a few weeks, and his track record was already poor. The kids were his permanently, though. I'm glad they'll have an education fund."

Quint tapped a finger on the table top. "We found one other thing that's interesting. One of the files in his computer was a database. It's a massive compilation of basketball teams, players, referees, and other factors. Now what does that suggest to you?"

Toni grinned, her suspicion confirmed. "Gambling."

"Right. If he was betting on sports, there's no telling what kind of characters he was dealing with."

Toni sighed. "Which broadens the possibilities even further. I think this case just became impossible."

"We're still checking area banks to see if any more accounts surface, and I'm sure you'll be thinking of things to check. Since we're working so closely on this, why don't you move in with me for the rest of your time here in Springfield? We could keep in contact more easily that way."

Toni snickered. "What you really mean is that you want to be able to keep your eagle eye on me."

"That, too," he admitted good-naturedly.

Toni considered a moment. "I only have tonight and tomorrow night left of this week, and I hate to move out on my in-laws too abruptly and risk hurting their feelings. How about if I land on you when I come back from the weekend in Clearmount? Next week is my last full week of classes. Finals are the twenty-eighth."

"That'll work," he agreed.

*

As Toni drove back to her in-laws' house, a kaleidoscope of facts tumbled through her head. Jesse Campbell had hurt a lot of people, meaning too many victims could be suspects. The man's violent death was affecting her more personally than she could ever have anticipated. What should she do?

Two things came to mind. First, John's assailant, who had been Jesse's bookkeeper, was a bookie. Second, the police had found a database in Jesse's computer that contained sports data. Both facts seemed to say that Jesse Campbell was gambling on sports, which was an especially bad thing if he had been betting on any games to which he had personal connections. Had he amassed a huge gambling debt and been killed by a muscle man? Although possible, it didn't ring right. He had money in the bank, and even if he didn't, killing him would mean never collecting.

Toni thought about the boys she had met in Ozark, wondering how much they knew. She was sure the police were checking those lists of names from Jesse's flash drive. But, now that she had an inkling of what was going on, she couldn't shake the feeling that she needed to give those two another try, see if she could get them to talk to her. But how?

She pulled into the Donovan driveway and called John. Before doing anything else, she needed to check on him. He answered promptly.

"How are you feeling?"

"Stiff and sore, but I'm driving okay. How about you? Are you sleuthing?"

"Not at the moment. I'm weighing what to do next. I just wanted to be sure you're getting along okay. I'll talk to you later."

"Whatever you do, be careful," he admonished just before she disconnected.

Toni sat for a few moments, rapidly formulating a plan. Then she gathered her bags and went inside the house, still being careful of her foot. No one was home. She dumped her satchel in the kitchen. Then she wrote a note, telling the Donovans she was going to run some errands and didn't know what time she would be in and to not delay the evening meal for her. Propping it on the counter, she grabbed a Coke from the refrigerator and returned to the van.

She drove to a thrift shop she remembered on Glenstone and bought a shoulder length auburn wig. Then she hunted around and found a pair of plain reading glasses. When she got back to the van, she put both of them on and checked her image in the rear view mirror. Her appearance was now quite different. The boys had only seen her once for a very brief time. She shouldn't be recognized.

When she got to Ozark, Toni parked a block away from the Harcourt house where her van would not be noticeable, just in case it might be recognized. Halfway up the walk to the house, she heard a yell and then a big splash. She veered across the yard to the wooden fence at the back of the house that, surprisingly, was not locked. She pushed it open and peered inside.

Two young men were at the large ground level pool that was surrounded by a concrete apron. One was in the water, the other poised on the diving board.

Toni recognized Vince Harcourt as he went into a bounce on his toes. The dive he executed was a thing of beauty, arcing high and going down to enter the water in a clean slice.

Toni stepped through the gate and closed it, and then walked across the lawn onto the concrete. Two white chaise lounges flanked a patio table. She stopped near one of the chaises and watched the young men frolicking in the water.

Glancing down, she spotted two pairs of heavy sandals below the tables, with wallets stuffed inside them. Pants and polo shirts were tossed across the other chaise. Two sweaty bottles of water sat on the table.

Suddenly Vince Harcourt turned in the water and noticed her. "Hey, what are you doing here?" he shouted, treading water and pushing his wet hair back out of his eyes. He was almost too handsome for his own good, but his manner and tone were unpleasant. Spoiled rich kid was Toni's assessment.

"I'm a reporter, and I'm doing a story on student finances. I'm looking for Vince Harcourt," she said, giving him her hastily devised cover story.

"That's me, but I don't want to talk to any nosy reporters."

"I got your name from a list of high school students planning to enter college soon. I'd really appreciate a few minutes of your time," she persisted, edging over to the empty chaise and perching on it. "I don't mind waiting a bit."

Glancing over, she noticed a small card under one of the bottles of water. It was getting wet from condensation, but she could see through the glistening liquid that it was a business card. A little smeared, all she could distinguish was the word Game. Curious, she shifted her body and inched nearer.

"I said I'm not talking to any reporter," the cocky Mr. Harcourt shouted. "Get lost!"

"Okay, okay," she said, jumping to her feet awkwardly and giving the table a bump that she hoped looked accidental. The water bottles toppled.

"Oops," she said, grabbing at the bottles and fumbling with them. She positioned herself between the table and the pool and palmed the card as she set the bottles upright. When she stepped back, she shoved her purse onto her shoulder and slipped the card under her thumb on the notepad and turned around.

"Sorry to be a klutz. Enjoy your swim." She skedaddled.

Back in the van, Toni shoved the card inside her purse, put the vehicle in gear, and took off. She had struck out with Harcourt. Hopefully the next kid would be more cooperative. Relying on memory, she retraced the route to the address of Dean Patrick, hoping he was home.

She was in luck. As she rounded the corner and rolled up before the house, Dean himself was just getting into the little brown Corolla parked in the driveway. She pulled up behind him, blocking the drive. She didn't think he would have noticed her van when she was here before, but there was no time to conceal it. Grabbing her notepad, she hopped out.

"Hello, I'm looking for Dean Patrick," she said, walking right up to the edge of the open door as he was settling behind the wheel.

The look Dean directed up at her held no sign of recognition. He frowned. "I'm Dean, but I'm on my way to work."

"I'm a reporter, and I'm working on a story about student finances. Your name was on a list of high school students preparing to enter college, and I was hoping to get an interview with you. What time do you have to be at work?"

The young man glanced at his watch. "Well," he said hesitantly, "I'm not actually due for almost an hour, but I'm going in early so I can have a snack at McDonald's before the first game starts. I umpire Little League games at the ball park."

A big boy, he no doubt required lots of snacks. Toni gave him an over-bright smile. "How about if I follow you to McDonald's and talk to you while you eat?"

He considered for a moment. "I guess that would be okay."

Chapter 12

Toni backed her van up and let the kid out of his drive. Then she tailed him closely up the street. Soon she realized he was heading for highway 65. He hadn't said he was going to work in Springfield. That was fine with her.

When he pulled in at the McDonald's on Battlefield, Toni parked next to him and met him at the door. "I appreciate you doing this. I know you're a busy person. The fact that you have a summer job already tells me you're a good subject for my story."

She could almost see his chest swell with importance. Good. If stroking his ego a little would make him talkative, she would stroke liberally. "Why don't you let me treat you to a meal?"

"Sure," he said, grinning at the offer of free food.

He ordered a double cheeseburger, a large order of fries, and a root beer. Toni ordered a large iced tea and paid the bill.

" Now, who did you say you are?" Dean asked when they were seated in a booth in the back corner of the main room.

"I'm a reporter, and I'm working on a story about student finance," she repeated, hoping he didn't ask for the name of her paper or organization. She continued quickly before he could do that. "I'm interested in finding out how high school students deal with finances and how they plan to pay for college. Since you already have a job, I assume you plan to continue working."

Dean shoved a wad of fries into his mouth and chewed, seeming only mildly interested in what she was saying. "I'll have to," he said when he could speak.

"Some students are fortunate enough to have a college account that their parents have been saving for them," she said conversationally.

"Not me," he said with a shake of his stringy-mop covered head. "We live in a big house, but we don't have a lot of money. My dad died when I was six, and my mom doesn't work or manage money very well."

"I hope you don't make the mistake so many students do by running up big credit card bills," Toni continued her phony spiel. "Putting tuition bills on a credit card is a very bad idea. The interest you'll pay will eat you alive. Are you checking into financial aid and scholarships? There are a lot of resources out there."

"I've been to see our school counselor, and my mom has been checking on what the different schools cost," he said between bites. "I'm hoping to get an athletic scholarship."

The perfect opening. "Oh, so you're an athlete. That's great. Has your coach recommended you to any schools yet?"

He frowned. "My coach was killed a few days ago."

"Oh, I'm sorry," she prattled. "I hope there won't be problems with any paperwork he might have started for you. Were you close to your coach?"

"Yeah, pretty close." He glanced down at his burger for a moment, and then took another bite. Grief wasn't hindering his appetite.

"Were you his assistant or anything like that?"

"I ran some errands for him sometimes." He continued to find his food more interesting than the conversation.

"What kind of a guy was he?"

"He was neat. Funny."

"Funny? In what way?"

"Let's see," he said, seeming to concentrate on memories. Then he laughed. "He was sharp. I remember one time he had me switch jerseys with Tim Bishop during halftime in the locker room. Tim was in foul trouble, see."

What she saw was a simplistic way of cheating. She had trouble controlling her expression. "That's pretty slick," she managed to say.

He seemed encouraged. "Another sweet trick he had was to secretly tape the other teams in their locker room before the game and during halftime to learn their strategy. Someone would go get the tape after the team went out on the court to play, look at it, and then go back out in the gym and report to coach."

He paused, as if realizing what he was revealing. Then he shrugged. "Hey, he's dead. So talking about this stuff now can't get him in trouble. Right?"

"Right," she forced herself to say.

Satisfied with her response, he went on. "I remember hearing about how he had a guy shave some points so he could..."

This time the boy came to an abrupt halt, realizing he had said way too much. He wadded up his wrapper and stood. "I gotta go. I have to get to the field and gear up." He gathered his litter and headed for the door.

When Toni got back to the house, she slipped out of her sandals and worked her foot around experimentally. The poor little toe was black and blue, but she could bear to touch it.

She dumped her purse on the sofa and peeked into the kitchen. Barb Donovan was there. It was only two-thirty, but she was already working on the evening meal. "I'm back. Do you need any help?"

"No, I'm fine," Barb responded. "Why don't you relax for a while? You've been working awfully hard for someone who's on summer vacation."

"Maybe I will." A nap did sound good.

But when Toni stretched out on the bed, she found that she was antsy. As pleasant as it felt to lie there and do nothing, she felt a need to be active, to do something more toward the investigation. But she didn't know what to do. Then she remembered the card she had stuck in her purse. She went back to the living room for her purse and returned to her room.

She had to pull her wallet and several smaller items out before she found the card where it had slid under an empty bank envelope. It was smudged from being wet, but it was now dry. The smudging didn't really matter, though. All the information printed on it were the words Game Room in a large fancy green font, and a web address in smaller letters under it.

Curious, Toni went to her father-in-law's office

where his computer was already booted. She logged onto the Internet and typed in the web address. What came up was an innocent looking game site. She saw icons and names for innocuous looking games like hangman, spades, hearts, solitaire, chess, and free cell. It certainly didn't look important.

Under the Game Room heading was a paragraph stating that this was a place for southeast Missouri students to hang out. It had a typo in it.

At loose ends, Toni began opening the games one by one, not sure why she was wasting time like this. When she had checked them all out, she started to close the browser. Then she noticed a small graphic in the lower left corner that looked like a logo or trademark. On closer examination she saw that the picture was a simple outline of a door. She moved the computer mouse over it and was surprised when the pointer indicated the icon was a clickable graphic. She clicked on it.

What appeared on the screen was an online gambling setup for area sports. Toni recognized the names of area schools. Too excited to fully comprehend the details, she scanned through the contents. It followed the design of a professional online gambling site, but the writing, including a couple of misspelled words, made her think an amateur had designed and posted it.

Toni sat frozen, considering the implications. Then, concentrating in an effort to remember what she had learned in her high school's professional development workshops, she clicked on the View menu and selected Source Code. She remembered being shown how meta tags looked and that they contained keywords meant to attract search engines to them. She saw nothing related to gambling.

"I think that could mean this site was not designed to be found by search engines," she muttered to herself. "Which means that anyone going to it has to know exactly what he or she is looking for—which means they only know about it through personal contact." That explained the business card. Someone was distributing them. Just how big an operation was this?

Toni closed the browser and grabbed the card. She hurried back to her bedroom, got her purse, and fished out her cell phone. "I'm going back out for a while," she called to her mother-in-law on the way out the door, dialing Quint.

"I just wanted to see if you're home," she said when her brother answered.

"I'm here."

"I'm on my way over. I'll be there in ten minutes." She disconnected and got in the van.

She found Quint sitting in a lawn chair by his apartment door, clad in jeans and a black tee shirt. He stared at her as she approached, not smiling. "What's up, Quizzy?"

"Let's go inside and I'll show you. Is your computer on?"

"No." He looked puzzled, but he didn't ask questions.

While his computer booted, Toni told him about her latest encounter with the boys at Ozark.

Quint's eyes rolled as she explained how she had approached them. But by the time she got to the point of Dean's comments, skepticism had turned to sober attention.

"Here," she said, handing him the card. "Go to this web site."

Quint sat in front of the computer and typed in the address. When the game site came up, he frowned, unimpressed

"They really are just games." Toni move closer to see the screen over his shoulder.

He clicked on one, and then another, just to see for himself.

Toni placed a finger on the small graphic in the lower corner. "Click on that."

He did. When he saw what came up, he whistled and leaned forward. "This is no small thing. It looks like a sophisticated setup."

He scrolled down through the site, studying it. Then he turned to face Toni, his expression troubled. "I think we have a high school gambling ring right here under our noses. From the looks of this, it's being run along the lines of an organized crime operation. I've heard about these rackets springing up in bedroom communities, but I had no idea there's one here."

"Do you think there's any possibility it's connected to organized crime?"

Quint's mouth thinned. "I don't know. I hope not. But I need to relay this to the detectives."

*

As she drove back across town, Toni tried to think how to go about identifying Jesse Campbell's killer. Facts and possibilities whirled in her head, but nothing fit together. All the things she had learned seemed important, but she wasn't sure how to connect them.

Knowledge. It occurred to her that she could never acquire too much knowledge. It was too late to go to the library, but the Internet was loaded with information.

After supper with Barb and Dan Donovan, Toni explained to them that Quint had asked her to spend her final week of classes with him and thanked them for letting her stay with them so much that summer. She explained that she would move to his apartment when she returned from the weekend in Clearmount.

The Donovans understood and didn't blame Toni for seizing the opportunity to spend time with her brother now that his rotating shift of crazy hours had improved and he could host company better.

After helping Barb clean up in the kitchen, Toni excused herself and went to her room. She took a shower and spent the evening searching out and reading about teenage—even middle school—gambling. It horrified her to read of the rising rate of compulsive gambling among teens and pre-teens. Cited as the fastest growing teen addiction, some researchers estimated a million of the approximately eight million compulsive gamblers in America to be teenagers. The problem was linked to risky behaviors like heavy drinking, carrying weapons, sexual activity and fighting.

As she read, Toni's anger escalated. It was bad enough that her boys were frightened for her, and that a friend had been mugged. But it was infuriating to learn that a coach had been getting teens hooked on gambling. It looked like he might have gotten what he deserved.

But it was still murder. And no one should get away with that. It made shivers go up Toni's spine to realize that her own boys, who would be in seventh and fifth grades that fall, were old enough to be aware of, or even involved in, this growing trend.

Forcing herself to calm down, Toni suddenly needed to hear their voices. She logged off the computer, took her cell phone off the charger, and called them.

"Hi, Mom," Garrett's voice answered after three rings. "We miss you, but we're fine. Grandma and Grandpa aren't tired of us yet. Anything else you want to know?"

"Brat," she accused with a laugh.

"Billy Radford is having a birthday party next week, and I'm invited," he went on. "I need to buy him a present."

"Does that mean you want me to shop for something?" She knew a hint when she heard it. Now she had to figure out what to get for a boy turning ten years old.

"Yeah. Thanks, Mom. Here's Gabe."

There was a pause, and then, "Hi, Mom," from her older son.

"How was your day?"

"All right, I guess."

In front of her, the muted television was showing a commercial. Toni watched a heat advisory scrolling across the bottom of the screen, warning that temperatures were expected to be over a hundred degrees the next two days.

"...so I need new ones before school starts."

Toni shook her head, having missed part of what

he was saying. "New what?" she asked blankly.

"Mom! Weren't you listening?"

"I'm sorry. I was distracted," she apologized. "Would you mind repeating it for me?"

"I said I need some new clothes and shoes before school starts," he repeated in a long-suffering tone.

Toni sighed. "Is asking for things the only reason you two talk to me?"

"Yep."

"Smarty. Okay, we'll try to get in some shopping this weekend." She paused for a moment. "Are you hanging out with your buddies quite a bit?"

"Some," he said off-handedly.

"I'm curious," she said, trying to sound casual. "I know you and your pals go swimming and ride your bikes during the summer. But what do your classmates do for fun during the school term?"

"Oh, they hang out, go to ballgames, and other stuff at school."

"Do they play a lot of games at home?"

"Sure. Everybody has video games and TV, things like that."

"What about card games or online games?"

"All that," he confirmed.

How could she get him to tell her what she really wanted to know? "Do they ever play poker or anything like that?"

There was silence for several moments. "Mom, you're after something. What is it you want to know?"

Count on Gabe to see through her. She sighed. "All right, I want to know if poker or other forms of gambling are going on with the kids there in

Clearmount."

"Sure. It's no big deal," Gabe said. "They watch poker on television, and a lot of them play it after school. Some even bet on sports online."

"Do they play for money?"

"Of course. That's the fun of it, winning money. Most of the games are on Friday nights, but it's getting more popular."

"How do you know this?"

"It's easy. During school you just walk along the halls and find out who's playing where. Some of the kids play at lunch and in study halls. Of course, the teachers don't realize they're playing for money. They think they're just killing time after their homework is done."

A picture of the students playing cards in the student union flashed across her mind. "Have you played in these games?" she asked carefully.

"A couple of times. So I know how to play poker, if that's what you're asking. But I'm not hooked on it or anything. I like basketball and baseball better."

Toni breathed a sigh of relief. Hopefully her boys had enough common sense to avoid that kind of thing. "The sports are much healthier," is all she said. They would have a serious discussion later, when it could be done face to face.

"I gotta go, Mom. Your baby boy is messing with my stuff."

"Okay, run along. I'll call again tomorrow night. Love you, kid."

"Love you, too. Bye."

Toni tried to call Kyle but got no answer. He was

probably some place where he couldn't get cell service.

*

Wednesday morning Toni headed for school with her brain still on overload. She had collected herself enough to pack a sandwich to gulp between lecture and lab. Her toe was feeling much better, so she forced thoughts of murder suspects and gambling from her mind and lectured from the front of the room. It went well.

At eleven o'clock she gave the class a five minute break and downed her sandwich. Then, during the respiration lab, she made her way around to the table where Nicole was working and leaned over to whisper in her ear. "Can you stay and chat with me for a couple of minutes after class?"

Nicole glanced up. "I can do that."

Toni moved on, facilitating the work at each table. While everyone else gathered their personal items and left the room, Nicole remained in her seat. When the students were gone, Toni returned to Nicole's table and took a seat facing her. The young woman looked tired.

"Is there something wrong?" Nicole asked.

"Oh, no," Toni said. "I didn't mean to alarm you. Your work is fine. If you do as well on the final as you have on everything so far, you'll have an A."

Relief flashed across Nicole's face. "Good. I've been working hard and loving the class. If nursing is this interesting, I know I'll like it. But keeping up with a job and a kid has me looking forward to a break."

"Believe me, I understand," Toni said. "I hope

you don't mind my bringing up your former coach's murder again."

Nicole shrugged. "I don't see how I can help, but ask anything you want."

"I've been doing some checking on Mr. Campbell's background," she began. "To the best of your knowledge, were his years at Branson successful?"

"He was a good coach," Nicole said without hesitation. "I think he had winning seasons every year he was there."

"What was his exact position with the district?"

"He was head basketball coach for the ninth grade and Junior Varsity teams."

"Do you know how long he was there?" Toni knew from the resume that it was five years, but she wanted to hear Nicole's confirmation. She was trying to gauge the accuracy of the girl's memory.

Nicole thought a moment. "He was new the year I was in eighth grade and was there until the year I graduated. So that would have been five years."

Toni didn't know how to phrase the next question tactfully, so she just asked outright. "Do you know for sure that he was fired?"

"I'm not a hundred percent sure," Nicole said, tipping her head in thought. "I was just a student and had no inside track, but one day when I was putting up a bulletin board in the hall outside the teachers' work room, the door was open, and I overheard a couple of staff members talking about it. They didn't know I could hear them. They were talking about him having resigned just as he was due for tenure. I didn't even understand about tenure at the time."

Tenure was as near to job security as a teacher could get. In the schools of Toni's personal knowledge, five years was the standard time a teacher had to work in the same district to gain that important protection from summary dismissal. Tenure was often criticized for allowing teachers to remain in the profession after becoming unproductive, shoddy, or incompetent. Schools were reluctant to grant it unless absolutely convinced that a teacher was a 'keeper'.

Toni also knew that teachers the districts didn't want to retain were commonly given the opportunity to resign rather than have an involuntary termination on their record. It sounded as if that had been the case with Jesse Campbell.

"What about the inappropriate relationship with a female student? Are you sure that really happened?"

"I'm positive it happened," Nicole said, her tone confident. "Sonya bragged about it."

"Do you have any idea how Jesse's wife reacted when the story got out?"

"I never heard any stories about her making a public spectacle of herself or anything like that," Nicole said after a brief pause. "She had two young kids to consider. The youngest one was born not long before Coach lost his job. I heard she left him, but then went back to him. Sonya's boyfriend wasn't so forgiving, though. He dumped her."

"Were there ever any charges brought?"

"No. Sonya said her parents found out and wanted to sue Jesse, but she wouldn't cooperate. She said it was her first fling with an older man, and she wasn't going to bring charges against him for something she had wanted. Besides, she was eighteen—at least by the time the story came out."

Toni wished she knew more about this girl. "Can you give me Sonya's full name and tell me how to find her?"

"Her name is Sonya Finch. The last I heard she was working at a nightclub here in Springfield, the Goldenrod."

"Do you know her parents?"

"Their names are Wilma and Ed Finch, but I don't know for sure where they live. So far as I know they're still in Branson. I think they lived somewhere in the country outside of town. I remember Sonya complaining about having to ride the bus when her car was in the garage. She was mad because her parents wouldn't drive her to school."

Toni noticed Nicole glance at her watch. "If you need to go to work, that's fine. I appreciate your openness."

Nicole nodded and gathered her books. "I have a few minutes, but I need to stop by the campus book store. Just for the record, I think the coach was asking for trouble when he started cheating on his wife. But that doesn't give anyone the right to kill him. I hope you find who did it. Good luck."

When Nicole was gone, Toni put the room in order. It was one-forty-five when she walked out into the heat. On her way to the parking lot, she dug her cell phone from her purse.

"Hello from Springfield," she said when her principal answered his office phone. "Don't you have a secretary today?"

"Hi, Toni," Ken Douglas responded pleasantly. "Paula's down in the main office getting some forms for me. What can I do for you?"

"Do you know anyone personally at the Branson High School who would be willing to give you an overview of Jesse Campbell's history there?"

He chuckled. "Still sleuthing, huh? I don't have any personal ties with anyone there, but I'll call and see if I can get the principal or superintendent—whoever's available—to talk to me."

"Thanks."

"How's it going?" he asked before she could end the call.

Toni unlocked the van door and nearly strangled on the enclosed heat as she slid under the wheel. "I'm spinning my wheels," she said, digging for her keys. "I'm finding that there are more people than just your friend who have reason to hate Campbell. Grant's wife isn't the only affair he had. I've been told that there was a relationship with a student while he was at Branson."

Ken's sigh was audible. "That's what you really want to know about, isn't it? That kind of thing is an administrator's worst nightmare. Okay, I understand. I'll get back to you soon and let you know if I have any luck."

As she disconnected, Toni started the van and flipped on the air conditioning. She tossed the phone in her purse and lolled her head back against the seat, waiting for the air to cool enough that she could bear to close the door and handle the hot steering wheel. She debated what to do next. She wanted to go looking for Sonya Finch, but she also wanted to talk to someone at the Glendale school. By three o'clock the summer staff would likely be going home.

When she was able to breathe, Toni closed the van door and drove off the parking lot. She worked her way to the southeast part of town, turned onto Ingram Mill Road, and soon pulled into the drive of Glendale High School.

She got out and went to the main entrance. Inside, she saw a hallway display of scarlet red, white, and Columbia blue school banners with pictures of their falcon mascot on them.

She imagined Jesse Campbell striding through these halls and interacting with the students. His death surely had been a major topic of discussion with the summer staff. She saw a small sign that said OFFICES and had an arrow pointing up the hall. She walked that way until she saw a door bearing a name plate that said PRINCIPAL on it. She opened it and stepped inside.

Scanning quickly, Toni saw an office that made her think every principal's office in the world must look the same. There was a desk out front, with offices behind and to the side of it. The desk was unoccupied.

She identified the door with the label she wanted and tapped on it.

"Come in," came from inside.

When she stepped into the room Toni saw a man who looked to be in his late forties or early fifties. His hair was whitening and thinning, and his face was round and full. Of medium height and a little too heavy, he wore wire-rimmed glasses. "May I help you?"

"My name is Toni Donovan. I teach science at the Clearmount High School, and I'm looking for the principal here."

The man stood behind his desk and extended a hand, his face brightening. "That would be me. I'm Roy Kissell. Do you have an application for me?"

Chapter 13

Toni went blank for a moment. "Oh, you mean an employment application."

The man's face lost its glow. "Yes. Isn't that why you're here? We advertised an opening. I assumed that was why you've come."

"Sorry to mislead you," she apologized. "I wasn't aware of that."

He dropped into his chair, his dark eyes assessing her. "No problem. What is it you need then?"

"I've been looking into the death of a former coach of yours, Jesse Campbell. My son discovered his body in the lagoon at Sequiota Park," she explained in a rush.

"Is there any official reason I should talk to you?" His authoritative voice and manner had become a bit intimidating.

"Not really," she said, opting for honesty. "My brother is on the local police force here and is working with the detectives on the case. As for me personally, I'm a compulsive fact collector."

The faintest hint of a smile tugged at the corners of his mouth. "You really are a science teacher then?"

"I am. At the Clearmount High School. But this summer I've been teaching a class at OTC for a regular instructor who's on maternity leave."

"I see," he said, seeming to weigh her intent. "So you're conducting a personal investigation. What are you looking for?" He gestured for her to sit.

She did. "I've been checking back through Jesse's work history, and I wanted to ask about his time with you here. Were you the principal while he was on this school's staff?"

The man nodded. "I've been here for twelve years, so I remember him well. In fact, I hired him. I was shocked when I heard of his death."

"I've seen his resume, so I know this was his first full-time coaching position," Toni said. "What I don't know is how he got along here. How would you rate his success?"

"Jesse first came to us as a student teacher from MSU," he said slowly, as if still making up his mind how much to tell her. But he continued. "He really impressed Lyle Mahoney, the coach who was his mentor. When Lyle resigned that spring to take a position at a junior college, he recommended that we hire Jesse to replace him. What we did was promote the assistant coach to head coach and offer Jesse the assistant position, which he accepted."

"I assume you were happy with him?"

"We were. He was young and inexperienced, only twenty-one, which is why we felt he should not be hired over the experienced assistant we had. He did a great job and stayed with us for two years. He was popular with the students and staff and became friends with coaching staff at other schools. After getting a couple years of experience under his belt, he accepted an opportunity to move up at another school."

"That would be Branson, right?"

"Yes. He became head coach of their younger boys."

"Did he develop any special friends here that he kept in touch with?"

Mr. Kissell considered the question. "I'm not sure. He might have. I didn't personally keep in touch with him. I only made note when his name came up in conversations or appeared in sports articles."

"Was he married or single when you hired him?"

"He was single, but he married during the holiday break that first year. His bride was a girl from his hometown. They had a baby the next year."

"What about the students? Did Jesse get along with them well?"

"As I said, he seemed to get along with everyone."

"Did he have any student assistants, or did an assistant coach rate a teacher aide—or whatever you call them here," she added with a smile.

"Actually, he did have one—both years he was here. The boy took care of the details of game preparations, lined up people to run the clock and keep the game books, a lot of little extras. So Jesse needed an assistant as much as the head coach did."

Toni thought about that. "Do you happen to remember the name of the student who assisted Jesse? He might be someone who would have kept in touch."

The principal's head bobbed slightly. "As a matter of fact, I do remember the boy's name. His mother works in the elementary school as an aide. His name is Barry Kuzman."

Bingo. A connection had finally been made. Toni was glad she had come. "Thank you for your time. You've been helpful," she said without elaboration.

"We were disappointed when Jesse left, but we understood." Mr. Kissell said as he stood and extended his hand.

Toni understood, too. It was a typical progression. Beginning teachers acquired a couple years of experience and moved on to something more lucrative if they got a chance. She also understood from this principal's glowing evaluation of Jesse Campbell that he lived with his head in the sand, or he was choosing to hide the rumors about Jesse from her. There was no point in bringing up what she had heard. She accepted his handshake and left.

Toni was unlocking the door of her van when her cell phone rang. She stopped and dug it out of her purse.

"Your story checks out," Ken Douglas said. "Jesse Campbell was at Branson five years as head coach for their ninth grade and Junior Varsity basketball teams."

Toni finished opening the door and crawled into the vehicle. It hadn't had time to get too hot yet. "I'm in a parking lot and it's hot out here. Just a minute while I get the motor and air going," she said while juggling the phone and digging for her keys. "Okay, go on," she said moments later over the sounds of the motor and air conditioner.

"I spoke to the principal, and he was pretty forthright when I identified myself and told him that someone investigating the case questioned me," Ken explained. "He said he didn't see any reason to hide anything at this point."

"So what about the termination? Was it voluntary or forced?"

"Forced. The guy gave them winning teams, so they liked him. But when they were faced with convincing evidence of dalliance with a student, they felt they couldn't risk keeping him around. There was never a formal charge, but they were afraid to grant him tenure and possibly have it happen again. They told him his contract wouldn't be renewed, but that he would be allowed to resign. Everything you heard is true."

Toni sighed deeply as she disconnected. She knew there were efforts in progress to close loopholes that allowed problem teachers to move from one school district to another. It was commonly called 'passing the trash' when districts allowed a teacher to quietly leave a school, failed to report problems to state authorities, or failed to check with state officials before hiring a teacher. The new school district might get the truth, but not the *whole* truth about the person's background. They might learn the dates of service and whether the person was dismissed, but no other information.

Toni drove to Quint's apartment. When she pulled into the visitor parking spot near his unit, she called John. "Would you like to ride home with me for the weekend and not have to drive that far with your sore arm?"

"Sure. That'll also save me a tank of gas." He chuckled. "What time will you pick me up?"

"Right after class. We'll grab lunch on the way

out of town. See you then."

She tucked the phone back in her purse and exited the van into the still oppressive heat. She gazed longingly at the pool about fifty feet across the lot. No, she didn't have time for a swim, she reminded herself.

"Got any Coke in your fridge?" she asked when Quint answered the doorbell.

"I think there's one with your name on it," he said dryly.

She stepped inside the cool apartment and went straight to the kitchen. "It's cooking out there," she said as she pulled the fridge door open. "I'm parched."

Quint leaned against the sink and watched her while she popped the tab and drank. "What's on your mind, Quizzy?"

Toni made a hand gesture toward the living room, taking another swig. She followed him and plopped onto the sofa. "I've talked to the principal at Glendale and someone who knew Jesse when he was at Branson. I also had my principal talk to the Branson principal and confirm what I heard." She summarized the facts.

Quint cocked his head to one side, his brow arched, when she finished. "You're really into this sleuthing, aren't you?"

She shrugged. "I guess so. And I feel like we're following a trail that's getting near an answer."

"I've been on the phone," he said smugly. "I don't go back to work until tomorrow night, but I decided to check in with the detectives. We were right about Mrs. Campbell."

"You mean she didn't do it?"

He nodded. "Under interrogation her story didn't hold together. She finally admitted she was trying to take the blame to protect her ex. Her story was a little garbled, but the gist of it, according to Detective Green, is that she made a mistake by getting involved with Jesse, and then she didn't know how to get out. When they got caught and Jesse insisted they get married, she agreed. She knew Grant was angry and hurt and was going to divorce her, whatever she did."

Toni nodded in understanding. "Jesse had other affairs. The difference that time was that it was his buddy's wife. He thought he should marry her, probably from guilt."

"You're right. Sheila was miserable over losing custody of her kids, so when it looked like Grant was the chief suspect, she panicked. She thought he really did do it, you see. She knew her kids need him, and she's eaten up with guilt."

"She wants to reconnect with her kids," Toni said intuitively. "I wonder if there's any chance of reconnecting with Grant."

"Stranger things have happened," Quint allowed.

Toni considered that for a moment, but then her mind switched tracks. "How would you feel about going out with me?"

He gave her a knowing look. "You mean play bodyguard while you poke around somewhere?"

"Nothing dangerous," she said. "Are you familiar with a place called the Goldenrod?"

"Sure. It's a restaurant and nightclub. Is that where you want to go?"

"It's where the girl Jesse messed around with at

Branson is supposed to be working."

His expression cleared. "I guess we could go to dinner there. They serve food—and other things. I'd rather go with you than sit here knowing you'll go alone if I don't."

He glanced at his watch. "It's way too early to eat. Why don't we go for a swim first?"

It sounded wonderful. "I'll have to run get my bathing suit."

After a quick trip to the Donovans to get the suit and tell her in-laws that she would be eating with Quint that evening, Toni reveled in an hour of frolicking in the water with her brother. Not only was it cooling, but it was mentally refreshing, temporarily suspending thoughts of all things serious.

"Are you getting hungry?" Quint asked about five o'clock.

"Hungry enough." She reached for the rail to pull herself up the steps.

When they were changed and ready to go, Toni grinned at Quint. Wearing light colored pants, a short sleeve white shirt, and dark loafers, he looked nothing like a cop. That was good.

Quint drove. The building he parked next to was long and flat roofed. A huge neon sign stood at the perimeter of the lot, a bright yellow goldenrod glowing next to the club's name.

Toni smiled to herself as she accompanied her handsome brother inside. It amused her to think they would be taken for a couple. The ceiling was low, the décor an effort at glamour and glitz that fell a bit short. To the right was a large arched doorway with a sign over it that said BAR. The room beyond it was dimly lit with flashes of neon making intermittent streaks of colored light across the walls.

There were twenty or so tables in the restaurant, about half of them occupied. They made their way to an upholstered corner booth and sat across from one another.

A blonde waitress, who looked no more than eighteen or twenty, approached with menus and an order pad. She wore a skimpy black and white fake leather outfit. "May I help you?"

"Is Sonya Finch working tonight?" Toni asked as she accepted a menu.

"She's working the bar right now. I'll tell her someone is looking for her. Maybe she can stop by to see you when she gets a break."

"Thanks. I'd like a large iced tea, a salad, and the grilled chicken special."

Quint ordered a steak, baked potato, and coffee.

When the waitress left, Toni studied their surroundings. The clientele seemed fairly affluent. She wondered if there was any gambling, drug dealing, or sexual activity going on there. "You're off duty, so I'll do the questioning," she informed Quint.

He grinned. "Enjoy yourself."

Their waitress returned with a loaded tray. "Is there anything else I can get you?" she asked when their food was before them.

"Everything looks good," Quint said.

For the next few minutes they ate in silence. They were just finishing when a waitress entered the main room from the bar. She was tall and slim, with straight dark hair to her shoulders and thick dark lashes. She wore the same skimpy outfit as the restaurant waitress. Her makeup was heavy, and long silver earrings dangled from her lobes. She held a camera.

When she saw them watching her, the girl paused and snapped a picture. "Sandy said there's a good looking couple out here asking for me," she said brightly, white teeth flashing. Her voice was low and husky.

She held up the camera. "The picture's only a ten spot."

Quint reached for his wallet, but Toni forestalled him. "I'll take it," she said, reaching for her purse. She pulled out a ten and shoved it toward the girl, regarding it as payment in advance for any information they might glean.

The girl tucked the money into her bra, pulled the picture from the camera, and handed it to Toni. "Thanks from Sonya."

"I'm Toni, and this is Quint," Toni said with a hand gesture. "I understand that you went to high school in Branson."

"Sure did, sweetie," she said, stepping nearer. She looked from Toni to Quint and back. "Does that make me famous?"

"I also understand that you were intimately acquainted with Coach Jesse Campbell."

Sonya's smile disappeared, and she took a step backward. "Hey! What is this?"

"Just some friendly fact gathering," Toni said. "Since you knew him so well, we were wondering if you might have any idea who hated him enough to kill him."

"Who sicced you on to me?"

"You weren't very secretive. The story got around."

"I'll just bet," she said with a snort.

Toni watched as a flash of anger crossed her face, and then changed to something more like arrogance. Sonya edged up close to the table.

"He was an important part of my education. He knew how to show a girl a good time, and I was goofy about him. I have no regrets," she said with a toss of her head.

This was a pretty fast and loose gal—or at least she wanted to be perceived as such. Toni exchanged quick glances with Quint. He dropped his lids in a gesture that she interpreted to mean she was on her own. She motioned for Sonya to sit across from her. Surprisingly she did.

"Who broke it off?"

"He did," Sonya said with a shrug. "But I understood. He was looking at big trouble, and his wife was unhappy with him—not that I could blame her, I guess. Anyhow, he told me we had to keep a lot of distance between us. The principal and super called me into the office and asked me a bunch of questions. I basically told them to take a hike and gave them nothing they could use to fire him. They had to find other reasons to not give him a new contract."

Toni figured protecting her lover had probably given the girl a sense of martyrdom. "Were there any more girls from the student body involved with him?"

Sonya gave her a sharp look, as if questioning her brightness. "No way. I'd have scratched their eyes out."

"Did your parents know about it?"

"My mom worked at the school, so she found out and told my dad. And, yes, they were upset. But they're getting over it. They retired last year and moved to Florida. They tried to get me to move with them, but I wasn't about to leave here when I'm just getting into the kind of work I want to do." She glanced around the room. "Not waitressing. This is just while I'm getting launched."

"At what?"

She picked up the camera and waved it. "I work for a modeling and photography agency. I get some practice here on the photography, and I'm starting to get some modeling assignments." She didn't say how many.

"Do you know anything about Jesse or your classmates being involved in gambling on sports? Did he ever say anything to you about such a thing?"

Sonya's brows went up, her eyes rounding. Then she shook her head, making the long earrings swing wildly. "Never heard of such a thing. Well, it's been nice meeting you, but I have to get back to work." She bounced to her feet and sashayed away.

"Either she's a very good liar, or she knows nothing about the gambling--and I think it's the first," Quint said as they returned to his truck. "The next time she sees me it'll be in uniform."

"Do you think she overplayed the lighthearted part a little bit? Did she cover for Jesse, let him dump her, and then get even?"

"I don't know," Quint said as he started the engine. "But I'm going to let the detectives know about our little visit. I just hope they appreciate our tips and don't hassle me about you poking around."

That evening Toni curled up on the couch to grade papers. At eight-thirty she called the boys and chatted a while. Then she called Kyle and discussed their plans for the weekend. Before ending the call, Toni shared with him that she thought they needed to have a heart to heart talk with the boys about the danger of getting caught up in any kind of gambling.

Thursday morning, bleary eyed from grading papers so late, Toni slipped on a pair of periwinkle blue palazzo pants and a bright blue blouse. She pulled the top of her hair back and secured it with a clip and let the rest of it fall free. After applying some light makeup and small hoop earrings, she chose a pair of thick soled navy sandals that felt reasonably good on her bruised toe. Then she joined the Donovans for a breakfast of eggs and toast.

"I'll pick John up and head home after class," she explained when they finished eating.

Dan gave her a warm hug. "We've enjoyed having you around this summer."

Barb's embrace was a bit stiff.

Chapter 14

Ten minutes before class was to begin, Nicole Warren entered the room and approached Toni's desk. "Did you talk to Sonya?" she asked softly as students walked past them.

Toni looked up at the serious young woman. "Yes, I did. I don't know if I learned anything helpful, but I think it's important to talk to as many people as possible who had personal knowledge or contact with your former coach."

Nicole nodded. "Does she know I gave you her name?"

"I didn't tell her where I got it."

At her assurance, she could see the tension drain from Nicole's shoulders. It made Toni wonder why so much tension. "If you hear anything about a gambling ring, will you tell me about it?"

Nicole's eyes darted around, and she seemed uneasy. "I'll do that. Mrs. Donovan, I hate to ask this, but will I be able to make up any work I miss if I don't stay for class today? My daughter is sick, and I need to take her to the doctor. She's in the car with my mother."

"You can if you bring me a signed note from the doctor," Toni assured her, sympathy surging through her for the young single mother.

"I'll be sure to ask for one."

"We'll be covering chapters twenty-two through twenty-four on the urinary and reproductive systems today and Monday. Read and study them thoroughly, and I'm sure you'll be fine. Now go take care of your daughter. I hope it's nothing serious and she's fine by tomorrow. I'll be thinking about you."

"Thank you, Mrs. Donovan," Nicole said, her eyes shiny with restrained tears.

When Nicole was gone, Toni greeted the class and began the lecture. "Lab finals will be next Wednesday and written finals on Thursday," she announced when she finished. Then she opened the door for them to exit. And found Quint leaning against the wall, dressed in sweat pants and a tee shirt.

"This could become a habit," she teased when he crossed the hall toward her.

"I wanted to catch you before you leave town. Got a minute?"

"Of course." She motioned for him to enter the now empty room. She sat at her desk and began clearing it.

Quint took a seat facing her. "The detectives have been busy. There are a couple of things I thought you'd like to hear."

"Go on." She pushed papers into her satchel. "I can function and listen at the same time."

He grinned. "I know. Okay, for starters, officers Durbin and Chilton located and arrested Barry Kuzman."

"Good. I hope they found out what's going on."

His grin turned smug. "They got out the cat-o-nine tails, or maybe it was the sharp talking negotiating detectives. However it went, they persuaded Kuzman to tell them about the high school gambling ring in hopes of lightening the charges against him. He's young and fairly new to this mafia style life, so he's scared."

Toni shoved another stack of papers into the satchel. "Ouch. That smarts." She grabbed her finger and squeezed it.

There was a small paper slit on her left index finger, with blood seeping from it. She stuck it in her mouth, and then blew on it.

Quint just shook his head. "The detectives have also been checking the background of those two teens you talked to in Ozark."

"All right!" She made a fist of the hand with the cut finger and pumped it. She was all attention now, paper slit and satchel packing forgotten.

"Young Mister Vince Harcourt, besides being an arrogant rich kid, is a computer nerd. He can't spell worth spit, but he's a whiz with computers and makes A's in all his classes except communication arts. I'm guessing he's the Webmaster of that site. He was probably recruiting someone when you showed up at his pool."

"That makes sense. The card was part of the promotion."

"As for his role beyond that, I'm not sure. It's hard to imagine a kid that age being a mastermind of the operation, but anything's possible."

"That was more likely Jesse Campbell," Toni theorized. "If that's true, two things can happen now. Everything can fall apart, or there could be a power struggle for control. What about the other kid, Dean Patrick?"

"Mr. Patrick isn't on the scholastic level of Mr. Harcourt, but they spend a lot of time together, according to the detectives' sources. If this operation is as big as I'm beginning to suspect, it has kids working as runners, recruiters, collectors, enforcers, and no telling what else. And that's alongside the online operation. My guess is that Dean Patrick fills one or more of those roles."

Quint pushed to his feet. "I know you need to get on the road. See you Sunday."

Toni finished tidying the room and went to the van. She called John as she left the parking lot and told him she was on the way. He was waiting on the front porch, his bags beside him, when she arrived at the house where he was staying.

"Are you in a big hurry to get home?" she asked as he tossed his bags in the back seat.

He peered over the seat at her. "There's nothing pressing, other than being anxious to see Jenny. Why?"

"Do you mind taking a detour? I'd like to swing around through Nixa and see if I can find anyone who'll talk to us at the construction company where Jesse worked."

John grinned and shut the door. As he climbed into the front seat, he was careful with his injured arm. "Could that detour start by way of a burger joint? It's noon and I'm hungry."

"I am, too. Would you settle for a drive through? It would save us time."

"Good enough."

They got sandwiches at McDonald's and ate on the road.

"The company's supposed to be located just this side of town. I looked up the address and then asked a student from Nixa how to find it. There's supposed to be a sign where we're to turn off," Toni explained as she drove.

They had no trouble following the directions to Dolman Construction. A trailer with an office sign on it sat in front of an asphalted parking lot for trucks and other equipment, most of them bearing a Dolman logo. There was a barn-like structure behind it that looked like a maintenance shed. Someone in a hard hat walked toward the shed from the back of the trailer. A cement truck roared into the lot.

Toni parked in front of the office trailer between a red Honda and a black pickup. "Want to start the questioning?" she asked John.

He grinned. "You trust me?"

"Sure. Why should I have all the fun? Besides, you need the experience."

John's large frame vibrated as he laughed. "Okay, let's go." He cradled his arm to his abdomen as he climbed out of the van and led the way up the wooden steps.

The office they entered was a utilitarian reception area. To the right was a closed door with a nameplate that said PAUL DOLMAN. To the left was a wide open doorway through which they could see a kitchen and a hallway behind it. In the center of the room, a red haired woman sat at a cluttered desk. She looked to be in her late forties or early fifties and wore a no-nonsense double-breasted navy dress with gold buttons down the front. The nameplate on the desk bore the name Gretchen Horner.

She looked up. "May I help you?"

"I'm John Zachary, and this is my colleague, Toni Donovan," John said. "A friend of mine used to work for this company. He died tragically a few days ago, and I'm looking for information that might help us find out who killed him."

The woman's expression changed from a mixture of welcome, to annoyance at having her concentration broken, and then to one of enlightenment. "You mean Jesse Campbell?"

"That's right."

"I've read the stories," she said with a sad shake of her head. "He seemed like such a nice young man when he came to work here."

"We're hoping you can give us some information," John repeated in a persuasive tone.

"I can't imagine what I could tell you." She pulled her glasses off and rubbed the bridge of her nose.

"How long did Jesse work here?"

The woman thought a moment, and then went to a file cabinet behind her. She worked her fingers along the tops of a row of folders. Then she pulled one out and resumed her seat. After a quick glance inside, she looked up. "He was here about two and a half years, twenty nine months to be exact."

"During the time that he was here, did he get along okay with the work and the crew?"

"His work was fine. He was dependable and a hard worker," she said. Then she paused, a shadow of unease crossing her face.

"What about his relationships with the other workers?" John pressed on. "Did he get along with them all right?"

"I believe so," she said without elaboration.

"Were there problems on jobs or anything like that?" Toni asked when John hesitated.

Gretchen Horner eyed them uneasily. "There may have been," she said finally. "But I don't feel comfortable talking about employees."

"This is a *former* employee we're talking about, a man who was killed by someone," Toni pointed out. "If you know of any conflicts he had with anyone, don't you think it would be appropriate to tell us so we can check it out. I assure you we aren't looking to cause trouble for anyone who wasn't involved. We just want to find out the truth."

The secretary replaced her glasses and stared at them for several long, deliberating moments. Then her chin lifted. "There was one job where there was some trouble. It happened not long before Jesse quit. The crew was working on an expensive remodeling job that took quite a while. The husband worked and the wife stayed home with a couple of young kids." She hesitated.

Toni sensed what had to be the story. "Jesse had an affair with the wife, didn't he?"

She nodded. "The only reason I know is because he got caught. I mean the husband found out, and he came here looking for Jesse. There was a fight, and the crew had to pull them apart."

"What is the man's name?" John asked.

Gretchen hesitated again. Then she reopened the file and read for a bit. When she finally looked up, she just stared at them in silence.

"We're sharing our information with the police," John said. "If you don't tell us the man's name and how to find him, you'll have to tell them."

"Oh, what the heck," she said suddenly. "The name is Malcolm Burk, and here's the address." She opened the file and covered the information above the address with an index card.

Toni grabbed her pen and notepad from her purse and wrote it down. "Can you tell us the quickest way to find it?"

The directions she gave them seemed simple. When she finished, they thanked her and left.

At the edge of town Toni turned on the street Gretchen had said to take. A half mile later she made a right onto the correct street and found the house number. The residence looked like most of the other houses in the neighborhood—dark brick, a picture window, a double garage, and a small yard. The difference was that this yard needed mowing. Badly. She pulled to the curb.

When they knocked at the door, a man opened it. "Yeah?" He peered at them through bloodshot eyes. "Whatcha want?"

"Mr. Burk?" John said.

"Yeah." He shifted his weight and swayed slightly.

"We're John Zachary and Toni Donovan. May we talk to you a few moments?"

The man stared blearily and made no move to admit them. "What about?"

He was disheveled, looked to be in his late thirties or early forties, and had large dark circles under his eyes. He was probably six feet tall, but he was so slumped it was hard to tell. His skin was peeling from sunburn, indicative of outdoor work.

"We understand that you knew Jesse Campbell," John said.

The man's body jerked at the name. "You bet I know who the snake is. So what."

"We're looking for information that could help us find out who killed him."

The man stared at them, and then his face and mouth went slack. "I didn't make it to work today. Musta knowed you wuz comin'."

"Will you tell us about your fight with Mr. Campbell?" Toni asked.

His face contorted. "That lowlife came here to build an addition onto this house like my wife wanted. Then he started sniffing after her. I caught 'em together."

"We heard there was trouble of that nature," John said, speaking carefully, his gaze locked on the man's face.

"She was stupid enough to fall for his line. He never had any intention of marrying her. I kicked her out."

"Couldn't you have worked things out?" Toni asked.

His head moved slowly back and forth. "Already did once. This time proved I couldn't ever trust her again. The divorce was final this week. She got main custody of the kids."

"I'm sorry," Toni said. "I'm sure you miss them."

His chin sank to his chest, his breathing ragged.

"Yeah," he muttered.

"We understand that you had a fight with Mr. Campbell," John prodded after giving him a moment to recover.

"Yeah. I punched the guy," he growled. "Shoulda done more."

"Do you have any idea who wanted him dead?" John persisted.

His shoulders came back up a little. "A lot of people—including me. But I didn't do it. Someone did me—and the world—a favor. If you get it figgered out, let me know so I can send a thank you card."

With that, he slammed the door.

They returned to the van and headed home.

They rode in silence for several miles. "I don't think he did it."

"Why?" Toni asked when John spoke.

"I think he hated Jesse enough to have killed him, but he's so drunk and loose lipped that he would have bragged about it if he had done it."

Toni kept her eyes on the road. "I think you're right."

John's sigh this time was one of loss. "I thought I had found a friend to hang out with. It's hard to believe what kind of guy Jesse turned out to be. He broke up marriages and dallied with a female student—maybe more than one."

"Don't forget that his winning record seems to have been accomplished with the aid of cheating, and it looks like he was deep into gambling."

"He may have been drawing kids into it," John added in disgust. "I'm afraid to find out what else he may have been doing. It seems like motives and suspects are cropping up everywhere."

"It'll narrow down," Toni said with conviction. "Some of these people are capable of the kind of rage evidenced in the crime. Some aren't. The police—or us—will hit on something that will clear up the picture."

Toni's thoughts meandered over what she had learned—and still wanted to learn. She wanted to know more about that web site. Where was it being headquartered? Who owned it? She was a computer user, but far from a technology expert. Suddenly it occurred to her that she knew someone who was.

The previous year three of her students had discovered a skull not far from the school grounds. Those boys had gotten involved in identifying the victim and figuring out who killed him. One of them was a computer genius. She would call Jeremy Barnes when she got home.

It was about five-thirty when they reached Clearmount. Toni delivered John to his house and then drove straight to her own home. Her dad's truck was parked in the driveway.

Seeing no one around, she gathered her bags and went inside. She didn't see anyone, but she heard sounds coming from the kitchen. She dumped the bags on the floor and went to find her mother removing a casserole from the oven. It smelled wonderful, and Toni was smart enough to appreciate the help.

"Where are the boys and Dad?"

Faye put the casserole on top of the stove and hugged Toni. "They hiked through the woods to the swimming pool. Russell knew you were coming, but he said if they weren't back by the time you got here, it would give you a chance to unwind a little."

Toni nodded. "Sounds like you two have everything under control. If you don't mind, I want to change into something more comfortable and make a couple of phone calls."

"Why are you limping?" Faye asked as Toni headed to her room in her careful walk.

Toni turned and gave her mother a stern look. "Will you promise not to bring up my past if I tell you?"

Faye's eyes dropped to Toni's foot. "Again?"

Toni nodded, and then giggled. "I was in a hurry."

Faye's head moved back and forth. "Toni, dear, you've got to stop mistreating those poor little piggies. How many times does this make now that you've damaged them? Five? Six? Sit down and let me take a look." She pointed at a chair.

Toni complied, knowing better than to argue with her mother, who would see it sooner or later, one way or another. "I think it's only the fourth."

Faye squatted and examined her toe and the discoloration that had spread up over her foot. "Well, it's obvious you smashed it pretty good," she said, touching it in a gentle probe. "The colors are vivid, and trying to splint it would be a waste of time. Just keep your weight off of it as much as possible while it heals."

She got to her feet. "Go on and change. I'll make a salad. Take your time," she admonished, aiming a meaningful glance at the toe.

Toni did just that. She changed into knee-length shorts and a cotton top and called Kyle to ask just when he planned to be home. He told her to look for him about five or six o'clock the next day.

When that call was finished, Toni got out the phone book and looked up the number of her former student's parents.

"He's in Cape Girardeau. He's taking a summer class, and then he hangs out in that little office he and his two buddies set up for detective work," his mother said when Toni asked for Jeremy. Her voice held a touch of disdain, as if she thought three boys setting themselves up as detectives was a noodle-head idea.

Toni disagreed. Those three boys had helped solve a murder case right there in their hometown. They might be young and inexperienced, but they were enthusiastic about their goal and were taking criminal justice classes to learn proper techniques and procedures.

"How about his cell phone? Would you mind giving me that?" she asked, thinking it would be her best, and probably only, chance of catching the boy. She doubted he and his pals had a land line in their little office yet.

When Mrs. Barnes gave her the number, Toni thanked her, disconnected, and dialed it.

"Heartland Investigations," was the perky response she got.

"Hello, Jeremy. This is your past catching up with you."

"Oh, hi, Mrs. Donovan," he said, recognizing her voice. "What can I do for you?" There was what sounded suspiciously like a note of disappointment in his voice. He was probably hoping for a client.

"Help me answer a question, I hope. I've gotten involved in something..."

"Are you working on another case?" he broke in, his voice perking with interest.

"I'm afraid so. I'm teaching a class in Springfield this summer, and when my husband and boys came up for a family reunion a couple of weekends ago, we found a body at the park where the reunion was held."

"You're looking for the killer," he exclaimed with excited certainty. "What kind of information do you need researched?"

Toni could visualize the tall skinny boy, about a hundred twenty pounds and glasses askew, hunkered over a computer. Jeremy was not the self-avowed leader and spokesman for the trio of wannabe sleuths from last year's forensics class. Nor was he the quiet mechanical genius. He was their technology guru.

"It's right up your alley," she said. "I'll pay your going hourly rate if you can locate where a web site is being operated from."

"Sounds like a piece of cake, but I don't want to charge you." He meant because she was their mentor and favorite teacher.

"You're in business, aren't you? I'm a client." She spoke firmly.

There was a pause. "Okay, if you really want it that way. Do you have the URL?"

Toni gave it to him and then provided some explanations. "It looks like just a game site, but the image map in the lower left corner of the home page brings up a gambling setup. I want to know everything you can find out about it, who's running it, owns it, that kind of dope."

"Do you want me to call you back on your cell or your home phone?"

"Better make it the cell, in case I'm out."

"I need to get home to my personal computer for this," he said. "I've got some programs on it that we don't have here at the office yet. I'll get back to you." He ended the call.

Chapter 15

"Hey, Mom. We've been swimming. Look what I found," Garrett called as he came rushing into the house through the back patio door. He held out his baseball hat. It contained about a dozen golf balls, making it resemble a bird nest of oversized eggs.

Toni just smiled and gave him a hug. "What did you do, get out of the pool while Gabe and Grandpa were still swimming?"

He nodded and backed away, his eyes bright. His hair was wild from being wet and air-drying without benefit of a comb. All he wore was blue swimming trunks and sandals.

Her dad and Gabe came through the door. "That boy has been scavenging the golf course again. I do believe he's happiest when he's finding things," Russell accused good-naturedly. He wore a tee shirt over his swim trunks.

"Hi, Mom," Gabe greeted her with a brief hug. His trunks were red and, like Garrett, his chest was bare.

"Glad you made it home," Russell said, claiming his hug. "Of course, I kind of hate to let you take my buddies from me. I'm glad you have another week."

"He just likes running around with them," Faye

accused with a shake of her head. "They're good for him."

Toni relaxed. Knowing her parents truly enjoyed looking after the boys made her feel better about leaving them so much this summer. But she was looking forward to the end of class and returning home permanently.

"I'm glad there's only one more week," she said aloud. "Finals will be Wednesday and Thursday. I plan to spend this week with Quint and then come home for good."

Gabe was at the refrigerator, getting a root beer. "I've made a list of the things I need for school. We are still going shopping, aren't we?" He popped the tab.

Toni watched his Adam's apple bob as he drank, and was amazed at how fast he was growing. It seemed he must have shot up a full inch this summer. Which meant he probably really did need new jeans, and no telling what else.

"We'll go tomorrow," she promised. "Anything we don't find that you need, I'll look for in Springfield next week."

The evening meal was pleasant, good food that Toni didn't have to fix, and accompanied by lively conversation. The boys asked about her week and were disappointed that she hadn't figured out who killed the man they found in the park lagoon.

"You still have a week to catch the killer," Garrett said with confidence.

Russell paused with his fork halfway to his mouth. "You seem pretty sure, young man."

Garrett just nodded. "Mom's good at puzzle

solving."

Russell's eyes danced. "You're right. I remember when I first realized that."

Garrett's eyes rounded. "When?"

"Well, let's see. She was about four I believe. Bill was only two at the time, and Quint wasn't around yet. They liked to play in the bottom of our bedroom closet."

"Yours and Grandma's?"

"Yep. Faye kept shoes lined up in there, and Toni and Bill would push them to one end and use our closet as a little playhouse. We kept telling them to stay out of there, but they kept going back. I hated the thought of spanking them just for playing in a particular place. So I decided to fix the door." He paused to sip from his coffee.

"How?" Garrett's question was impatient. Gabe's attention was also rapt.

"I got a hook and eye type fastener," Russell continued. "Toni stood there and watched every move while I nailed the hook to the door and the eye to the doorframe. When I finished, I fastened the door shut."

"What did Mom do?"

"She disappeared," Russell said solemnly. "I thought she was upset. So I was surprised when she came trotting through the living room a few moments later, carrying a broom."

Gabe laughed. "A broom?"

"Yep. She made a beeline right back to the bedroom. I followed to see what she was doing. She took the handle of that broom and stuck it up under that hook and started pushing at it. It took her a few tries, but within a couple of minutes she hit it just right. That hook popped right up, and she opened the door."

"What did you do to her?" Garrett asked, glancing at his mother in amusement.

"Nothing right then. I had to go tell her mother about it and have a good laugh first. Then I sat her down on the sofa and explained that if she messed up that closet again, I would start keeping my hunting boots and gear in her closet."

"Did she mess it up any more?"

"Nope." He gave his grandson a steady look. "So I guess you could be right in thinking she'll figure things out in Springfield."

Faye put her empty coffee cup down and stood. "Okay, that's enough history for now. Let's clear this table and go home."

They each carried their empty table service to the kitchen counter, and Toni loaded the dishwasher. Ten minutes later her parents were gone. She was so tired she wished she had spent her summer relaxing instead of working.

After the boys were in bed that night, Toni climbed into her own bed, breathed deeply, and fell asleep.

Friday morning the phone woke her.

"Sorry to roust you," Kyle said when she mumbled a hello. "I wanted to let you know that I'll be late getting home. I just got word that I have to attend a meeting at headquarters this evening." He didn't sound thrilled about it.

"Do what you have to," Toni told him, coming awake. "But don't break the speed limit when you do head home."

When they disconnected, Toni checked the clock. It was only six-thirty. She turned over, went back to sleep, and didn't crawl out until nine. The boys were still sacked out. She started breakfast, or brunch, knowing the smells would draw them. About ten they had bacon and eggs and pancakes. Then they were ready to go shopping.

"Will Dad be home in time for supper?" Gabe asked as they climbed into the van.

"He called this morning and said he has to attend a meeting this evening. He won't be home until late. Since he won't be here in time to eat with us this evening, let's shop in Farmington and eat out before coming home."

"That's an awesome plan," Gabe declared with eagerness. Garrett seconded it.

It took an hour to get to Farmington, and the first item to find on their expedition was shoes. From there they progressed to clothing, and then to classroom supplies. It was five o'clock when they finished and went to a steak house to eat. They left there at six-thirty and were home at seven-thirty.

As Toni entered the kitchen, the phone rang.

"I've been trying to call your cell phone," Jeremy said in a rush when she answered.

"I've been to Farmington," Toni explained. "You probably rang when I was out of range, which is most of the way. Have you found what I need?"

"I have enough to help you," he said, his voice turning business-like. "I looked over that site and found the IP address hidden behind the hostname. I ran a trace on it, and sent a ping signal to the computer. When it sent a signal back, I got a name for who registered and operates the site. But it's probably phony." His youthful voice dropped from restrained excitement to disappointment at the last.

"You're probably right," Toni said. "It's an illegal operation, so real names aren't going to be used. How can we find out who it is?"

"I tried to contact the person, but had no luck," Jeremy continued. "I got the name of the DNS server that provides the IP address for the site, but they won't give me any information."

"Give me the name, and I'll call the police in Springfield. I bet they can get it."

"The host is MOSpace, and the registered operator of the site is Matt Webber," Jeremy said.

Toni grabbed a pen and jotted down the information. "Thanks for the help. If you'll tell me your fee, I'll put a check in the mail."

Jeremy cleared his throat. "Uh, I didn't spend all that much time on it. Most firms charge fifty an hour, so we only charge forty. I didn't spend quite an hour on it. Does twenty-five sound all right?"

"It sounds fine," Toni said. Actually, it sounded like far less that he should be charging, but more than she should be spending on a case that meant nothing to her personally other than satisfying her growing curiosity. She suspected she was the first paying client for the boys and their fledgling enterprise. They were only nineteen years old, and college students always needed money.

As soon as she hung up the landline, Toni used her cell phone to call Quint. She was surprised when she got an answer, since he was already on duty. On the other hand, she knew he set his cell phone on vibrate and kept it in his pocket in order to not disturb anyone.

"What's up, Quizzy? And make it quick. I'm cruising the streets."

She gave him a quick repeat of her report from Jeremy. "Can you follow up on it?"

"I'll pass along the information and let you know any results."

Toni grinned as the phone went silent.

Sounds from the boys' room told her they were occupied. She curled up on the couch and turned on the television. She scanned the channels, but found nothing that interested her. A few minutes later she turned it off and went to take a shower. Then she peeked in on the boys. "I'm too tired to wait up for your dad, so I'm going to bed. Don't stay up too late."

"We won't," Gabe said. "We'll wait up for him."

"If he's not here by midnight, you get in bed. Both of you," she admonished sternly, looking from one to the other.

"Okay," Gabe promised for both of them.

Toni had just crawled into bed when her cell phone rang. She grabbed it from its charger next to the bed.

"Your young man from Ozark, as suspected, is the owner and operator of that site," Quint said briskly. "The name Matt Webber looks like his cute version of Webmaster. I just picked up an arrest warrant, and we're going after him. Talk to you later."

"You have such a unique hang up style," Toni said into the silent phone. She put it down, stretched out under the rotating ceiling fan, and let her body go lax. She was sound asleep when she was roused by the sound of the garage door rising and a truck pulling into it. She went to meet Kyle as he entered the house, noting that the kitchen clock read one-thirty.

"When did you leave St. Louis?" she asked, welcoming his arms around her.

"About eleven-thirty," he said wearily. "It was a long meeting."

She gave him a brief kiss. "You have to be beyond tired. Come on to bed."

"Soon as I have a shower." He picked up the bag he had dropped on the floor.

When he crawled in beside her a few minutes later, Toni snuggled up next to him, happy to have him home.

*

"What do you want?" he snapped into the phone, pacing in agitated steps.

"I need something done." The words were cool and deliberate.

He paused. "What kind of something?"

"A mouth shut up."

"Not by me, you don't. Do your own dirty work. You can't expect me to do it for you."

"Oh, yes, I can. Do you remember where you left the knife?"

The coldness of the words made him freeze in shock. He swallowed hard. "Are you saying you have it?"

"I am. You do what I need, and I'll keep it to myself—and mark your debt paid."

"How did you get it?"

"I was in the car with Jesse when he went to

meet you that night. I waited for him, but he was gone so long that I wanted to leave. But he hadn't left his car keys. I went looking for him, and heard the two of you arguing." There was a pause for him to grasp the significance.

"I don't believe you. You never heard a thing," he tried to bluff. *"And I don't need to work off any debts."*

"Oh, yes, you do. You're wallowing in gambling debts. I know because I keep the records. You found out Jesse was banging you-know-who again, and you were threatening to tell his new wife. Jesse laughed at you and wouldn't cut you any slack or give you more time. You went at him with this knife I'm holding. I saw you stab him and run off through the woods. I was looking in the water for his car keys and found this instead."

"You think you can take over," he snarled. *"But you can't. Others have the same idea."*

"Watch me. I expect the job to be done before Monday." The phone line went dead.

He fumed, and then began to pace again, frantic to figure out a way to get it done.

*

Saturday morning everyone was up by eight, too pleased at having the family complete again to waste any more time in bed. They were just finishing breakfast when Quint called.

"We picked up Vince Harcourt last night," he said without preamble. "We went after him about an hour after you called. He wasn't home, but his mother finally told us where he could be found. We busted him about ten o'clock and brought him in for a grilling."

"Did you get anything out of him?"

"Not much, but just before his lawyer arrived he gave us a name. It's one we already know—Barry Kuzman. I think the kid's just trying to lay blame at someone else's door. I suspect there's a power play going on now that the coach is dead."

"You mean Jesse Campbell really was the kingpin, and now others want to take over?"

"Right. I think Vince sees giving up Barry as a way to eliminate competition."

Toni shook her head in sympathy. "Sounds like more problems than solutions. You have your hands full."

"Don't be a pain," he muttered. "See you tomorrow night—or sometime Monday."

"Okay," she said to the silent phone. Little brother could use some instruction in telephone etiquette.

"I have to run down to the garage and have Benny check the brakes on my truck. They're squealing," Kyle said as he left the table.

"Can we go with you?" Garrett asked.

Kyle gave his youngest a raised brow look.

Garrett's shoulders jerked. "Oops. May we go with you?"

"Sure. Come on."

Kyle got as far as the doorway and stopped to look back at Toni. "Oh, your dad sent me a text saying he wants us to come up tonight for barbecue and homemade ice cream. What should I tell him?"

Toni laughed. "You shouldn't have taught him how to text. Now you'll have to talk to him all the time. Tell him we'll be there about six. If that's okay with you, that is."

He shrugged and pulled out his phone. "Will do."

Toni watched her husband go on out the door. He hadn't said a word about the meeting that had made him so late getting home. His manner toward her was hard to read. Something was bothering him, and he was avoiding telling her about it. Should she press, or wait until he was ready to talk? Knowing Kyle, he would level with her, no matter how hard it was. But not until he was ready. She would wait.

When they arrived at the Nash home that evening, Russell met them at the door. "Good to have you home," he greeted Kyle. "The ice cream is made and waiting for us. I have something I want to show you after we eat."

Faye came from the kitchen carrying a platter. "It's ready, so let's go ahead and eat. Then we can visit."

Her barbecue pork steaks and potato salad were good country fare. After finishing off with ice cream, Gabe put his spoon down and pushed back his chair. "May we be excused? We want to ride Grandpa's ATV before it gets dark."

Toni aimed a questioning glance at her dad.

"They've been practicing. They'll be fine," he assured her.

"Watch the speed," Kyle cautioned as they dashed out the back door.

He and Russell took cups of coffee to the living room. Toni and Faye loaded the dishwasher and followed them.

Russell took a tape from the top of the

entertainment center. "Do you two remember that Faye gave me a game camera for my birthday last month?"

Kyle nodded. "I should. I helped her buy it. Have you been getting any interesting pictures?"

"I sure have." He popped the tape into the player.

In addition to following Cardinal baseball, Russell hunted wild game, but what he preferred to do was just tramp the woods and watch the wildlife. Faye had decided he might enjoy getting pictures of the deer that came up close to their house. The game camera would let him do that without spooking them.

The picture was dark at first. Then it turned bright, the camera having been activated. There was a moment of silence, and then the sound of approaching footsteps.

Expecting to see a deer walk into the picture, Toni and Kyle were stunned to see their two boys, hands tucked up under their chins with the fingers hanging down, come prancing into view. Toy reindeer horns protruded from their heads.

They pranced around in the picture a bit, turned, and pranced out of camera range.

Kyle was still chuckling under his breath when they got home.

"That's just what I needed," he said when he and Toni were alone in the living room. "It was a good pressure release."

Toni squeezed his hand. "Good. I've been feeling some guilt about leaving them so much this summer, but that tape proves they're not suffering too much."

They snickered together.

"You want the shower first?"

She shook her head. "I need to do a couple chores. You go ahead. I'll probably be finished by the time you're done."

He headed to the bedroom, unbuttoning his shirt as he went. Toni went to the computer and printed a copy of the test she had worked on earlier. She tucked the original in her grade book, ready for making copies in the workroom before class Monday morning. When Kyle came from the shower, she went to take her turn.

When she returned to the living room, Kyle was sitting on the couch. The boys were nowhere to be seen, but she could hear sounds coming from their room.

Her husband looked up, his expression somber. He reached over and patted the cushion next to him. "Come here."

Toni sat close to his side and slid an arm behind his back. "Why did you need cheering up? What's bothering you?"

Kyle sighed. "It was a gloomy meeting last night. We were told…"

"Whatever it is, we'll deal with it," Toni interrupted, sensing his need for reassurance.

He made an effort at a smile, but it wasn't quite successful. "You're sure?"

"I'm sure."

He studied her face a moment, gauging her sincerity. Then he cleared his throat. "I already told you the company is in trouble."

"Have you lost your job?" she asked bluntly, meaning to meet the problem head on if that was it.

He shook his head. "No, but I've been

reassigned. Effective the first of September I have to either move to the coast—or resign."

For a moment no words would form. "I'm sorry you've been put in this position," she said finally. "We'll do whatever you want. The boys are young. They'll adjust. The house won't be hard to sell, and I can find a teaching position anywhere."

Kyle pulled her to him, nestling her head under his chin. "Don't get in too big a hurry to pack," he said, his voice strained. "Let me think about it."

She nodded against his chest. "I won't say anything to the boys unless you tell me we're moving. School starts in four weeks. If we have to move, we need to make the transition as quickly as possible so they can enter a new school at the beginning of the term. I think that would be easier for them."

"Hey, I said don't jump too far ahead," he chided gruffly. "I've hardly digested the situation. Let me explore the alternatives. I know time's short, but I'll try to make a decision before next weekend."

"Will you be able to get home in time to bring the boys to Springfield Friday for a barbecue dinner like your mother asked?"

"I'll try. If I see I can't, I'll let you know."

*

Toni was troubled as she and John traveled back to Springfield Sunday afternoon. While John slept, her mind wandered. She was happy with her small town existence and didn't want to live anywhere else. But she would do whatever was necessary for the sake of her family. If Kyle couldn't do what he loved to earn a livelihood here, they would go where he could.

She and Kyle had become sweethearts when she was in the seventh grade and him the ninth. At a basketball game, she had lost her purse with her spending money in it, and he had helped her look for it. When they were unable to find the purse, he had bought her a Coke.

When Kyle graduated from high school two years ahead of her and left for college, Toni had been overcome with loneliness. They even tried dating other people, but both felt guilty for thinking of one another while on a date with someone else. Failing that, they had committed themselves for life, but delayed marriage until both of them finished college.

As soon as Toni completed her bachelor's degree and teaching certification, they had married, and she had signed a contract to teach at Clearmount. The first years had been hard, learning to balance teaching, working on her Master's in biology, and having babies. But they had learned to compromise when necessary and work through problems. Their love had weathered storms and kept them together, and Toni knew that Kyle considered the needs of his family above his own. In this case, though, she felt that his needs needed to be top consideration.

Toni's mind returned to the murder investigation. But thinking back over the facts she had learned made her feel like she was spinning her wheels.

Jesse Campbell had created a gambling operation of shocking size. He had also been a philanderer. Which of those had gotten him killed?

She began to categorize. Of the adults she had met who were connected to Jesse in some way, none of them struck her as a murderer. Grant Volner still seemed the one with the best motives—friendship betrayed and wife lost. But Toni didn't think he fit the profile. He seemed more victim than victimizer.

His ex-wife, Sheila, was too weak to rebuff Jesse's advances. Which meant she surely didn't have the strength to do something as violent as killing him. Even if she did, why would she lure him to the park to do it? Or use a knife? There were easier and cleaner ways, all of them closer to home.

The secretary, Joyce Franklin, struck Toni as stronger and more purposeful. The relationship between her and Jesse must have been ending as the one with Sheila Volner was starting. No, wait. There was the guy, Malcolm somebody, at the construction company in Nixa. When she spoke to him, he was pretty plastered, but she couldn't exclude him as a suspect. Should she take a second look at Joyce and Mr. what's-his-name? Burk, that was it.

Toni's thoughts moved on to students. Vince Harcourt and Dean Patrick were still in high school. Her gut said they were both involved, but they seemed too young and inexperienced to be the brains and muscle behind the gambling operation. Also, there had probably been hero worship for Jesse that had gotten them involved in the first place. It was unlikely they would have killed their hero. But they, or at least Vince, *could* be involved in trying to take over now that their hero was dead.

Toni knew by now that there were more high school students involved, but those were the only ones she had met and talked to personally. However, there were former students of Jesse's to consider. Barry Kuzman had been an assistant to him at

Glendale, his first teaching position. Then came Branson and the girls, Nicole and Sonya. At Kickapoo the secretary's son, Corey, had played basketball for Jesse. It was impossible for Toni to picture the girls stabbing Jesse, and difficult to see a knife in the hand of either of the young men. But she had to consider all of them as potential suspects. Except maybe Nicole. Toni would bet money that Nicole's act of bringing her that newspaper and asking about it had been from genuine concern. And she surely wouldn't have brought up the subject if she were guilty.

The rectangular green sign on the roadside alerted Toni that she was nearing Springfield. She delivered John to where he was staying. It was seven o'clock when she rolled the van into the visitor parking space in front of Quint's apartment. She scooped her purse and satchel from the passenger seat and got her suitcase and garment bag from the back. Feeling like a pack mule, she trudged to Quint's door and set the suitcase down, wishing he were home. She dug into her purse and found the key he had given her.

Just as she clicked the lock of the door, her cell phone rang. She grabbed her suitcase, hurried inside, and dropped it at the door. Everything else she tossed on the couch and fished her phone from the front pocket of her purse.

"Toni," Quint said as soon as she answered.

"What's up?" she asked, detecting a somber undertone in his voice.

"There was an explosion. Barry Kuzman's car blew up. He's dead."

Chapter 16

"He's dead?" Toni repeated stupidly. "I thought he was in jail." She dropped onto the couch, unable to grasp this news.

"He was released Thursday, right after you left town."

"What happened?" Visions of flying car parts, and worse, passed through her head.

"We're assuming he spent the morning in his apartment, probably sleeping. When he went outside and started his car, it exploded. The bomb was crude—but effective."

"When did this happen?"

"A couple of hours ago. I knew you were on your way in and would have no cell service most of the way, so I waited until I thought you could be in town to call you."

"I just got here," she mumbled, thinking how terrible it would have been to die that way. She hadn't known Barry personally, and what she knew about him was not good, but no one should die like that.

"I don't get off until two a.m. You'll be in bed then, and you'll be gone before I get up, so we won't have a chance to talk until you get out of class. Will you be coming straight back to the apartment?"

In other words, would she be going out snooping and possibly getting into trouble? His babysitting was so obvious.

"I'll most likely come straight here," she said, leaving herself some wiggle room. "I don't know what time I'll get here, though. Students sometimes stay after class with questions, and because finals are so near, there will probably be more of those than usual."

"I have to go," he said. "See you tomorrow."

Toni just sat there holding the silent phone, stunned and horrified at this latest development. There was no doubt in her mind that it was connected to the other murder. Besides Barry, the one other person she was positive was involved was Vince Harcourt. Now, who did she know who was linked to both Vince and Barry?

Dean Patrick popped into her mind. Barry had mentioned Dean by name, and he attended the same school as Vince. She dialed John.

"Your friend, Barry Kuzman, will never mug you, or anyone else, again," she said when he answered. "He was killed this afternoon."

John emitted a long whistle. "That's awful."

She related what little she knew. "I want to talk to Dean again because he's the one person I know who has links to both Barry and Vince. Would you be interested in running out to Ozark with me?"

"Sure," he said without hesitation. "Where should I meet you?"

"I'll pick you up in thirty minutes. I want to grab a sandwich first. I just got here and I'm starving."

After a quick turkey and cheese sandwich, the only thing Toni found in Quint's fridge, it didn't take long to go get John and drive to Ozark. She was beginning to feel a familiarity with the neighborhood.

There were no cars in the driveway at the Patrick residence, but Toni knew they could be parked in the double garage. She rang the doorbell.

Dean's mother opened the door and stared a moment before recognizing Toni. "You've been here before. What do you want now?"

"Just to speak to Dean for a moment," Toni said, remembering that she was supposed to be a college rep.

The woman stared at her long and hard before seeming to decide she and John looked harmless. "He's not here right now. He got a phone call earlier that upset him, and he left."

"Do you know where he might go when he's upset or needs time alone?" Toni asked, trying to sound sympathetic.

There was no answer.

"Mrs. Patrick, there was an explosion this afternoon that killed a young man of Dean's acquaintance. I don't know how close they were, but I'm sure your son is suffering from shock and grief. We want to find him and be sure he's all right."

The woman swallowed. "He goes to Springfield a lot. He hangs out at the gym in the winter and the ball fields in the summer. He umpires Little League games and plays in an older age one at the Ewing Complex. There are five or six fields there. I know he didn't have a game today, but sometimes he hangs out and watches other teams play."

"Does he have a cell phone?"

She shook her head. "He did, but he lost it a couple of days ago. He was upset when, for some reason, the phone company wouldn't give him an immediate replacement."

"Thank you, Mrs. Patrick."

They took their leave and headed back to Springfield. "It's a long shot, but let's drive out there," Toni said, weaving into the left lane and passing a slow moving truck.

John just nodded.

When they rolled into the complex, only one game was underway, but cars were parking at a couple more of the fields, boys climbing out of them carrying baseball gloves.

The players in the game in progress looked to be junior high age, too young to be Dean's pals. But they went over to check it out anyhow. A few yards from the bleacher seats they stopped and scanned the faces in them.

"I don't see him," Toni said, turning away in defeat. Just then the door of one of the buildings that housed restrooms opened. When a figure stepped out, Toni halted and looked closer, hardly able to believe their luck.

"Is that him?" John asked.

She nodded. "Let's watch where he goes and try to get a seat near him." She started walking toward the boy.

They slowed when Dean rounded the seats and worked his way to the bleachers not far from those they had passed minutes earlier. He climbed to the bench next to the top and sat.

Toni and John waited a moment to be sure he was settled, and then followed him. Toni sat next to the boy, and John settled on the other side of her. The late July heat was still over eighty, but an occasional waft of breeze stirred the air.

Dean's muscular body leaned forward in a dejected pose, his chin on his fists. He squeezed his eyes tight, obviously in pain.

"Dean," Toni said quietly.

He glanced over, not happy at having his space invaded. Suddenly his eyes widened. "Don't I know you?"

"We met once. I'm with the college," Toni said, hoping he would not ask which college, or in what capacity. "My colleague and I are also working with the police department on another matter."

"You're here about Barry," he said dully, his nasal voice evidence he had been crying.

"That's right. Are you willing to answer some questions?"

He shrugged, dropping his eyes to stare at his hands that were laced together so tightly his knuckles were white.

"What was your relationship with Barry?" she asked.

"We were just friends," he muttered without looking up.

"I think you were more than friends. You both spent a great deal of time with Coach Campbell."

Dean's eyes closed, and his mouth tightened, but he didn't look up or speak.

Not quite sure what approach to take next, Toni shifted the subject. "What about Vince Harcourt? I know you go to the same school. What else do you do together?"

He remained silent.

Toni let her breath out slowly. "Okay, Dean. Here's how it is. Barry has been killed. Vince has been arrested. Your name has been linked to both of them. Now tell me again that you were just friends with them, and nothing more. But keep in mind that I know Jesse Campbell was involved in some bad things and Vince and Barry were both working for him."

For several more long seconds Dean still didn't reply. Then he raised his head enough to stare out over the ball field, but she was sure he wasn't seeing the game. He turned and faced her, his eyes clouded with unshed tears.

"I'm scared," he murmured, his body shivering involuntarily.

"Why are you scared?" Toni asked, resisting the urge to comfort him. She wanted to keep him talking. He was a young adult who had gotten caught up in something that was going to force him to mature and face consequences. Rapidly.

"Everything was working fine," he said so low she could hardly hear him. "But then Coach was killed. Now Barry's dead, too. I'm not sure what's happening."

Toni listened closely, trying to absorb every nuance. "Can you tell me just what *is* going on? How did this thing get started?"

Dean moved his head back and forth, as if bewildered. "Most kids play cards. It was four or five years ago, when I was in middle school and junior high, that it got more popular. A lot of parents go to Atlantic City and Vegas to play, and when they're home they let us play in their houses where they can keep an eye on us. Some schools even have supervised gambling at their post prom school parties."

"How often do these games happen?" she asked before he could ramble off track.

Dean shrugged. "Pretty much every night. It's easy to find out where there's a game and who's playing. Even Coach..." His voice cracked. "Even Coach used to have games in his garage. Kids play in the lunchroom and the restroom, all kinds of places. But some of us aren't that crazy about cards."

"So you started betting on sports," Toni said when he didn't continue.

Dean straightened from his hunched position and leaned back against the bench behind them. "That and Internet gambling."

"What kind of stakes are kids wagering?"

He hesitated before speaking. "It started out as quarter antes and two dollar bets. But it soon moved up to a dollar ante and five dollar bets. Then it kept growing. Some bet hundreds, or even thousands, of dollars on basketball and football games."

"What if they lose and can't pay?"

The boy's eyes darkened, and he winced ever so slightly. "Bookie runners deliver messages and try to collect," he said haltingly.

"Are the messages threats? Is there physical violence?"

Dean nodded. "Both. I heard that one kid was snatched and dropped off in the woods alone."

"So he would get lost?"

He shook his head in misery. "It was punishment for a bad debt. But he found his way home."

"How did it get to this?"

"I don't know," he mumbled brokenly. Then he cleared his throat. "It all started as fun and recreation, but then it started going bad. I don't know when everything went out of control."

Some of the tension went out of Toni now that Dean seemed to be delivering truth. "How is the operation set up?" she asked, hoping he wouldn't clam up at the question.

His eyes squeezed shut, and then reopened. "I don't know a lot of details. I'm just a flunky, one of the younger workers. There are kids from high schools and colleges all around here who work as bookies, collectors, runners, and things like that. Betting on sports is the big thing. It's easy to play. You can bet over the phone with no money down. There's an eight hundred number to get the odds on games. It changes every couple weeks or so, and there's a special code."

"Give me an example."

"Well, if you want to bet ten dollars, you say 'give me two times'. For twenty-five dollars you say 'give me five times'."

"What about the Internet?" John asked, joining the conversation. "Isn't there a web site that you and your friends use?"

Dean's eyes widened in surprise. "You know that, too?"

"We've seen it," Toni said. "We think your classmate, Vince, is the webmaster."

"He is. It's really coming apart, isn't it?" Dean moved his head back and forth again as he grasped the gravity of the situation.

"What was your role?" John asked. "Were you an enforcer?"

Dean's head jerked up, and his hands raised, palms forward. "Oh, no! I'm just a runner. All I've ever done is deliver messages or pick up things."

"Do you have any idea who killed your friends?" Toni asked. "Is there any chance they owed big gambling debts and were killed over it?"

"That makes no sense," he shot back. "Coach was the boss. He didn't owe anybody. And Barry was his main man. Nobody could touch them."

"But they did," Toni pointed out. "Do you know who all is involved?"

"No way. My own school has over four thousand students, and some of the others have more. The ones involved come from all of them. They meet one another sometimes, but never in a big group. New ones are always showing up, and others move away or drop out."

"Do you know who's in charge of the overall operation now?"

Dean shook his head. "I can't even guess."

Toni exchanged glances with John, silently asking if he could think of anything else to ask. He indicated with a head shake that he couldn't.

She turned back to Dean. "I have to tell the police about this talk, and I'm sure you'll hear from them. I hope you'll be totally honest and help in any way you can. It will go better for you if you do."

*

Toni was haunted by the vision of Dean Patrick's forlorn figure, still sitting on the bleachers, when they left the ball field. She shared his fear and felt a sense of helplessness. And rage. She had trouble sleeping that night.

Monday morning she dressed in white slacks and a pink T-top, bolted a donut and glass of milk, and left for school while Quint slept.

"Our final lecture will cover the urinary and reproductive systems," she announced at the beginning of class, noting Nicole Warren just slipping into a seat. Her face was set in a distracted gaze, and a frown creased her forehead. Something was troubling the young woman.

Forcing her attention from Nicole, Toni proceeded with the lecture. But she glanced back at the young woman every few minutes. Each time Nicole's eyes were glued to her, almost trance-like. The two hour lab that followed kept Toni from watching the young woman closely, since she had to keep moving around the room.

She wasn't surprised when Nicole remained seated at the end of lab. Toni went to the door and saw the class out, issuing reminders of the next day's unit exam. When they were gone, she closed the door and went to sit across the work table from Nicole. "What's wrong? Are you worried about the exams?"

Nicole nodded, and then shook her head back and forth. Her smile was forced. "I'm worried, but not about the exams."

"I'm sorry. I didn't mean to pry," Toni apologized.

Nicole extracted a piece of paper from her purse.

"Here's the doctor's note I owe you."

"Good. Now you can make up the quiz you missed Thursday. Is that what was bothering you?"

Toni opened the note and glanced at it. Then she looked closer. The required documentation indicated that Nicole's three-year-old daughter, Morgan Sandoval, had been seen the previous Thursday in the office of Doctor Meyers.

"Your daughter's name is different from yours."

"Warren is my maiden name. I took it back after I divorced Mitch Sandoval. He's why I'm worried," she added nervously, lowering her gaze.

Toni hesitated, unsure whether to probe into her student's personal life. "Is there anything I can do?" she asked gently, hoping to put her at ease.

"Be careful," Nicole said, nearly strangling on the low words.

Toni went on alert. "Why? What are you trying to tell me?"

Nicole looked up. "Mitch is…can be mean."

"Did he abuse you?"

Nicole nodded. "It started a few weeks after we got married. I was afraid to stay with him, and afraid to leave him. I was pregnant."

"I understand. But you finally did leave him. What changed?"

"I stayed with him as long as I could. I had Morgan, and things got better. But then he started hitting her. He called it spanking. But it was more. I sold everything I had of any value and hired a good lawyer. I won custody of my baby. Not that he wanted her," she added bitterly. "He didn't want the responsibility."

Toni watched the way Nicole wet her lips with her tongue, sensing genuine fear in her.

"I saw him watching this building after class last Thursday," Nicole said after a long hesitation. "Then he was here again today."

"Why do you think he's watching you? Is he stalking you?"

"He's not watching me," Nicole said, raising her head. "He's watching you."

Toni frowned. "That doesn't make sense. I don't even know him. You're the one with reason to be afraid of him."

"I *am* afraid of him," Nicole said forcefully. "But I watched him. He didn't even see me arrive today. He was totally focused on you. That's why I was almost late. When I spotted him, I ducked out of sight and waited for him to leave."

Toni was mystified.

"He's dangerous," Nicole continued. "I just found out from a friend that he's involved in the gambling operation you're investigating. I think he's some kind of enforcer." Her eyes glittered with unshed tears.

A clutch of fear made Toni go weak. "Do you think he's connected to your former coach's death? Or the one yesterday?"

Nicole shuddered, but she didn't ask what death Toni meant. That meant she knew about Barry Kuzman. "I don't know," she said. "But I think he's capable of a lot. And I'm afraid for you. Promise me you'll be careful."

"I will," Toni promised. "I'm staying with my brother this week, and he's a local police officer. I'll talk to him."

Nicole took a deep breath and gathered her books. "Good. I have to go to work."

Chapter 17

As she drove back to Quint's apartment, Toni kept an eye on her rear view mirror, alert for anyone following her. Seeing nothing suspicious, she chided herself for being paranoid. It was Nicole that her ex was watching, not a teacher he didn't know. That had to be it. Just the same, she took a circuitous route, winding through a residential area, looping around to Route 65, and then to Battlefield and through more residential streets before getting on Ingram Mill Road. She checked her rear view mirror again, and looked every direction before pulling into the apartment complex.

Quint lay sprawled on the sofa watching a ballgame when she entered. "You're looking energetic," she kidded him, forcing herself to not limp. If Quint knew she had injured another toe, he would tease her unmercifully.

"I got up about eleven and went shopping," he said. "Then I hurried back so I would be here when you got in. We have a few edibles in the place now."

"Does that mean you're going to bring me up to date on the case?" she asked over her shoulder as she took her purse and book satchel to his guest bedroom.

"It does," he called after her.

She returned and claimed his recliner where she

could face him to talk—and he couldn't hang up on her. "What kind of progress are you making?"

"A lot of watching and checking without definitive results." He pushed upright and placed an arm along the back of the sofa. "We're finding that it's a bigger operation than we imagined possible. The card playing is small in comparison to the sports betting. These kids are wagering big money."

"Which is attractive to organized crime," Toni mused, wondering if they could possibly be connected to any crime family.

"The operation does mirror adult organized crime," Quint said. "We're looking for any ties."

His head moved from side to side. "In urban America we find drugs. In suburban America, we find sports betting. Internet gambling is illegal, but that's a generous interpretation of the law. I don't know of any arrests that have been made for merely placing bets online, but this sports betting is bad for students. More kids get into gambling through sports than any other gambling activity. What doubly troubles me is finding out that athletes are nearly twice as likely to be problem gamblers as non-athletes."

Toni nodded. "I've been researching and reading some sad stories."

"We've talked to several school administrators in the area. None of them were aware of these activities. I guess I can't blame them too much, since we didn't know either."

"How cooperative are they being?"

"They're willing to work with us. One reason is because when student athletes place bets with a bookie, they not only break the law, but they jeopardize their eligibility. Once they do that, the bookie is in control. If a student athlete gets addicted and deep in debt, point shaving gets offered as a way out."

The mention of bookies brought Barry back to mind. "I guess I didn't realize how big a role a bookie plays. I thought he was low in the pecking order."

"They use students or runners to collect debts and parlay sheets and give them a commission for it," Quint explained. "Gamblers pay commissions for information related to sports teams—player injuries, game plans, discipline issues, stuff like that. Which brings us to the database we found in Jesse Campbell's computer."

Toni's interest ratcheted up another notch.

"It's a massive thing that would excite any statistician. It lists players from every school and will predict which players will guard each other, track tendencies of referees, and factors all kinds of things into forecasting game outcomes."

Toni's mouth pursed, and she emitted a long whoosh of air. "That would be a valuable tool for the guy's business. No wonder he was making money. He probably sold information as well as placing personal bets."

"We found a list of referees who work in the area, as well as some who work professional games. A few of the names had a small star by them."

"Sounds like Jesse had plans to move to bigger things," Toni speculated.

"We're wondering if those marked refs are ones who will do things like take bribes for making calls that will affect the point spread in games, or ignore fouls and call make-up fouls to give additional foul shots to a particular team."

"I remember reading a story about a coach who was killed because he was going to come clean about illegal gambling and game-fixing," Toni said thoughtfully. "Do you think that could be what happened to Jesse?"

Quint considered for a moment. "I suppose it's possible, but I seriously doubt it. I haven't seen any record of contacts between him and anyone in law enforcement."

"I guess he was prospering too much to do anything like that," Toni agreed. "Well, what about that website? I haven't checked lately. Is it still active?"

Quint nodded. "When Vince Harcourt was arrested, the detectives questioned him, but didn't search his house and confiscate his computer. They want the site to stay up while they look for who is taking over control. Someone didn't want Barry talking to us anymore, and they're hoping they can learn from the activity on the site."

"What else are they doing?"

Now Quint grinned. "You'll like this. They created an undercover identity and opened a betting account on the site."

She pumped a fist. "Yeah, that should get them some interesting facts."

Suddenly Quint sobered. "So what did you do last night? Where did you go?"

Toni went silent, taken off guard by the question.

"I called here not long after I reported to work and got no answer."

"John and I went to talk to Dean Patrick again," she admitted, meeting his gaze. "Dean was the only person I could think of with ties to both Vince Harcourt and Jesse Campbell."

Quint leaned forward on his knees. "Tell me everything he said."

She did, beginning with the drive to Ozark, having to return to Springfield to find the boy, and then relating the conversation almost verbatim, amazed at her clarity of memory.

"So you see," she said when she finished, "everything Dean told us matches the facts you just told me."

"Okay, all-knowing big sister, I guess you did all right. Is that all you did?"

"That's it. But another matter has come up."

He rolled his eyes. "Spit it out."

"You remember my telling you about Nicole Warren, the girl in my class who recognized that I was at the park when Jesse Campbell was found?"

He thought a moment, and then bobbed his head. "You mean the one who was in Campbell's class in Branson."

"That's her. Well, she stayed after class today to warn me that she saw her ex-husband following me."

His gaze sharpened. "Does this ex have a name?"

"Mitch Sandoval."

Quint's eyes squeezed shut for a moment. "He has a history dating back to junior high that includes purse snatching, bullying, and other nice stuff. Why do you think he's following you?"

"I don't know that he is. I kept my eyes open and came home by a route like a rat maze. I didn't see anything that looked like I was being followed."

"What did this Nicole tell you about Mitch? Is he involved in the gambling ring? It sounds right up his alley."

"She said she thinks he's some kind of enforcer."

"Fits him to a tee."

A frisson went up Toni's spine as the vision of Mitch Sandoval hitting Nicole and her daughter flashed across her mind. She sucked in a deep breath of air.

"Okay, I know I'm just your baby brother," Quint said grimly. "But I'm telling you to be very careful. You're obviously making someone so uneasy that they have a goon watching you. Don't underestimate this guy, and don't be traipsing around alone."

"I have to go to work," she pointed out.

"It's only for three more days, thank goodness. I never thought I'd want to run you out of town, but right now I wish you were back home where you would be safer. I'll follow you to school in the morning and meet you after class."

Toni shook her head. "You don't need to do that. I'll call John. He won't mind coming by and following me to school. His class starts thirty minutes later than mine, and he won't mind being a little early. He gets out later than I do, but I have to stay late tomorrow to set up for Wednesday's lab final."

Quint debated silently for a few moments, and then relented. "Okay, call him."

When Toni called John and explained, he didn't hesitate to be her escort. "Precautions seem like a smart idea to me."

When Quint left for work at three-thirty, Toni curled up on the couch with some paperwork. In the middle of grading a paper, her eyes drooped and her head jerked, fighting sleep. She put the papers down and crashed.

At six o'clock the phone woke her. She checked the ID. Quint. Checking on her again. "I'm here," she answered.

"You better be. Have you eaten yet?" He sounded relieved, and in better spirits than when he had left.

"No, I fell asleep on the couch."

"Good. That's probably just what you needed. If you can hold off until about nine, I can meet you and feed you, like any decent host should do for his guest."

"I'm not a guest. I'm a sibling mooching a bed. But I am hungry. Where should I meet you?"

"You shouldn't. I'll pick you up," he said firmly. "I'll call when I'm on the way."

"Okay, I'll…" She stopped when she realized she was speaking into a dead phone.

By the time Quint had called and Toni heard him pull up in front of the apartment, she thought her stomach must be touching her backbone. She darted out and climbed into the patrol car. "Is it okay for me to ride with you on duty like this?"

"I told my superior I needed to feed you, and he okayed it." He spoke over his shoulder as he backed out of the parking space.

"It seems the only time I get to have a decent talk with you is at a quick meal like this," Toni said when they were about halfway through dinner at the Golden

Corral steak buffet. "I feel like I'm in your way."

He grinned. "I think the detectives are learning to like having you in my way. They like the tips I've been feeding them so much they offered to buy your supper. Not mine, just yours."

Toni cocked her head to one side. "Does that mean they trust me a little?"

He sobered. "I think so. No, I know so. Just before I called you, they were going through a box of odds and ends they took from Jesse Campbell's home desk. One of them suggested I let you join our little guessing game."

"So this turns out to be a business dinner, huh?" She was intrigued, and pleased at their willingness to seek her input. She also welcomed access to any new information. "What are we guessing?"

Quint put his fork down and reached into his pocket. "It's a torn receipt with an unreadable signature." He handed her a rectangular piece of paper. "There are three questions. What is it for? Who signed it? And does it have any significance?"

Toni studied the paper and saw what he meant. It looked like it was from a business receipt book, but there was nothing to identify it. The top portion was torn off, as if it had been ripped out in a hurry, or just carelessly. Only the lower two thirds of it were there. It was made out to Jesse Campbell, showing that he had paid someone seven hundred fifty dollars. It had been signed in a hard-to-read scrawl that looked like a first name of Edna. On closer study she decided the last name might be Rankin.

"Got any ideas?"

"What do you think this number is?" She pointed

to the memo line at the lower left corner, neglecting to verbalize a guess at the last name.

"Our best guess is that it's the number of the check he wrote, but they haven't found anything to match it in any bank records."

Toni examined the signature and number again, committing them to memory. "I'll sleep on it," she said, handing it back to him.

Before she went to bed that night, Toni tried to call Kyle. She was worried about him and wanted to hear his voice. She needed to assure herself he was all right, and assure him that her support was firm. But all she got was an automated message saying he was unavailable.

She felt a little better after calling the boys and chatting with them and her parents.

*

Tuesday morning Toni pondered the matter of the receipt as she watched John's car in her rear view mirror on the way to school. What kind of things cost seven hundred and fifty dollars? Suddenly she thought she might know. She doubted that the apartment Sheila Campbell lived in at Ozark could be had for that, but there were a lot of apartments available in the area in that monthly price range. Springfield was bigger, making it a better location for a secret business headquarters—or place for liaisons with women. Could that number on the memo line be the number of such an apartment? If it was one his wife didn't know about, Jesse probably paid for it in cash.

Toni wished she had time to pursue the line of thought more, but she had a job to do. She pulled into the parking lot and dialed John, waving at him as he pulled up a dozen yards from her. "I'll be done with class by eleven, but I have to do lab prep afterward."

"Just call me when you're ready to leave the building," he said from the other side of his door window, grinning at her through the glass. "I can be here in minutes." He watched her until she got to the door of the building. Then he waved and drove away.

It was an easy morning, since all she had to do was monitor the exam. The students came to the desk one and two at a time as they finished, placed their exams on the corner of the desk, and left. By eleven o'clock the room was empty.

Toni spent the next two hours setting up for the next day's lab final. Models of the heart, eyes, ear, trachea, male and female reproductive organs, and a kidney were on display. Each work station was outfitted with microscopes with slides positioned on them, a urine dip stick, and cat bodies for dissection—like a kitty morgue, she reflected whimsically.

As she finished putting up pictures that identified blood types, John entered the room.

"I wasn't busy, and I guessed at how long it would take you." He grinned. They had been fellow teachers long enough to know the routines.

"Since you're being so good about this, would you mind if I make a stop at the campus book store on the way home?" she asked.

"No problem."

At the bookstore, Toni located a textbook designed for a business technology class, paid for it, and was back in the van in less than ten minutes.

From Quint's parking lot, she watched John drive away. Before going inside, she checked the index of the textbook, thumbed to the chapter on proper telephone technique, and stuck a piece of paper between the pages to mark it. Then she gathered her belongings and entered the apartment.

"I was beginning to wonder about you," Quint called from the kitchen. He came to meet her, carrying cold sodas. "I saw you pull up."

Which meant he was concerned enough to be watching for her. Toni felt bad for not thinking to call him.

His phone rang as he put the drinks on the coffee table. "Nash."

He listened a moment. "Okay." He disconnected.

Toni grinned. She was pretty sure he had ended the call before someone could finish their last sentence. She handed him the book she still had in her hands.

Quint took it and read the title, his brow creasing in puzzlement. Then he noticed the bookmark and opened it. When he saw the chapter title, the corners of his mouth deepened. "Are you trying to tell me something?"

She nodded. "Your technique could use some improvement. But I'll keep loving you whether it does or not."

He laughed, but then turned serious. "That was my sergeant. I'm supposed to be off tonight, but they're shorthanded. I have to go in to work."

Toni hated that Quint had to work on his night off, but part of her was secretly glad to have the apartment to herself. As soon as he left, she grabbed the phone book and flipped to the yellow pages. When she found the listings for apartment rentals, she was daunted. There were so many that she couldn't think how to tackle them, other than to work through them alphabetically.

She started to dial the first number, but hesitated. She had already spent way too much time on a case that was no business of hers. Now it looked like it wouldn't be solved before she left town. Why should she waste any more time on the matter?

But I'm still here right now. And I'm invested in the case.

She checked her watch. It was only four o'clock, and there were no more lesson or lab preparations to do. Everything was completed. Her finger moved, almost of its own volition, back to the phone. She began dialing.

"May I speak to Edna Rankin?" she asked when a man answered after six rings.

"Who?"

"Edna Rankin," she repeated, hoping she had deciphered that second name correctly.

"There's no one here by that name."

That was the pattern of the calls. But, rather than becoming discouraged, Toni was emboldened by an old familiar surge of stubborn refusal that wouldn't allow her to accept defeat. She began punching at the phone, willing it to yield an Edna Rankin.

Perseverance finally paid off.

"Just a moment. I'll get her," someone said at the Sunrise Apartments.

Toni stared at the phone in surprise.

"This is Edna," a voice said, making Toni realize

she needed to say something.

"Hello, Mrs. Rankin," she said, suddenly remembering those telemarketing calls she hated so much. "This is your lucky day. Your name has been chosen to receive…"

"Not interested," the woman cut her off. The line went dead.

Toni checked the address. She wasn't familiar enough with the city to know just where it was, so she went to Quint's desk and rummaged around until she found a city map. She located the address in the southwest corner of town.

Stuffing the map in her purse, she left the apartment, checking to assure herself that no one was sitting in any of the parked cars watching her. Seeing no one, and feeling paranoid for even checking, she got in the van and headed across town.

The neighborhood was comprised of modest homes, businesses and apartments. Toni missed the entrance to the apartment complex and had to swing into the lot of a car wash to turn around and go back half a block. She parked toward the center of the units and sat there a bit to survey the premises. She noted a breezeway two doors down. Just then a couple came walking through it and headed up a set of stairs to the second level. They wore bathing suits and carried towels.

Each unit had a small balcony with a wooden safety fence around it. None of the numbers matched the one on the receipt.

Toni exited the van and marched to the breezeway, as if she knew exactly where she was going. She walked through it and found herself inside a courtyard. Apartments surrounded it on all four sides, like a small fort. There was a pool house in the center of it, surrounded by parched grass that wouldn't need cutting any more if they didn't get some rain. She could see a pool inside through the greenhouse-like clear walls.

She turned right and walked parallel to the pool house, scanning the door numbers on both levels. When she reached the corner, she followed the sidewalk to the left and scanned all the doors across that end. At the next corner, she made another left and started walking slowly along the back row of units. She found the number she was looking for on the upper level in a location where occupants had an excellent view of the courtyard entrance and close proximity to the pool.

Toni's heartbeat picked up with the excitement of discovery. It had to be Jesse Campbell's apartment, one where he conducted business—and monkey business.

Chapter 18

Toni glanced around, wondering where to find an office or apartment manager. Looking back at the breezeway, she decided it must be out front. She started to cut across the yard, but came to a stop as she reached the pool house. At the far end of the small building was a door with a nameplate on it that said OFFICE.

Toni went to the door and found it locked. But then she saw a small sign beside it that said MANAGER UPSTAIRS. A small arrow pointed to the right. She went to that corner of the building and found a set of stairs going up the side of the building. She climbed them and found a single apartment sitting directly at the top of it. The name Edna Rankin was etched on the nameplate next to the door. Toni knocked.

The door opened to frame a tall, portly woman who looked to be in her fifties. A kitchenette was visible behind her. She wore a loose caftan and a floppy brimmed straw hat. Flyaway strands of gray hair peeked from beneath it in a thick fringe. Her eyes were pale in a round fleshy face.

"Hi, are you the apartment manager?" Toni asked.

"Landlady, apartment manager, whatever," the

women said in a voice that made Toni think of a witch's cackle. "I'm Edna Rankin."

"My name is Toni Nash," Toni said, impulsively using her maiden name. "I'm looking for an apartment, and a friend recommended this complex."

"I have three units vacant out front," Edna said, jerking her head in the direction of the breezeway. "Would you like to take a look at them?"

"I'd prefer something back here." Toni swept her hand in an arc that indicated the inner courtyard.

Edna frowned. "Everything's full in here."

Toni tried to cover her dismay.

Edna's brow creased. "How big a hurry you in?"

"Oh, I don't need it immediately. I don't start my new job until the first of the month. I took a couple of days off to come look around."

Edna pursed her lips and studied Toni. Then she took on a conspiratorial demeanor. "I have a unit that's paid up till the end of the month, but it'll be vacant before then. The tenant was killed, you see. So he's not coming back."

Toni feigned surprise. "That's awful. Is there a family who will have to move out of the apartment?"

Edna shook her head. "No, he wasn't married. I don't know about his family. Never saw or talked to him much."

"So his belongings are in the apartment?" Toni asked casually.

"Not for long," Edna said. "His fiancé is in there right now, cleaning it out."

That took Toni by surprise. "Is she alone?"

Edna didn't seem bothered by the question. "No, she has two young men helping her. I should be able to get in there in a day or two and start getting it ready for a new tenant. Of course, you might not be interested, knowing that the last person who lived there got hiz-self killed." She ran her eyes over Toni, judging her take on such a situation.

"Oh, that wouldn't bother me," Toni said blithely. "I don't believe in ghosts and such stuff."

"Good. If you want to come back in a couple days, I could let you see it then."

"I'll do that," Toni said, anxious to escape now that she knew someone was in that apartment. "Thank you for your time."

Fiancé? Toni hurried down the steps, thinking fast. Jesse Campbell had just gotten married, and she doubted that any of his side dishes had any thoughts of marriage. Someone was in a hurry to get their hands on his possessions.

As she reached the bottom of the steps and rounded the corner of the pool house, Toni pulled out her cell phone to call Quint. But a glance up at the balcony of that apartment brought her to a standstill. Two big guys were out there gathering the barbecue grill and deck chairs. One of them was Dean Patrick. She didn't recognize the other one. As they went back inside the apartment with the stuff, she rushed across the grass and through the breezeway to where, sure enough, there was a moving van parked near the stairwell.

Knowing the two young men could appear any moment, Toni slid into her van and dialed Quint's cell.

"Nash," he snapped. "Make it quick, Toni. I'm on duty."

"This is duty," she snapped back. "That receipt was for the rent on an apartment in the Sunrise complex. I'm there now, and there's a woman and two guys cleaning it out. You need to stop them before they get away with a pile of evidence."

"Get out of there," he ordered sternly. "I'm on my way. Where are you exactly?"

"I'm in my van in the parking lot."

"Okay, stay put—but out of sight. Don't you go near those guys. Hear me?"

"Gotcha. There's a moving van parked near the stairwell. I'm sure it's theirs." She was talking to air.

Toni's heart pounded frantically as she sat watching the moving van and debating about going back to the courtyard where she could see the apartment.

Suddenly she saw lights flashing and a police cruiser turning into the parking lot. Another followed it. Her phone rang.

"I see you. Stay there," Quint ordered.

Toni watched as he stepped from the first cruiser. Someone joined him from the one that pulled to a stop next to him.

"It's number two-forty-eight, and it's in the inner section overlooking the pool," she said, speaking fast.

"We'll get it."

Toni gripped the steering wheel so hard she wouldn't have been surprised to hear it crack. She hunched down and peered over the top of it, scanning the length of the complex and concentrating on the stairwell. She wanted to go where the action was, but she knew the officers didn't need her help, or to be distracted. And she needed to play lookout for them.

No sooner had that thought crossed her mind than movement caught her eye to the right. A woman came running around the corner of the far end of the building, her arms loaded with what looked like books and folders. Her back was to Toni, and she wore a red baseball hat with her hair pushed up under it. She sprinted to a car at the end of the lot, yanked the door open, and tossed everything into the passenger seat. As Toni climbed out of her van to get a closer look, the woman jumped in the car, backed up, and went squealing out of the lot.

Toni ran up the sidewalk, trying to get a closer look, but the car disappeared from sight before she could get a look at the driver's face. She made a mental note that the car was a dark green Cougar, and then wanted to kick herself for concentrating so hard on trying to identify the woman that she failed to get a license number. Her gut said Jesse's *fiancé* had just made a getaway.

She was on her way back to her van when Quint and the other officer came through the breezeway, each of them escorting a young man in handcuffs. They marched them to separate cruisers and plunked them into the back seats.

Toni went to Quint, intending to tell him about seeing the woman leave, but he forestalled her. "We have to get to the station," he said, getting into his vehicle.

The window swished down, and he spoke through the opening. "I want you to go back to the apartment. I'll talk to you later, after we've dealt with these guys."

Toni didn't agree or disagree. She just backed

away and watched them leave. Then she marched back into the courtyard and headed for that apartment. She found Edna Rankin just locking the door of it. At Toni's approach the woman whirled around and frowned in recognition. "Are you the one who called the cops?"

Toni winced. "Yes. I'm sorry I deceived you. But I knew that the guy who lived here left a grieving widow. So when you said a fiancé was cleaning out the apartment, I knew something was wrong."

The woman's expression underwent a strobe-like series of changes, from anger to puzzlement, and then to curiosity. "You weren't looking for a place to rent. You were looking for this apartment. What's going on?"

"I'm trying to find out who killed your tenant," Toni said, deciding the time for honesty had arrived. "My son is the boy who found the man's body, and I've been working with the police."

Edna shook her head, her oversize body shaking along with it. "You say there's no fiancé?"

"No fiancé," Toni repeated. "That means someone is up to no good. Those young men were moving stuff out of an apartment that doesn't belong to them, or to that woman. Did she give you her name?"

"No. Like I told them two cops, she just introduced herself as Mr. Campbell's fiancé and showed me a ring on her left hand and the man's picture. No one else has showed up to claim anything, and I needed to get the place emptied. I shoulda been more careful."

"I understand," Toni assured her. "Can you

describe the woman for me?"

Edna straightened her shoulders and gave Toni a skeptical look. "Them cops said the detectives will want me to come down to the police station tomorrow and talk to them. I shouldn't be talking to you."

Toni took a deep breath. "One of those cops is my brother. I'm staying with him and working with him on the case. I have a theory about who the woman is, but I need confirmation. If you can do that for me, I'll be able to help the police find her."

Edna blinked, her pale eyes showing confusion. Finally she spoke, as if talking to herself. "What can it hurt if I describe the lady to you now, if the cops are just gonna ask me the same stuff?"

"Nothing that I can see," Toni said, wishing she really did have a theory about who had been in that apartment.

"She was tall and slim and had long dark hair, just like thousands of gals in this city."

"What was she wearing?"

Edna closed her eyes a moment, mused a bit, and then reopened them. "A sexy yellow tank top and jeans."

"What…"

"She had real thick eyelashes and wore a lot of makeup," Edna continued. "Oh, and she had on some kind of long dangly earrings."

A picture began to form in Toni's mind. It took her a bit to put a name to it. Then she considered the women she had seen fleeing the parking lot. The body fit, but the hair had been covered and the face obscured. "Thank you, Mrs. Rankin. You've been a big help."

Quint called as she was steering the van onto Ingram Mill Road. "You didn't go straight home," were the first words out of his mouth.

"I'm almost there," she said. "I'm a big girl. Don't worry about me."

"Well, how about you come by the station and talk to the detectives?"

Toni pulled into a parking lot and stopped. "Will I be grilled if I do?"

"Yeah, thumbscrews and the whole hard case treatment," he said gruffly. "But you can handle it."

She laughed, her apprehensions easing. "Will you stand guard over me?"

"Maybe. Will you get your butt in here?" He was starting to sound a little exasperated.

"Okay, I'm on my way."

*

When Toni walked into the police station, the officer behind the glass fronted desk was on the phone, but his eyes scanned her thoroughly. He was a young man, probably in his early thirties, sandy hair worn in a crew cut. She took a seat and waited.

"Thank you, ma'am. We'll have someone check on it right away. Yeah. Okay, ma'am. Thank you for calling."

He put the phone down and jotted something on a notepad before looking back at Toni. "May I help you?"

She nodded. "My brother is expecting me. His na…"

"Nash?" His eyes raked over her in sharper interest.

"Yes."

"He said you were coming. I'll get him." He picked the phone back up and punched a button. "Your sister is here."

He hardly had time to replace the phone before Quint appeared in the doorway to her left. He beckoned for Toni to follow him.

She trailed him to a small office about halfway down a wide hallway. She felt nervous as she entered the room and took in the sight of the man behind the cluttered desk. He was an older guy, a large black man with a thick shock of salt and pepper hair, a round face, and a mouth that turned down at the corners. He wore a rumpled white shirt, charcoal pants, and a green striped tie. There was a gold band on his left hand. He gave her a sharp assessing look and came to his feet. "Hello, ma'am."

"The name's Toni," she said, placing her hand in the one he extended across the desk.

He released her hand and pointed at a chair. "I'm Lieutenant Green. I understand you've been doing some independent investigating and feeding your brother here the info you find. I've talked to officers Durbin and Chilton, and they seem to think you have a good head on your shoulders." His deep voice was relaxed and easy.

Toni wasn't sure how to respond, so she didn't.

"She knows the chief of police personally back home and has helped him with a couple of cases," Quint volunteered.

The lieutenant nodded. "I've heard. Let's talk about this latest incident," he said to Toni, getting down to business.

Her stomach knotted, but she didn't hesitate. "I

found an apartment Jesse Campbell was renting."

"How did you find it?"

Toni glanced at Quint. He nodded that she should tell him.

"Quint showed me a torn receipt and asked if I could guess the significance of it." She explained her thought processes and how she had tracked the location of the apartment complex.

Lieutenant Green leaned forward on his elbows. "How did you know those young men were inside the apartment?"

Toni gave Quint a guilty frown. "I went to the landlady and told her I was looking for an apartment to rent, and that I preferred something inside the courtyard."

The corners of Green's mouth twitched ever so slightly, but he waited for her to continue. In her peripheral vision she could see Quint make an I-should-have-known shake of his head.

"She said she didn't have any empty units in there, but she had one that would be available after the end of the month. She confided that the tenant had been killed and that his fiancé was in there cleaning it out right then."

Both men came to attention. "Fiancé?" Green snapped. "There was no fiancé in there."

"We arrested two men. There was no woman," Quint added.

Toni raised her brows. "You took off before I could tell you what I saw. While I was following orders and staying in the parking lot, a woman came around the end of the building, threw an armload of books and papers in a car, and split."

The lieutenant observed the byplay, but ignored it and grabbed a pen. "Can you describe her?"

"I only saw that she looked fairly young. She was tall and slim and wore a red baseball hat. I went back and talked to the landlady after the officers left with their prisoners."

"That's why it took you so long to get here," she heard Quint mutter.

"Edna Rankin, the landlady, said the woman she let into the apartment was tall and slim, which matches the woman I saw. She said she has long dark hair and wears lots of makeup and long dangly earrings. That's all the description I got." For some perverse reason she didn't share her suspicion as to the woman's identity.

"What kind of car did she drive?" Quint asked.

"It was a dark green Cougar. I'm not good at models and such, so I can't tell you the year, but it looked no more than four or five years old."

The lieutenant made another note.

"What about the guys you arrested?" she asked, figuring it was time for some reciprocation. "I recognized Dean Patrick, but I didn't know the other one."

"His name is Mitch Sandoval," Quint said, his voice grim. Toni's gut tightened.

The lieutenant glanced from one to the other of them. "What?"

Toni explained about her student's warning. "Nicole said he's an enforcer and that he's dangerous."

"Both of them have clammed up," Green said. "We can hold them for twenty-four hours while we go after a warrant and get bail set. I'm sure they expect the woman, whoever she is, to come up with bail money."

"Dean's a juvenile," Quint pointed out.

"Yeah, I know," the lieutenant said wearily. "He's going to juvie and will probably be released to his parents."

*

Sandoval held the phone to his ear, tapping his fingers impatiently against the counter before him. "Get me out of here if you want your name kept out of it," he snapped angrily.

"Okay, calm down. Just sit tight. How much should I send?"

He told her.

"It'll be there. Just keep your mouth shut, and tell the kid to do the same."

"I can't. They took him to juvie."

"I'll take care of it. When you get out, I want you to keep watching that nosy teacher. She worries me. I saw her in the parking lot, and I'm sure she's tipping the police."

Chapter 19

When Toni exited the police station, she called John. "Want to take another ride with me?"

"Pick me up," he said, not asking where she was going. He was hooked on the case.

It was a little after six o'clock when they drove into the Goldenrod parking lot. "We're looking for a dark green Cougar," Toni said, scanning their surroundings.

"Are you looking for the one you saw at that apartment complex?" John asked. "You think it might be here?"

Toni nodded. "I didn't see the face of the woman in it, but I went back and talked to the landlady again and got a description of the phony fiancé. The woman was the right size and build to have been Sonya Finch. If it's her car, we might find it where employees park."

John grinned. "It's worth checking."

There was no green Cougar at the back section of the lot next to the highway. But there was one sitting between a red Mustang and a brown pickup at the south end of the lot.

"That looks like it," Toni said in satisfaction. "Let's go talk to Miss Finch again."

The restaurant wasn't very busy yet, but it sounded like business over in the bar was picking up. They bypassed the hostess and headed that way. The interior they stepped into was darker than in the restaurant. Toni was glad she hadn't come alone. The din was noisy, and the air permeated with smoke so thick she could hardly breathe. License plates from what must have been every state in the nation decorated nearly every inch of the walls.

People stood elbow to elbow along the long bar that extended across two walls in an L. Looking around, Toni spotted Sonya working the back section. "Could you eat a burger?" she asked John. "I didn't have lunch, and that looks as close to a meal as we can get in here."

"I'm hungry, too," John replied as they made their way to a table.

Sonya came sashaying to the table, wearing her incredibly short skirt and spaghetti strap top. She came to an abrupt halt when she recognized Toni, her smile turning to a scowl, and her eyes darkening.

"We'll have a couple of burgers and Cokes," Toni said blithely. "Put lettuce, tomato and mustard on mine." She turned a questioning look on John.

"Load mine with everything."

"I'll have someone else get it for you," Sonya said in a cold tone, turning away.

"You do and I'll have a nice talk with your boss."

Sonya spun around, glaring at Toni. She started to speak, but then clamped her jaw shut. She walked away.

When she returned with their drinks, Toni smiled at her. "I didn't realize you and Jesse Campbell were getting married, since he just got married this past spring." She put a meaningful emphasis on the last phrase.

"I don't know what you're talking about," Sonya snapped, her look venomous. She plunked the glasses down.

"She doesn't like us much," John said as the gal stalked away.

"Maybe if I poke at her enough she'll admit she was at that apartment."

"I think you need to be careful," John cautioned. "She already hates you. I don't want to see you get hurt."

Toni considered the warning, and then grinned. "I can't believe how cheeky I feel. But I don't sense any real danger from her. We're here in front of a lot of witnesses. She can't afford to do anything to me so openly."

When Sonya returned with their burgers, she slapped them down and turned to leave.

"I know you took a pile of papers from that apartment," Toni said before she could march more than two steps. "It had to be records and correspondence related to the operation Jesse was running." She spoke as if she knew all about it.

Sonya's hostility was so near the surface she could no longer control it. "Listen, lady," she hissed through clenched teeth. "If you came to harass me, you can take your pal and get out."

"I just want the truth," Toni shot back. "I want to know…"

"I don't care what you want to know," Sonya cut her off in a near shout, her face flushing beet red.

"And stop making up stories."

"I'm not making up anything," Toni said, leaning forward over the tabletop. "I saw you running away from that apartment, and I know you're involved up to your pretty little neck in Jesse Campbell's illegal gambling ring."

Fury flashing across her face, Sonya took three quick heavy breaths of air. "Shut up! Lady, I know how to deal with people with big mouths. Watch it, or you'll end up like Barry."

"Ah, so you admit you knew him—and you're involved with what happened to him." Toni waggled a finger at her.

In a lightning move, Sonya's arm drew back and came forward in a vicious swing.

Toni's reflexes were quick, but not quick enough. She tried to duck, but Sonya's fist caught her in the left cheek, the impact making her head rattle. She saw stars.

People turned to stare as the commotion caught their attention. Sonya's hand pulled back to swing again. This time John shot to his feet and grabbed her wrist as her arm came forward.

"Someone call the police," a female voice shrieked behind them.

A moment later the bartender arrived at the table. "What do you think you're doing?" he barked at Sonya.

"She's been harassing me," Sonya snarled, struggling to free her arm from John's grasp.

Two police officers barged through the doorway, paused for just a second to find the disturbance, and proceeded to the table. "What's going on here?"

Officer Durbin asked.

"She started it," Sonya accused furiously, pointing at Toni.

"I just asked her a question." Toni rubbed a hand over her burning face as she recognized that his partner was again Chilton.

Both officers did a double take as they recognized her. Officer Chilton's mouth made some strange movements, and Toni knew Quint was going to hear about this—real soon.

Sonya spun around in a sudden move that took the officers by surprise. When she started to run, Officer Durbin grabbed her arm. "Hold on there."

"Take your slimy hands off me," she yelled, jerking her arm.

Now both arms were grabbed and yanked behind her. "Okay, let's take this argument down to the station and get it straightened out. All of you," Durbin said, eyeing Toni and John.

He frog marched Sonya out of the bar, her protests loud and ongoing.

"You two come along. You can drive your own vehicle," Officer Chilton said. "But I'll be right behind you."

Toni looked with longing back at the burgers and Cokes they were being forced to abandon. It was still sweltering outside when they exited the building. It hit them with force. The after work traffic whizzed in each direction as they caravanned to the police station. Toni pulled up next to Durbin's cruiser, and Chilton swung in on the other side of her van.

Chilton hopped out and met Toni on the parking lot. "Quint's coming," he said quietly, taking her arm.

He escorted her in silence back to where she had been only an hour earlier.

Toni could see John looking over their surroundings. Inside, it looked like the day had gotten hectic. Every chair along the hallway was occupied. She felt conspicuous—and a sliver of fear. Durbin took Sonya to a room on the right side of the hallway, while Chilton took her and John directly to Lieutenant Green's office.

The man looked up as they entered, and his expression was not a happy one. "You're back," he barked, no longer friendly. He jabbed a finger at a chair.

She sat. John took the chair by the door. She heard footsteps, and Quint entered.

"You've helped us before, but now you're out of line," Green said, an edge of anger in his voice. "It's time to stop meddling and worrying your brother."

Toni slid forward in the chair. "I haven't been trying to worry anyone. I just had a suspicion I needed to check. And I didn't go alone," she added for Quint's benefit.

Her brother moved to the far wall and backed up against it, his arms folded across his chest. He stood watching them, his jaw clenched. But he didn't speak.

The lieutenant was visibly steaming and making no effort to hide it. "Why didn't you just tell us you thought you knew who you saw?"

Toni bit at her lip and flushed slightly. "I was only suspicious. I wanted to find out for sure before telling you. Incidentally, where is she?"

"Being questioned in another room. Now, give me a step by step account of this latest episode."

"After I left here I went and got John. We went to the Goldenrod for a burger, which, by the way, I didn't get to eat," she tossed in. Her head was beginning to pound from the combination of tension and lack of food.

"Back to the story," Green snapped.

"Sonya came to our table to wait on us," John spoke up. He went on to give a concise account of the incident, including Toni's threat to talk to Sonya's boss when she said she would get someone else to wait on them. Then he repeated Sonya's threat, word for word, and described how Sonya had hit Toni.

Green's index finger rubbed back and forth over his upper lip. "She belted you, huh?" He stared at Toni's still red and aching cheek. "That's good for assault. Do you want to press charges?"

Toni thought about that. It would cause Sonya some inconvenience, but it didn't seem wise to enrage her any more right now. She also wanted to be sure Sonya was free to roam the streets. Her gut said things were moving toward answers, and she wanted Sonya to do something that would incriminate her. She also didn't want any legal issues pending when she went home at the end of the week.

"No, I'm leaving town in a couple of days," she explained, and caught what she thought was a look of pleasure flash across the lieutenant's face at hearing she was leaving.

He leaned back in his chair and stared at her. "All right," he said, a bit reluctantly. "You seem to be rattling some cages. Why don't you leave it to us now?"

Toni got to her feet and placed her hands on the

desk, leaning forward. "I will if you'll get some more background on that gal. She's involved with those young men, and they're involved in the gambling ring. I'm convinced there's more to the connection."

Green's eyes shot sparks. "Are you telling me how to do my job?" he thundered, rising to his feet and coming nose to nose with her, his hands flat on the desk.

She backed away. "No, I'm just telling you she's in this up to her neck, and I don't want you to miss it."

Toni paused, out of breath and waking up to how aggressive she was acting. This wasn't her classroom. It was the lieutenant's. She took a deep breath. "I'm sorry. I didn't mean to get out of line, and I don't want to jeopardize the case. Are we free to go?"

Green backed down, too, and eased into his chair. "Yeah, you can go. And I'll do some deeper checking on the gal."

John and Quint escorted her out of the building and to her van. As John went around to the passenger side, Quint took Toni's arm and stopped her before she could get behind the wheel. "Is it useless to hope you'll go straight back to the apartment?"

Toni didn't want to lie, but she didn't want to make promises she couldn't keep. "I'm too hungry to take time to cook. I have to stop somewhere and eat. I think you should talk to Dean again. If you get him alone, he might admit it was Sonya with them."

He shook his head. "Yeah, yeah. You had no lunch, and your burger got left behind. Get out of here." He ignored the bit about Dean, turned and walked away. But Toni thought she saw the corners of his mouth curve a little before he got turned away from her.

"You hungry?" Toni asked John as she started the engine.

"Yes, but I need to get back to my room and work on a paper. It's due tomorrow, and I have a lot to do yet."

"Can't have the teacher bombing a paper." She put the van in motion.

After delivering John to his housing, Toni considered her growling stomach. But that thought was superseded by a vision of Nicole Warren. She pulled into a parking lot, dug out her book satchel, and extracted her grade book. She flipped to the back where she kept a list of her students and their contact information.

She found Nicole's number and dialed it.

"Warren residence." Nicole sounded harried.

"Hi, Nicole. This is Toni Donovan—your A & P instructor."

"Oh, hi, Mrs. Donovan. Morgan, put that down," she snapped. The sound muffled. Then it cleared up. "Sorry, Mrs. Donovan. I've got a kid having a bad day."

"I'm sorry I called at a bad time."

"Oh, it's fine," Nicole assured her, the background noise settling down. "Morgan's hungry, and I've been trying to study."

"Would you have time to meet me at Burger King? We could feed Morgan and ourselves some greasy fast food."

Nicole laughed. "She'd like that. So would I. How soon?"

"How soon can you get there?"

"Fifteen minutes?"

"I'll meet you." Toni pulled back onto the highway. At Burger King, she recognized Nicole leading a little dark haired girl across the parking lot.

"Can you tell me more about Sonya Finch?" she asked when they were seated in a booth with their food.

"I need ketchup, Mommy," came from Morgan.

Nicole aimed an apologetic look at Toni and reached for the ketchup.

"I have two boys," Toni said gently. "I'm child proofed."

While Nicole squirted ketchup over Morgan's fries, the three-year-old bounced in her seat, her ponytail bobbing up and down. She grabbed a fry and stuffed it in her mouth.

Toni smiled, remembering moments when her own babies were small like that. She missed it. But she also enjoyed the freedom afforded by their older independence.

"You asked about Sonya," Nicole said, her attention returning to Toni. "I don't really understand what you want to know. She liked parties, expensive things, and older guys."

"That's pretty comprehensive," Toni said with a nod. "Can you expand on it a little? Give me an idea how she thinks."

"Well, she thinks big. She wants the best of everything. I don't really understand her, and we were never best friends or anything like that." Nicole sprinkled salt on her fries.

"Did she do well academically?"

Nicole considered that. "I think so. But she didn't put a high priority on grades or education. She said she learned more from life experience, and she didn't plan to spend her life in a stuffy classroom."

Toni nodded. "She told me she considers her relationship with her coach in that light. What other of her life experiences do you know about?"

"She started dating older men during our junior year," Nicole said thoughtfully. "Then during our senior year she started talking about someone who took her to a casino just over the line in Oklahoma. Toward the end of the year—that would have been after she had to cool it with Coach Campbell—she got a job working there weekends. She was eighteen by then and could look and act even older. One day I heard her bragging about how good a shill she was. I'll admit she was good at influencing people to do things for her."

"So she learned the gambling business first hand," Toni mused. "Do you think she stayed hooked up with the coach?"

Nicole tipped her head to one side, her lips pursed in thought. "If she did, I wasn't aware of it. But it wouldn't surprise me. She got around, and she didn't seem to want permanence from any one man. She probably did."

Toni hesitated before the next question. "Do you think she's ambitious enough to want to take over the coach's business now that he's dead?"

Nicole chewed while pondering. "She might be, but I can't picture her murdering him," she finally decided.

"How about giving orders to someone else?"

"I don't know. But I do know she likes to be in charge." She gave Toni a troubled look. "Do you think she did it?"

"I'm not sure, but I'm convinced she's involved."

They finished eating in a thoughtful silence broken only by Morgan's happy chatter.

"Why don't I give you my cell phone number," Toni said as they prepared to leave. "That way, if you think of anything you think might be helpful, you can call me."

Nicole pulled out her own phone. "Give it to me."

As Toni quoted it, Nicole entered it into her address book and saved it.

After they parted in the parking lot, Toni checked her rear view mirror and pulled into the street. Once certain she was not being followed, she relaxed. She had an itch, a restless feeling she couldn't shake. Quint was at work, so the apartment was empty. She wasn't in the mood to visit Kyle's parents. She had tests to grade, but that wouldn't take long. On impulse she turned off the thoroughfare and looped south over to Lone Pine Avenue, wanting another look at the surroundings where Jesse had been killed.

When she arrived at Sequiota Park, she chose a parking spot where she estimated that Jesse Campbell's car had been found. From there, the crime scene was obscured by the island down the middle of the lagoon. She got out and walked across the lawn to the edge of the water. Then she walked alongside it until she was directly opposite where the body had been found. She stopped and stared across the water, remembering the sights, sounds, and smells of that experience. She studied the area, and then glanced back at where her van was parked, visualizing someone sitting in it. If someone had been there, he or she could have gotten tired of waiting for Jesse to return and come looking for him.

Another thought filtered through her mental processes. What about Jesse's car? Had the detectives found anything in it that might identify a passenger? Would they even talk to her at this point?

Her cell phone interrupted her thoughts. She jumped involuntarily and answered it without checking the caller ID. "Toni Donovan."

"Mrs. Donovan, if you're not home yet, please go there and stay," Nicole's trembling voice said. "Please be careful."

"What's happened, Nicole?" she asked, her nerves reacting wildly.

"Mitch just stormed in here and started asking questions about you. When I told him it was none of his business what I know about you, he…" A choking sound was followed by a sniffle.

"Did he hit you?"

There was a pause. "Yes, but I still didn't answer him," she said in a weak voice. "I told him I was calling the cops. He finally left, but I'm afraid for you. Please be careful."

"I will," Toni promised, her gaze darting around at the sparsely inhabited park. She saw two people on the bridge, and a couple more at the mouth of the cave beyond the bridge. Only three cars occupied the parking lot. The heat had people staying indoors rather than bringing their kids outdoors or to the parks.

A biker whizzed past her, making her jump. Then a car rolled slowly along the highway, making her realize how open and vulnerable she was if anyone was looking for her. It had been stupid to expose herself this way.

"Are your doors locked?" she asked Nicole.

"Yes," Nicole answered.

"Do you have some place you can go stay for a while?"

"I guess I can stay with my mother."

"I wish you would," Toni said, heading back to her van in a speed walk.

"Okay, I'll pack bags for me and Morgan. And I won't forget my textbook," she added, trying and failing to lighten her tone.

"You'll do fine on the exam," Toni assured her. "You've done well all along. See you in the morning."

Chapter 20

Toni's hands shook as she scooted behind the steering wheel and gripped it tightly. All the way to Quint's apartment she kept checking behind her. When she arrived, she couldn't get inside fast enough.

She tossed her things on the couch and sat beside them, her mind still reeling. It was several minutes before she was calm enough to think again.

Was there another adult involved in the running of the operation? If so, who? She couldn't visualize it being Sheila Volner Campbell. Not only was she a non-aggressive personality, but she had not been involved with Jesse long enough to have been in on the early stages of the gambling setup. But the Kickapoo secretary had preceded Sheila by five or six years. Could she have been involved in more than just a romantic relationship? She had clerical skills. She could have been a business manager. She had a son who could be a runner. Had their relationship really ended when Jesse took up with his best friend's wife? Had it ever ended?

Toni rummaged through her notes and lists, but couldn't find the number she wanted. She found a phone book, mumbling to herself.

"Michelle...Michelle what? Cran... Cras... Carin... Carringer. That's it. But what's her husband's name?"

She found a Robert Carringer that matched the address she remembered. She dialed.

"Mrs. Carringer," she said when a husky voice answered. "I'm the teacher who came by and spoke to you about the Jesse Campbell murder."

"It's Mickey," the woman corrected. "I remember. What can I do for you?"

"I'm not sure," Toni said, awkward now that she had the woman on the phone. "There have been some leads in the case. I'm finding out about some activities, and names associated with them, that make me wonder whether they're connected to Kickapoo."

"You mean Joyce Franklin," Mickey said bluntly. "What kind of activities are you talking about, other than sexual ones?"

Toni wasn't sure how much information she should share, but she couldn't get information without giving. "It looks like your former coach was involved in, or running, a teenage gambling ring. Students from different schools were working for him, and..."

"You want to know who the connection is at Kickapoo," Mickey finished for her. "Wow. This is heavy stuff, and it's news to me."

"Do you think your kids and their friends would tell you what they know?"

"I notice you didn't ask whether they know, just whether they'll tell. But you're right," she said on a sigh. "The kids always know what's going on in the schools and communities. Mike and Julie aren't in right now, but I'll talk to them when they get home."

"Thanks," Toni said. "I'll give you my cell

number so you can call me back."

When they disconnected, Toni tried to call Kyle again, but she still couldn't reach him. He should have noticed her missed call the night before and gotten back to her. But he hadn't. Was he avoiding her?

As she sat there worrying about him, her phone rang.

"Mom, that boy's driving me crazy," Gabe said. The words were sharp, but his voice was subdued enough for her to recognize fear underlying it.

"What do you mean, Son?"

"He's dreaming again, and saying crazy things."

Toni's gut tightened, and she gripped the phone tighter. "Where are you? What kind of things is he saying?"

"I'm just down the road from Grandma and Grandpa's house. I'm on the ATV. No, it's not moving. I'm stopped by an empty lot so I could call you."

He meant privately.

"He's hard to understand when he does that," Gabe continued. "He kind of mumbles. But last night he was saying something that sounded like, 'Watch the black car'."

"Okay, I'll watch for the black car," she said, speaking more brightly than she felt in an effort to put his mind at ease. "Remember to expect your dad home a day early so he can bring you to Springfield Friday."

He seemed excited at the prospect of another visit with his second set of grandparents. After the call, Toni considered what Gabe had said about

Garrett's dream, but she didn't know what to make of it. She tackled her paper grading and was putting the papers away when Mickey Carringer called back.

"I thought I was beyond being shocked, but this gambling thing has knocked my socks off," she said as soon as Toni answered. "I don't know where my kids get their information, and I try not to pry so deep they'll quit talking to me. According to my son, our secretary and Jesse Campbell did break up after he left the school. But she took up with him again sometime later."

"Does your son know if Joyce has been keeping books or anything like that for a side business?"

"I asked him that," Mickey said. "He doesn't know if she's involved or not. All I can tell you about her is what I've heard. The word is that her finances have always been shaky. If that's true, I can see how she could be tempted to pick up some easy extra money. But that's just conjecture."

"Do you know if gambling is widespread among the students in your school?"

"I sure hope not," Mickey said. "I'm going to talk to my brother-in-law about all this and see if he knows what his former buddy was up to besides women. He needs to find out how much involvement there is in his student body. This mess has already cost him so much, and this could make it worse if a bunch of his students are involved."

"Maybe he can help clean it up," Toni suggested.

Mickey didn't speak for a moment. "Being part of a solution might help him feel like he's regained some control of his life," she said thoughtfully. "Listen, I appreciate what you're doing, whether anyone else does or not. If I hear anything more, I'll call you."

Toni thanked her and ended the call. Then she stretched out on the couch and lay staring up at the ceiling. The next thing she was aware of was the clicking of the door. Startled from sleep, Nicole's warning about Mitch Sandoval shot a jolt of fear through her.

Her heartbeat slowed when she recognized Quint closing the door behind him. "What time is it?" she asked groggily.

"Two-thirty." He started removing gear from his belt.

She sat upright, coming awake now. "Was it a rough night?"

"Busy. Got any coffee made?"

"No, but I can have some by the time you get your shower, if you mean to take one."

He began unbuttoning his shirt. "I'll sleep better if I do. Could you manage some bacon and eggs with it?"

"Can do."

As promised, she had food and coffee ready when he returned from the bathroom a few minutes later, wearing a loose tee shirt and shorts. He sat across from her and picked up the hot cup by his plate. "That's good," he said after a healthy swig. He put his cup down and faced her, his expression solemn. "Did you come straight home after you left the station?"

Toni picked up her own coffee and drank slowly, not wanting to answer. But his manner said he was not going to be evaded. "I met my student, Nicole, for a burger. I was hungry."

He nodded. "Did she give you any helpful information?" He tackled his own food.

"She told me a little more about Sonya Finch as a high school student. Sonya dated older men, and one of them took her over into Oklahoma and introduced her to casino life and gambling. She worked weekends as a waitress and bragged to her senior classmates about what a good shill she was."

Quint looked up. "Is that all you learned?"

Toni tensed. "She called later and said her ex, Mitch Sandoval, showed up at her apartment and questioned her about me. She wouldn't answer, and he hit her." The last was said angrily.

"He's bad news," Quint said with a grimace. "He must have gone straight there as soon as he made bail. But we can't help her unless she presses charges."

"She told me she and her daughter would go stay with her mother for a while. I hope she stays there until this case is settled."

Quint gave her a slight grin. "I can tell you one thing that might give you a little satisfaction. The manager of the Goldenrod called the station and told the officer who answered to tell Sonya she's fired."

"Did you get any answers out of Dean or Mitch?"

Quint swallowed and sipped from his coffee before answering. "At first they both clammed up and refused to say who was with them in the apartment. But when Lieutenant Green questioned Dean alone, he finally admitted that it was Sonya Finch. So you were right about that. It was enough to get us a search warrant for her apartment."

"I bet she wasn't happy about that."

"She was fit to be tied, but Green and another guy from the squad searched it. They found a knife and what looks like records of the gambling operation. It's appearing more and more that she's our killer, but they have to test the knife to be sure it's the murder weapon and glean through that pile of folders and paperwork. They've also requested her phone records. The biggest fear is that she'll pull a disappearing act before we can get enough proof to charge her."

"What's the status on Dean and Mitch?"

"As expected, Dean was released to his parents. Mitch made his phone call, and a young man showed up with the cash to bail him out. He was free less than two hours after you left. That's why I said he must have gone straight from the police station to Nicole's place. Have you talked to anyone else?"

Toni nodded. "I called the Kickapoo art teacher I talked to before."

"Didn't you say she's related to the Ozark principal?"

"His sister-in-law. She talked to her kids, and her son said their school secretary and Jesse Campbell did break up after he left the school, but that they hooked back up again later."

Quint shook his head. "I can't believe that guy. He got around more than a hooker."

"Mickey said that secretary's finances have always been shaky, so maybe she was working for Jesse because she needed extra money."

Quint shrugged. "That's a strong possibility, and I admit it would be satisfying to poke around in her house, but speculation isn't enough to get a search warrant. This *has* been quite a day for searching, though."

"Oh?"

"The detectives confiscated everything they could find of interest in that apartment. But they didn't find much that was helpful."

"That in itself sounds suspicious to me," Toni said.

He drained his coffee. "I agree. There was no computer, but that's not surprising since laptops are so common. The top drawers of the file cabinet were empty, so someone emptied them. The others contained office supplies and unused receipt books. The bottom drawers were more interesting. They were stuffed with fancy phones and phone covers with sports logos on them."

That struck Toni as interesting. "I remember a story about some drug dealers who gave middle school and junior high students fancy shoes for passing drugs to their friends," she said while refilling his cup. "Fancy phones could be used the same way."

His eyes narrowed. "Give them fancy phones for recruiting their friends into gambling? You could be right. Of course, the detectives have probably considered that."

"The schools have a bigger problem than they realize."

"The department is trying to educate them," Quint said. "They've been calling on administrators and questioning them about their knowledge of gambling in their districts. Most of them are pretty naïve and tell us how disappointed they are at hearing of such student participation. One of the hardest things for the department is convincing parents of the students that there is anything criminal involved."

"They don't understand the seriousness of what their kids are getting into. They tend to say, 'Thank God it's not drugs'. They don't see that a gambling addiction is as much of a problem as a drug addiction."

"In some cases parents pay off their children's debts, but they still resist what they consider interference by school officials or law enforcement," Quint added.

"I know. If kids are caught and punished with detentions or suspensions, the parents go ballistic. Even assigning them to write essays and watch movies about the dangers of gambling meets with grumbling and resistance."

He gave an exaggerated sigh and focused on his food.

*

Wednesday morning Toni stared in the closet at the two remaining outfits she had with her that were suitable for work. "Eeny, meeny, miney, mo," she mumbled and reached for the simple white dress on the right.

Quietly, so as not to wake Quint, she dressed and tried to conceal the bruise on her face with makeup. It took a thick layer that felt stiff when she moved her facial muscles.

After a bowl of cereal, she left the apartment. John was waiting on the parking lot to follow her to school again. This time she welcomed his presence.

When they arrived at the school, Toni walked briskly to the entrance of the building, turned to wave good-bye, and watched him drive away. Then she hurried inside.

Lecture time was spent reviewing for the finals. All she had to do during the lab final was monitor while students worked. Fortunately, it was an all multiple-choice exam, so she could grade them with the scantron, an electronic grade scoring machine. As students finished and handed her their answer sheets one by one, Toni scanned them and entered the scores in her grade book. By the time all the students were gone except Nicole, who was obviously waiting to talk, she had everything caught up.

Nicole approached the desk and handed Toni her answer sheet.

"If you'll wait a minute, I'll grade it," Toni said, inserting it into the scantron. She grinned when she saw the results. "Ninety-six percent. I told you that you would do fine."

Looking up, she realized that Nicole was staring at her face, her composure rigid. Self-consciously she ran a palm over her bruised cheek.

"What happened to you?"

"I offended someone. We match now," Toni said, trying to make light of it.

"Was it Mitch?" Her voice was low and strained with tension.

"Oh, no," Toni denied quickly, and watched some of the tension visibly drain from Nicole.

"I'm glad it wasn't him."

"How about you?" Toni asked pointedly, indicating Nicole's own bruised face. "Has Mitch bothered you any more?"

The young woman gave a weary sigh. "I'm okay.

We stayed at Mom's last night. She says I should get a restraining order."

"That might be a good idea."

"Who hit you?" Nicole demanded. "I know you husband and boys aren't here. So it can't be a family problem."

"It doesn't matter," Toni said.

"It does matter," Nicole insisted worriedly.

Toni saw that she wasn't going to let it go, and she deserved honesty. She had answered all her questions and warned her about Mitch. "It was Sonya," she said with no further explanation.

Nicole's eyes rounded. "What happened?"

"I went to the Goldenrod and asked her some questions that made her angry." Toni stopped at that, uneasy about going into the details and having to explain about the apartment.

Nicole stared, weighing her words. After a few moments she apparently opted against prying any more. "I'm sorry that trying to help the police got you hurt."

"I'll live," Toni assured her. "But I appreciate your concern. I'm going to miss you."

Nicole smiled now. "Will you give me your e-mail address? I'd love to keep in touch."

"Of course." Toni jotted it on a piece of paper and handed it to her.

Nicole smiled, said "Thanks," and left.

*

It took an hour to tidy the room. Just as she was finishing, John breezed through the doorway. He wore khaki walking shorts, a red sport shirt, and a big smile, obviously happy about finishing up and going home to Jenny.

"Hi. Ready to go?" he asked.

"Yes. I'm also hungry," she answered, closing a supply cabinet door.

"Then why don't we stop by the Greasy Spoon. Unless you'd prefer the Slimy Fork. Or how about the Nasty Knife?"

Toni moaned at his silly puns and gathered her bags. "Anywhere you choose is fine."

"Who's driving?" he asked.

Toni hesitated at the door. "Both our vehicles are here."

"Right. But I assumed you'll want to go talk to a suspect after we eat. And you can't be running around alone."

"As a matter of fact, I've been thinking I'd like to talk to the coach's widow again," she admitted. "It's hard to believe she saw nothing and knows nothing, even if she wasn't married to the guy very long."

"Maybe she's had enough time to think about it and remember something helpful if asked the right questions," John said, implying that Toni could do that.

"I'll drive," she decided. "Leave your car in the parking lot, and we'll come back here for it."

They had burgers at McDonald's and went to Ozark. As she drove, Toni shared with John about Gabe's phone call and what Garrett had said. The irony was that, in their absorption with the conversation, they both forgot to check behind them for a black car.

"I'll sit out here and study," John said when they pulled up in front of Sheila Campbell's apartment complex, tapping the notebook on the seat beside him. "You have to give a final tomorrow. I have to *take* one."

She frowned. "Now I feel bad about monopolizing your time."

"No need," he returned easily. "I'm enjoying myself."

It made no sense to argue at this point, so she left the keys in the ignition so he could run the air conditioner and went to see if Mrs. Campbell was home. When she rang the doorbell, Sheila opened the door and peered at her through pale eyes that could have used some makeup. She was barefoot, wore jeans and a loose pink tee shirt, and held a half grown white and yellow kitten. Her expression morphed from blankness to recognition, and then to annoyance.

"What do you want?" she asked flatly.

"I want to talk to you again. May I come in?"

Sheila hesitated, but then she stepped back and widened the door opening. Toni followed her to the couch and sat on the opposite end of it. "That's a pretty kitten. I don't remember seeing it when I was here before," she said, attempting friendly conversation.

Sheila stroked the animal in her lap. "I adopted him last week. I thought the kids would like him. I'm hoping to get to see them more often," she added, her eyes and tone so full of longing that Toni couldn't help but feel sorry for her.

"I'm sure this whole experience has been difficult for you."

Her mouth trembled, and she lifted a fisted hand to rub against it. "It's been awful. The reality is still sinking in."

"I don't want to seem like a voyeur, but in order to understand what was going on in Jesse's life, I'd like to ask about your marriage," Toni said cautiously. "Were you two getting along?"

Sheila took several moments to respond. When she blinked, tears leaked from her eyes and trickled down her cheeks. She made a hasty swipe at them. "I'm not sure," she admitted in a tremulous voice. "The questions the police have been asking have convinced me that I never really knew him at all."

"Did you know he was keeping another apartment?"

"No," she said in a near whisper, moving her head slowly back and forth.

"Did you know about his involvement in gambling?"

"No," she choked, still shaking her head.

Toni stared at the wan and listless woman. She was either one incredibly naïve lady—or in a serious state of denial.

"You're sure you knew nothing about either one?" she pressed, watching for facial clues. "You never even suspected?"

More tears worked their way down her cheeks. Sheila compressed her lips and tried to speak. When no sound came out, she spread her palms in front of her. The kitten hopped off her lap and trotted from the room.

"Maybe," she finally whispered.

Chapter 21

Sheila took a deep, steadying breath and went motionless, as if lost in remembrances. She blinked as more tears escaped, but finally regained her composure. "Marriage vows didn't mean anything to Jesse. I mean, he knew I was married when he…when he…"

"Started an affair with you?"

Her nod was in short jerky movements. "I don't know why I let him get to me like that. I guess because he was Grant's buddy, I thought he was a good guy. But that's also how I know his track record. He could be very charming—and persuasive," she said, swiping at her eyes in self-anger.

"I never met him," Toni said quietly. "But I'm sure he must have been."

"Yeah, well, I fell for him, and look what it got me," she shot back, grabbing a tissue from the box in front of her on the coffee table. "I lost my husband and kids. I really don't understand why Jesse pushed me so hard to marry him."

"Because he felt guilty for destroying your marriage to his buddy?"

Sheila raised her chin, and her shoulders

stiffened. "That's right. I can see it now. I just wish I had seen it then."

"You knew he had affairs before you married. Did you know he was straying during the short time you were married to him?"

"I didn't want to think so, but I was beginning to wonder," Sheila admitted, speaking stronger now. "He took me with him to some of his haunts, and I met some of his former students. One evening when we were at a local hangout, I saw him talking to some of those students I had met. There was a tall dark haired girl I believe he said he knew in Branson, and two young men. One of them, a tough brawny looking guy, was also from Branson. I'm not sure where the other one went to high school. Anyhow, I got the feeling there was something between Jesse and the girl. But I had no idea he was keeping another apartment."

"Did you see any gambling in those haunts?"

"An occasional poker game," she said with a matter-of-fact shrug. "When I asked Jesse about those students, he told me they were members of some fantasy leagues—basketball and football—and they kept track of their teams on a web site. I know that kind of thing is popular, so I believed him."

Toni thought Sheila was finished, but she began to speak again.

"A few days after that I went out to lunch with a friend, and I saw that girl and one of the guys again, the smaller one with the highlights in his hair. They were in a booth close to us, and I heard them talking about Jesse seeing someone. It was confusing. There was the girl I suspected of being involved with Jesse, and she was talking about him picking back up with another woman. At the time I was still fighting for custody of my kids and didn't need any new problems."

Toni thought she understood. The woman had already lost her husband and was losing her children. To find out the guy she had gotten in exchange for them was already messing around with someone else had to have been devastating.

"I was weak," Sheila said bleakly. "I didn't say anything, didn't ask any questions. But, looking back, I've wondered if that conversation was about the woman he was seeing when he lost his job at Kickapoo."

Toni thought for about a second. "You mean the secretary?"

Sheila nodded, her demeanor not quite as remote as it had been. "I talked to a friend about it. Then she started asking around about why Jesse left Kickapoo. She heard about a hushed up affair with someone on the support staff. By that time I knew I shouldn't have married Jesse, no matter how much he pressured me to do it. But I was a coward and did nothing."

"I'm sorry things turned out so badly for you," Toni said awkwardly.

The woman drew a heavy breath. "Me, too. I'm not sure how long I would have stayed married to Jesse. I'm sorry he died the way he did. But the more I find out about him, the more I see how stupid I was."

Toni found herself feeling glad she had come. She wasn't sure how helpful it was going to be, but it seemed to be serving as a small catharsis for Sheila.

Verbalizing thoughts that had only been growing suspicions seemed to be freeing her in some indefinable way. The past acknowledged, guilt admitted. Maybe that would help her move forward.

Toni returned to the van where John sat slumped in the seat with his nose buried in his textbook, the engine and air conditioner running. He put the book down and straightened in the seat when she opened the door.

"Glad you kept it cool in here," she said, getting behind the wheel.

"I'm doing fine, so if you want to go anyplace else, feel free." His grin was a bit smug.

"Smart guy." She backed the van out of the parking spot and swung forward into the street, heading back the way they had come. Feeling safe with John riding shotgun beside her, and discussing her conversation with Jesse Campbell's widow with him, she didn't pay as much attention to their surroundings as she should have. As they made a turn at the end of the block, a dark car pulled out of a parking space a hundred yards down the street and followed them.

*

When Joyce Franklin opened the door, her eyes widened in recognition. "I don't want to talk to you," she snapped, starting to close the door.

Instinctively Toni shoved a foot between it and the door frame. "Let's forget about what you want and do what's smart."

Joyce glared at her through the partial opening, distrust marring her face. Her white-blonde hair was pulled back in a ponytail and held by a powder blue ribbon.

Toni placed a palm against the door and pressed firmly. "May I please come in?"

The woman's eyes flashed with annoyance, but she made no further attempt to close the door, obviously wrestling with herself. After a long moment of indecision she stepped back. "Make it short."

Toni followed her inside and took a chair while Joyce plopped onto the couch.

"I told you everything I know when you were here before," she said in an angry burst.

"But you didn't tell me the truth," Toni said, watching the woman's eyes.

Joyce blinked. "I don't know what you mean."

"You told me you hadn't seen Jesse Campbell in several months. Why did you lie?"

"I didn't," she protested in a tone that bordered on surly.

Toni wasn't going to back down. "Yes, you did. You said Jesse dumped you when he left the school, which may have been true. But you hooked up with him again later. People talk," she added pointedly.

"So what if I did. I sure didn't kill him." She was bristling now, recognizing that further lies would do her no good.

Toni eyed her closely, sizing her up. Joyce's small size, as well as her naïve personality, made it unlikely that she would have committed such a physical attack, or have been in possession of a hunting knife. But her honesty was in question. She probably knew more than she was telling.

"What did you really do after Jesse left the

school? Did you look him up?"

Joyce shook her head adamantly. "No way. I blocked him from my mind and moved on. Corey, my son, was a senior at the time, and graduation was a big thing for us. It gave me something to focus on and plan for."

That sounded like a fairly solid approach to Toni. "What about after that?"

Joyce ran a hand through her wispy, flyaway bangs. She still wasn't friendly, but she answered. "The next year Corey started college, and I missed him. I was lonely, but I kept busy. A friend was the cheerleading sponsor. I started helping her work with the girls after school. It occupied me, and I enjoyed the practices."

"But you and Jesse did connect again."

Joyce tilted her head, as if trying to guess how much Toni actually knew. She shrugged. "Schools are like little towns or communities inside a building. Everybody knows everybody else's business, and gossip flows fast." She sounded more resigned than bitter.

"When did you call him?"

"I didn't. I knew from the grapevine that he went to work for a construction outfit after leaving the district. I also knew when he started coaching again at Ozark, but I never called him."

Toni waited while Joyce paused, gazing around as if wondering where her life had gone out of control.

"Because of working with the cheerleaders, I kept attending basketball games, even though I no longer had a boy playing on the team," she said, more in control now.

Toni anticipated the next part of the story.

"Jesse showed up with his Ozark team to play us early in the season. It was one of our first games. Afterward he stopped me in the hall, and we talked a little. He asked how I was, how Corey was doing in college, things like that. That was all. But the next time he came for a game, he looked me up and asked me to meet him for a drink. I tried to resist him, I really did. But when he kept calling me, I finally gave in. He was like a disease for me. I couldn't resist him." Her eyes begged Toni to understand.

What Toni understood most clearly was that someone had cured that addiction, cold turkey, with a murder.

"I knew he got in a mess and felt like he had to marry his buddy's ex after her divorce. He felt guilty, I guess. But I'm sure he didn't love her," Joyce went on. "She's kind of wimpy."

So speaks the expert on love, Toni thought wryly. Any sympathy she had felt for the woman dissolved. Undoubtedly, Joyce believed Jesse loved her, and only her, while all evidence indicated that Jesse loved no one but himself. Well, maybe he had loved his kids. She could allow him that.

"Did you know he was operating a teenage gambling ring?" she asked, steering the conversation in a different direction.

"No. All I knew was how he made me feel," Joyce said with self-absorbed candor.

"Were you helping him with his bookkeeping?"

"I said I didn't know about any gambling ring," she snapped.

"How did your son feel about your affair?"

Joyce looked up at the ceiling for a moment, and then back down. "He said I was being dumb for letting him string me along. I guess he was right. But I couldn't seem to break free."

"Are you sure you never heard any talk about betting on sports or Internet gambling?"

Joyce gave a tight little laugh. "No, but I heard the boys laugh about some funny little tricks that helped them win ballgames. That wasn't serious, though, or gambling."

"You mean tricks like videoing the opposing teams in the locker room to get their play plans, or switching jerseys in the locker room when a player got in foul trouble?"

She looked surprised. "You know about that, too?"

"I do," Toni said in her sternest school teacher tone. "It may seem funny, but it's cheating. And small things have a way of leading to bigger things. In this case, it looks like a huge business has grown."

Joyce's face went lax. "I had no idea."

"Did you know if your son was friends with a young man named Barry Kuzman?"

Once again Joyce needed time to think, and didn't seem to have a lot of thoughts from which to draw. "I always knew his friends in high school, but when he started college I..."

Her voice trailed off, and then her eyes went wide. "Wait a minute! Are you talking about that guy who was blown up in his car?"

"That's him."

"I read the story in the newspaper, but I never

heard of him before that."

It was clear to Toni that she had gotten all she was going to get from this interview. Which she rated right around zero in value.

*

When she slid into the van, Toni slapped her hands against the wheel and looked over at John. "I think I finally understand why we have dumb blonde jokes."

He smirked. "I take it you've found one."

She snorted. "That lady was so besotted with Jesse Campbell that she forgot she had a brain. Why am I doing this? I'm just running in circles."

"Didn't she say anything at all that was helpful?" John asked in sympathy.

"She admitted to starting up with Jesse Campbell again after he began coaching at Ozark, but denied any knowledge of the gambling operation and said she had no idea whether her son was friends with Barry Kuzman. She's so unobservant that I tend to believe her."

"Maybe it just isn't meant for us to know the answer before we go home," he said with a commiserating head shake.

"I guess you're right." Toni put the van in gear and pulled into the street.

"You're spoiled," he accused. "You're two for two as a sleuth, and you can't handle defeat."

"But the possibilities won't stop running through my mind," she grumbled. "I can't seem to let it go."

John's mouth quirked. "I understand. My mind is also refusing to quit. I was just sitting here wondering about the murder weapon. The police found a knife in

Sonya Finch's apartment. That has to make her a prime suspect. But do you think she did it?"

"I think she has the temperament for it, but I'm not totally convinced she did it," Toni answered thoughtfully. "I think it would have taken real strength to kill a physical fitness type like Campbell. Maybe she could have caught him off guard. But why?"

John tapped his fingers against the door frame where his arm was resting. "Maybe a better question is, what was the guy doing in the park that night? Was it a clandestine meeting for a tryst? Or was it business?"

"I don't think Sonya cared who knew she was messing around with him, married or not, and no matter how many other women he was stringing along. So I doubt it was a tryst. Toni said, merging into highway traffic. "So what was the motive? Something tells me it had nothing to do with his coaching job. Money is behind a high percentage of crimes, and Jesse was raking in a lot of it. There was also a lot of anger in the way he was killed. I think it had to be related to his moonlighting job."

"That got him killed in the moonlight," John added, chuckling at his terrible pun.

For a few minutes they rode in silence. Then Toni glanced in the rear view mirror as she steered into the right lane to take the ramp up ahead. In the distance behind her she noticed a dark car make the same lane change.

She exited the thoroughfare and glided to a stop at the red traffic light at the top of the incline, glancing back at the car as it rolled nearer. When the light changed, she shot forward, swung left onto Sunshine, and sped down the street.

John came upright in the seat. "What's wrong?"

"I'm being paranoid. I saw a black car change lanes behind us, and I'm over-reacting," Toni said, not slowing down. She changed lanes and made a quick right into a residential area.

"You're not being paranoid," John assured her. "You're exercising wise precautions."

Toni wound through the streets and finally exited onto Chestnut. As she drove into the campus parking lot and pulled up next to John's car, she scanned the empty vehicles there.

"I don't see anyone sitting in any of them," John said, voicing her thoughts. He opened the passenger door and climbed out, but he didn't walk away yet. "If you want to take a scenic route to the apartment, I approve. I'll stay right behind you until I know you're safely inside your brother's apartment."

Toni gave him a grim smile. "You're a good friend."

When she drove off the lot, John stayed right on her tail. Neither of them saw the car parked on the lot of a gas station at the far side of the street, the driver slumped low, watching them.

Chapter 22

When they finally reached the apartment, John met Toni at the door of the van and walked her to the door, refusing to just drive away as he had done before.

"Spend the evening here with your brother, where you'll be safe," he cautioned firmly. "And be honest with him. Tell him you think someone followed us. Promise?"

Toni nodded, not mentioning that she didn't see Quint's pickup anywhere in the lot. "I'm sure I just overreacted back there, but I appreciate your concern."

"Call me if you need anything." He watched her go inside before he left.

Tired and facing defeat, Toni kicked off her shoes and flexed her toes, relieved to be able to do so with only a twinge of pain. She dumped her bags in the guest room and went to the kitchen for something cold to drink. The apartment was quiet and surprisingly tidy. Quint must have been spending at least a little of his days off around the place. So where was he?

She was just returning to the living room, popping the tab on a soda, when he arrived. Wearing jeans and a tan polo shirt, he looked comfortable and relaxed. She held up her drink. "Want one?"

"Yeah. It's hot out there. Something cold sounds good."

"What have you been up to?" Toni asked over her shoulder as she went to get it.

"Had to run a couple of errands," he said vaguely.

When she returned and handed him the soda, he studied her. "What's up?"

Sometimes she wished her brothers weren't able to read her so well. "My imagination got the best of me. I thought I saw a car following me," she admitted, her voice a little strained. "I guess I'm getting paranoid."

"Don't underrate your gut feelings," he said irritably.

"I think I'm letting my son influence me," she said with a shrug.

He went still. "Has Garrett been dreaming again?"

Toni nodded and tried to appear casual. "Gabe called and said he was dreaming and mumbling something that sounded like 'watch the black car'."

"The car you thought was following you was black?"

She nodded again.

"That kid has an eerie track record. Cancel any plans you might have for going out this evening." His tone brooked no argument.

"Yes, little brother," she said meekly. Then she perked up. "Okay, who's cooking?"

He grinned. "I'll put some steaks on the grill out back and pop some potatoes in to bake while you take a shower if you want one. Then you can make us a salad. I have ice cream in the freezer, and I bought some strawberries today that I'll let you slice if you're nice to me."

"Sounds good." She had been taking care of a family for several years now, and suddenly her baby brother was taking care of her. Truth was, she found she kind of liked it.

By the time they sat down to eat, Toni had regained some clear-headedness.

"Tell me about your day," Quint invited as he applied steak sauce to his meat.

Their mealtime chatter was pleasant and included talk of their family. Russell's hearing concerned them, as did his other health problems. Gabe would enter junior high in about a month, and Garrett's growing propensity for finding things fascinated Quint.

"It's been fun having you here this week," he said as he took his plate and cutlery to the sink after they finished eating. "I know you're disappointed at not solving our murder case before leaving, but I admit I'm glad you're going back where you'll be safe."

"I can't stop thinking about it," she said, running water in the sink and squirting detergent into it. "We didn't make a big mess, so I'll wash these few things instead of running the dishwasher."

He grabbed a dishtowel. "I'll dry."

"What have the detectives learned about that website? Did their secret participation net any helpful information?" she asked, unable to leave the case alone.

"Unfortunately, all they learned was how to place bets and how the runners ferry money to winning bettors and collect debts for distributors. They wanted to put surveillance on the Harcourt kid and gather more evidence on him, but because of the fast escalation of the case and a second death, they decided to abandon the website activity and search his residence."

"Did they find anything incriminating or explanatory?"

"They confiscated his computer and a bunch of papers from his desk. I'm not sure what they've learned from it."

"It takes time to examine that kind of material and know what it represents," Toni allowed, placing a mug in the dish drainer.

"The medical examiner says the knife found in Sonya Finch's place is the murder weapon, but that doesn't prove she killed the guy. There were two sets of fingerprints on it, hers and an unknown. The detectives had the foresight to save a drinking cup she used Tuesday while the two of you were there," he explained, picking up the mug. "They were able to match a set of prints from it to one of those on the knife. But they got no hits from AFIS on the other set."

Toni got the picture. "Those may belong to the killer, and it might be someone who hasn't done anything that would result in being fingerprinted. Do you think it's someone who's too young to have a record?"

"Could be." He placed the mug in the cabinets.

"What about in that apartment of Jesse's? Did

they take prints there?"

"Too many. They've found Sonya's, Dean's, and Mitch's. But we knew they were in the place. It's the collection of unidentified prints that are dead ends. It's the same with trying to trace those fancy phones. When they asked school administrators if they had noticed seeing a lot of extra phones around, they just laughed. So many kids have phones these days that there's no way of knowing who has new ones or where they got them. Plus, it's summer vacation, and the kids aren't around right now."

"That's all hard to accept, but easy to understand," Toni said, draining the sink and wiping it. "I wish I could see some records, like bank accounts, phone records, credit card statements."

Quint hung his dishtowel on a rack and faced her, his expression reflecting uncertainty over whether to say something. Finally he spoke. "If—and I say if," he repeated, holding up a palm, "I were to take you to the station tomorrow after you finish at the school and ask my superior and the detectives if they'll let you look at some files, will you be nice to them?"

A smile spread across her face, and she grabbed him in a tight squeeze. "I would treat them like royalty," she promised in pleased exuberance.

"Okay, okay, I hear you," he said, edging back. But he was grinning.

Toni released him. "I'll do my best to not get you fired."

They spent a pleasant evening of camaraderie that Toni thoroughly enjoyed. Quint went to bed about ten, but she stayed up to watch the news and weather. When she turned the television off, sounds drew her to the window. She gazed out at people cavorting in the pool and thought longingly of her boys racing through the woods to the pool at the country club to beat the heat.

There was little other activity in the courtyard or parking lot. When a car cruised slowly past the complex, her muscles tightened. As it came even with her line of vision and she saw that it was blue, the tension ebbed from her. With a sigh she turned and went to her room.

Just as she was crawling into bed, her phone rang. She grabbed it from the night stand.

"How's my girl?" Kyle asked.

"Missing you," she said wistfully. "How are you?"

"Let's talk about you first. How is your class turning out?"

"It's been a good experience, and I think the students have done well, but I'm ready for it to end. I miss you and the boys, and I prefer my own job."

"I know Kara appreciates you pinch hitting for her."

"It's been fun spending time with her, too."

Toni pushed herself up against the headboard of the bed. It was good to hear from him and know he was all right. She was being careful not to be the one to bring up the subject of his job. She didn't want to pressure him.

"Have the police arrested anyone yet?"

Toni sighed. "No. It looks like it's not going to be solved before I leave here, if ever."

"I hear the disappointment in your voice. Has Quint been taking good care of you this week?"

"He fed me steak this evening. I've enjoyed the time with him."

They talked a few more minutes about inconsequential things, neither of them broaching the subject hovering between them.

"I tried to call you Monday night and again last night," she said when they seemed to wind down. "I was starting to get concerned about you."

There was a moment of silence. "I've been really busy. I worked some extra hours so I can get home early this week. It looks like I can make it in by tomorrow night and bring the boys up Friday morning."

"Have you talked to them this week?"

"No, I've been on the move and…preoccupied. I'll give them a ring next."

"Good. Gabe called me the first of the week to tell me that Garrett was worrying him."

"He must have been dreaming again if it upset Gabe enough to call you. What was he doing or saying?"

"Gabe said he was hard to understand, but it sounded like he said 'watch the black car'."

After a slight pause, he asked, "What significance have you attached to it?"

Toni attempted to keep her tone light. "It has made me think a time or two that I was being followed by a black car. But I'm being careful," she hastened to assure him.

"Toni, I don't want you taking any chances. If there's even a possibility you're being followed, don't leave the apartment."

"I have to go to school," she reminded him. "But

don't worry. John has been following me to school in the morning and meeting me after class."

"Good."

There was another pause. "Toni, I know I should have called you back before this," he finally said. "But I really have been busy—and thinking. I didn't call because I'm still not sure what to say to you."

"It's all right," she said quietly. "You have a lot on your mind, and it's too important a decision to rush."

"I'm exploring the alternatives," he continued. "But I don't want to make a decision until I've finished my research." His words ground to a halt.

"Why don't you call the boys and chat with them awhile?" she suggested. "I bet that will make you feel better."

"I will."

When they ended the call, Toni turned off the light and snuggled down. But she slept fitfully.

Big yellow eyes followed her everywhere, watching her every move. She tried to outrun them. She tried to hide from them. But they dogged her everywhere.

She was in the van, sailing down Kansas Expressway, when suddenly the eyes zoomed up behind her, and she realized that it was the headlights of a black car. Terrified, she slammed the accelerator to the floor and shot forward. But she couldn't outrun it.

Toni woke with her heart pounding and her skin clammy. It took her several moments to get oriented and look at the glowing numbers on the digital clock. Six o'clock. She peeked out the window and saw a man carrying a black lunch box getting into a battered pickup. The working world was up and about.

She gazed up at the skyline. The sun was making its morning climb, but it looked like there might be some light puffy clouds drifting from the south. Hopefully they would bring the needed rain, but she wasn't too optimistic about it.

Donning her robe, Toni went to the kitchen and found Quint leaning against the counter with a steaming mug of coffee in his hand. He was barefoot and wearing faded jeans and a tee shirt. She halted in the doorway.

He set the mug down. "I decided to get up and see you off to school. I have coffee and cinnamon toast made. Care for some?"

"Sounds great." She took a seat at his table.

"Can you join us and Kyle's family for barbecue tomorrow?" she asked as they both nibbled at their toast.

"What time?"

"I think they plan to eat around two."

"I have to work tomorrow night, but I could stop by and mooch a free meal before reporting for duty."

"I'd better get going." She drained her cup and stood.

Minutes later Toni left the apartment and found John waiting in the parking lot. As she watched him follow her up the street, a sense of foreboding washed through her. She gave her shoulders a shake, as if she could physically dispel it. It didn't work.

*

By the time final exams were about finished, Toni was gripped by a mixture of relief at having completed a challenging task, and something like withdrawal pains. This summer teaching experience had been different from her regular job—less discipline, more in-depth and longer assignments—but about equal in paperwork.

Most of the students had turned in their exams and left the room well before the allotted time expired. Nicole Warren waited until last to say a private good-bye. With tears in her eyes, she thanked Toni for the class and promised to keep in touch.

When everyone was gone, Toni looked around the empty room and felt a bit sad that she would probably never see it again. But it was time to move on. She tackled the grading, and then averaged all of them. That done, she made sure all equipment, materials, and models were tucked into their proper storage places and all the tables wiped.

She picked up a protective drape and approached the skeleton in the corner of the room. "Well, Mr. Bones, let's wrap you up until your next class," she said to the inanimate model. "You've been very cooperative and helpful."

She started to pull the drape over it, but paused. Tipping her head to one side, she asked whimsically, "So what's your opinion, Mr. Bones? Do you think the police are going to find the coach's killer? Or should you and I stick around and help?"

She paused again, as if listening to an answer. "Okay, I guess they're on their own. I have to go, and you're not talking."

"I'll miss you," a gruff voice said.

Chapter 23

Toni gasped and jumped back. Then she whirled to face Quint, who stood leaning against the door frame. Not in uniform, he looked comfortable in jeans and a white polo shirt.

"Does Kyle know you talk to spooks?" he asked, chuckling.

Toni shook her fist at him. "You stinking little brother. One of these days I'll..." Her voice trailed off as images of his teasing when they were children flashed through her memory. He had been such a cute and impish little boy—and she had adored him. She still did.

In a sudden movement, she lunged at him and planted a huge smacking kiss right on his cheek, startling him. "I'll teach you to make fun of me."

As she started to kiss him again, he grabbed her hands and trapped them in front of his chest. "Hold on there, girl. If you attack me again, I won't feed you."

Suddenly their gazes locked, and the playfulness disappeared. "You're babysitting me," Toni accused.

"So?" He produced a faint grin.

"It's all right. You need to feel like you're taking care of me while I'm on your turf. You've always had a hero complex."

He shrugged. "Well, you're the only sister I have."

Although considerably younger than her and Bill, Quint had always been determined to do anything his older siblings could do. And he had. Toni recalled seeing him swatting baseballs with Bill and his friends when Quint was hardly big enough to hold the bat. With his big brown eyes, perpetual energy and winning nature, the older boys had let him tag along and play with them—and entertain them.

Toni still loved him dearly, but her emotions were mixed about having him feel responsible for her. She reached up and touched his chin. "I'm a big girl. You don't need to miss sleep and interrupt your routine because of me."

"Yes, I do," he returned simply. "Kyle would have my head if I let anything happen to you. Now, are you about done in here?"

She wrinkled her nose at him. "I just have to finish putting Mr. Bones to bed."

Lunch was a stop at Taco Bell. By one o'clock they were at the police station. Toni parked her van next to Quint's pickup.

"I'll take you to meet the chief first. We'll see if he'll approve my looking at the files with you along," Quint said, meeting her at the van door. "Lieutenant Green is off today, so you don't have to be nice to him after all."

"I'm not sure this is worth our time. I just keep hoping we'll spot a missed detail," Toni said, as Quint escorted her to the chief's office and opened the door to peek inside.

The man at the desk was not a big man, but it

was hard to judge his height with him seated. Light brown hair was swept straight back from his forehead, and deep set eyes peered at them from behind wire rimmed glasses. He beckoned for them to enter. "What are you doing here on a day off, Nash?" he asked, his tone deep and even.

"I'd like to introduce my sister to you," Quint said, stepping on inside the office. Toni followed and stood at his side. "Chief, this is my sister, Toni Donovan. Toni, Chief Rick Anderson."

The chief stood and reached across the desk for a handshake. "Good to meet you, Toni," he said, releasing her hand. Then his eyes sparked in recognition. "You're the teacher whose boy found our latest murder victim."

Toni gave a slight nod. "I'm afraid so."

He resumed his seat and leaned back in the chair, "What can I do for you?" He directed the question at Quint.

"I'm off duty, but I'd like to look at the files on that case."

The chief's brows lifted slightly, and his eyes darted to Toni. "You mean you'd like her to see them."

"Yes."

His fingers tapped idly against the arm of his chair. "She came up with a couple of helpful ideas already, right?"

Quint nodded. "That web site and the apartment."

The look he gave Toni was hard to read. "You think she might find something else?"

"I don't know," Quint said frankly. "But I figure it can't hurt to let her try. She's leaving town tomorrow."

"Okay." The chief reached for the phone and punched a button.

"Pull the files on the Campbell case," he instructed someone. "Put them on Green's desk."

"You can use Green's desk since it's empty today," he said when he hung up.

Quint took Toni to the familiar office. "You use the desk," he instructed, taking a chair in front of it.

As she settled in the seat, an officer entered and dumped a bundle of files on the desk. "Hello, Nash," he said, his voice not exactly warm. "What makes you think you can do better than the people who are trained for this kind of work?"

"I don't," Quint returned easily. "My sister here is a scientist, and surely another brain couldn't hurt. Toni, this is detective Boyd Wagoner."

The man gave her a skeptical glare. "Don't get anything mixed up," he snapped before leaving the room.

Toni ran two fingers across her brow in a gesture of relief. "I don't think that one's happy."

Quint shrugged. "Don't worry about it. That one's never happy. Dig in."

Toni picked up the files. There were five of them, a huge one on Jesse Campbell, smaller ones on Sonya Finch, Vince Harcourt, Dean Patrick, and Mitch Sandoval. She looked up at Quint. "You want one?"

"I think I'll let you do the work." He eased back in the chair, his legs extended and feet crossed. Then he pulled out his cell phone and began composing a text.

Toni started through the files, skimming to get an

idea what was in them. There were copies of detectives' reports, with written memos regarding interviews with each of the suspects. When she finished the overview, she went back and began to read in detail the items that interested her the most.

In Sonya's file she zeroed in on the phone bill that had been methodically checked and color coded. Calls to one number were highlighted in yellow, another in pink, and some in lime green. A key at the top indicated that calls to Mitch Sandoval were in yellow, ones in green were designated as Dean Patrick, and the pink ones were Corey Franklin. She counted twenty-two made to Mitch, only eight to Dean, and two to Corey. Mitch apparently was Sonya's main man, probably a lover as well as a business associate. All the calls had occurred within the last two and a half weeks—since Campbell's death.

She checked the bills in the other files and did a comparison. All three guys had called Sonya—Mitch several times, Dean and Corey only once each. There was no question that those four were connected, but the police already knew that.

Toni put the phone bills aside to examine the credit card bills in each file. They showed the normal charges—gas, groceries, restaurants. Nothing looked revealing, which didn't surprise her, since she knew that it was illegal for credit card companies to accept charges for online gambling.

A bundle of printouts with a label indicating they were from Sonya's computer were more interesting. The first sheets were a list with a heading that said RECEIVABLES-OVERDUE. Toni assumed these money amounts had to be gambling debts owed to Campbell.

She was amazed at the length of the list. As her eyes ran down the three pages, the names and amounts boggled her mind. She noted all three of Sonya's cohorts, or whatever they were to her, on the second and third pages. Dean was only in for a couple hundred dollars, but Mitch and Corey owed over five thousand each.

Beneath that list was a stack of correspondence that made it clear that, while Jesse ran the operation, Sonya managed the day to day functions and kept track of information related to wagers, runners, and bookies. There were even copies of letters documenting mediations involving disputes between bettors.

After reading through them, Toni laid those files aside and opened the Campbell one. The autopsy report was on top, so she read it first. Quint had told her what was in it, but it was still interesting reading. The pathology report indicated nothing remarkable aside from the stab wounds. The time of death was judged to have been between ten p.m. and midnight. Lab tests showed a minimal amount of alcohol in the victim's system, but no drugs or poisons. Death was due to multiple stab wounds caused by a single edged knife with a six or seven inch blade. A detective had noted on a sticky note that the knife had been found with two sets of prints on it, Sonya and an unknown. There was nothing there that Toni didn't already know.

The next items were the ones she had been hoping to see. A trace report on Jesse Campbell's car stated that silver nitrate had been found on the handle of the passenger door, both inside and out. Someone had been handling film. An image of Sonya Finch snapping pictures at the Goldenrod flashed in Toni's mind. She saw no notes indicating the detectives had made that connection.

Sonya had been in that car. But when? If it had been the night of the murder, had she witnessed the murder? Committed it? That didn't seem right. Aided the killer? That seemed more likely. The one thing Toni was growing more certain of was that, whether she had done it or not, Miss Finch knew who *had* done it. She had probably kept up an affair with Jesse since high school, and over time become involved in his gambling business.

Toni placed that sheet face down on the desk and moved on to the next one. The tech portion of the report indicated that keys to the vehicle were found under the floor mats, and fibers and debris had been taken from the floorboard.

She paused to ponder. Why were the keys still in the car? Jesse surely wouldn't have left them there if the car had been unoccupied. Someone—Sonya was Toni's guess—had been with him. She began to visualize a scenario. Jesse had slipped the keys under the mat and walked across the park to meet someone, not feeling threatened. His passenger must not have noticed him putting them there. When Jesse didn't return, the passenger went to look for him—and witnessed the killing. Whatever the reasoning, the knife had been removed from the crime scene.

That reason suddenly became clear to Toni. Sonya had been looking for the car keys, thinking they were in Jesse's pocket. When she didn't find the keys, she took the knife. Then she left. But how did she get home? She must have called someone to come get her. Toni thought it had to be one of those three young men.

She dropped that sheet and shuffled back to Sonya's phone bill. When she located it, she ran her finger down to the date of the murder. Then she moved down to the time that would have coincided. There it was. At ten-thirty-seven, Sonya had made a call to Mitch Sandoval.

Feeling pleased at that little discovery, Toni went back to the reports and resumed reading the remaining interview notes and memos. When she finished, she picked up the bundle of photographs. There were shots of the body and crime scene, taken from every angle. Since she had been present at the scene, the pictures were not shocking to her.

There were also pictures of the car, taken from different positions and depicting the area around it. Then there were pictures of the interior. There was a shot of the keys lying beneath the floor mat that was being held up by a corner.

Toni started to put everything back in the folder when the last photo made her pause. She picked it back up and stared at the debris pictured on the floorboard. She turned it sideways and studied it more closely. The small item at the edge of the mat next to the passenger door looked like a piece of candy. Under careful scrutiny she could make out a small marking on it, probably a brand name. Squinting hard, she thought what she was seeing could be the base and one side of the letter M. What kind of candy started with the letter M? Suddenly Toni's breath caught. It looked to her like part of an M & M.

Quickly she thumbed back through the written report and reread the list of debris gathered from the floorboard. It said a small piece of candy had been tested and male DNA found on it.

Closing her eyes, she thought hard. Then she remembered who she had seen eating M & M's. She shook her head and opened her eyes.

"Here's someone who just keeps popping up," she muttered to herself, thinking how many times he seemed to be around. "We haven't been paying enough attention to him."

"He was in that car," she continued her one-sided conversation. "I don't know when, but he was there. It was probably sometime when he was delivering or picking up money or bets, but he's involved more deeply than anyone realizes."

In front of her, Quint had slumped in his chair and fallen asleep. He stirred and opened his eyes. When he looked at his watch, Toni checked her own—and gasped at the realization that it was after three o'clock.

"I didn't realize we had been here so long," she said with a grimace.

He straightened in the chair. "No problem. I got a little nap. Was your time well spent?"

"I think so," she said, putting the files back in order.

On their way out, Quint stuck his head in the chief's doorway to thank him and tell him they were leaving. Back at the apartment, they parked side by side in the lot.

As Quint was unlocking the door, Toni's eyes strayed with longing to the pool where a couple was swimming. Quint noticed.

"Okay, let's go for a dip and cool off."

The water was cool and relaxing, and they spent the next two hours playing in it. But Toni's disturbing thoughts still nagged her. When they pulled up onto the edge of the pool and sat with their feet dangling in the water, she brought it up to Quint.

"I think there are a couple of things you could follow up on," she began slowly. "I wish I could do it myself, but I'm out of time."

"You noticed something," he said, reading her expression.

"I did," she said without much excitement. "But they're things the detectives have probably already noticed, and I wasn't privy to their discussions."

"Tell me anyhow."

Toni explained about the silver nitrate on the door handle. "When you and I went to the Goldenrod together, Sonya Finch had a camera hanging around her neck and was snapping pictures. She said she works for a modeling and photography agency."

He nodded. "I remember. That means she handles film and gets silver nitrate on her hands. You think she was in the car. But we can't prove *when* she was there. I admit it's one more connection, though. Anything else?"

"Photos of the car show that Jesse's keys were under the floor mat. I think Sonya was looking for them when she took the knife from the crime scene."

Quint listened without comment while she explained in more detail. "I think she must have called someone to come get her. I took another look at her phone bill and found that she made a call to Mitch Sandoval at ten-thirty-seven that night. I think he's her right hand man and probably the killer." She also described the letters and records indicating how deeply Sonya was involved.

Quint moved his mouth around in thought. "I'll pass the thoughts along to the detectives when I report for work tomorrow. Maybe it'll help and make me look good. It might even help me make detective someday."

She kicked at the water, splashing him. "Do you think you'd like that?"

He thought a moment. "Yeah. I think I would."

Her stomach growled, embarrassingly loud.

"Let's go inside, and I'll order pizza delivery," he suggested, smirking.

"Canadian bacon, pepperoni, mushrooms and lots of cheese," Toni ordered, getting to her feet.

As they disappeared inside Quint's apartment, a black car drove past the complex.

*

As they devoured pizza and sodas in front of a televised ballgame, Toni held up a slice. With cheese stringing down, she tipped her head and worked her mouth around the gooey stuff.

"This is good," she said, chewing with relish. "But I should have made us a salad to go with it, add a little green to our diet."

"I don't feel like a rabbit tonight, and who cares about diet," Quint said just before taking a big bite.

As they ate, Toni still couldn't shake the thoughts that weighed on her. Every time she tried to banish them from her mind, a new snippet would occur. She finished the slice and wiped her mouth and hands with a napkin. "It's a shame."

"Huh?"

"It's a shame Jesse died that way. From all I've read and heard, he had a lot of potential."

Quint gave her a rueful grin. "Still can't let it go, huh?"

She made a grimace and shrugged. "It's unreasonable, but I keep remembering that lifeless body and thinking what a waste it was."

"And you can't bear the thought of someone getting away with murder," he added with a knowing gleam in his eyes.

"He was smart and athletic, but marriage vows meant nothing to him. Then there's still something else about the whole case that angers me. His children didn't deserve any of this. His killer needs to be caught—for their sake."

"He was playing with fire," Quint pointed out.

Toni exhaled heavily. "I know. He was a jerk for getting students involved in such a mess. He deserved punishment, but not murder. Where did he go off track?"

Quint's face creased in thought. "I don't think it was from lack of a good home life when he was growing up. Would it help to go back over what we know? I'll begin. All indications are that his childhood was very normal growing up in Sedalia."

"Where he and Grant Volner were close friends," Toni continued. "Their relationship continued on through college and more. I assume they still kept in touch while Jesse was starting out at Glendale. He had a good experience there, won a lot of games, got married, and then moved on."

"But he kept in touch with some of his former students there, one of whom we know eventually became a bookie for him."

"I feel some guilt over Barry Kuzman's death," Toni admitted.

Quint's eyes creased in surprise. "You have nothing to feel guilty about."

"My brain knows that, but my emotions are confused. I helped find him because he hurt John. Then he was pressed for information. And when he started to talk, he was killed for it."

"It was his fault for the life he was living and the people he was dealing with," Quint said.

"I know that, but it stinks. I'm sure he wasn't the only Glendale graduate Jesse had working for him, but he's the only name I can identify. His next school, Branson, seems to be where he moved from small tricks to betting on games and stepping over the line with female students."

"The individuals you've met who were from there were…" He stopped for her to supply the names.

"Sonya Finch, the girl he had an affair with; Nicole Warren, my student here at OTC; and Mitch Sandoval, Nicole's ex and apparently one of Sonya's current lovers and flunkies," she enumerated for him.

"There's no question that Sonya and Mitch are involved," Quint said. "I know you like Nicole, and she seems to be innocent. But are you absolutely convinced that she is?"

"She has given me information and shown a real

concern for my safety. She's also genuinely afraid of Mitch. I can feel it radiating from her."

"But what's the motive for Sonya and Mitch?"

"She wants to take over the gambling operation," Toni said, thinking out loud. "There's big money to be had."

"You think she killed both Jesse and Barry then?"

Toni rubbed her eyes in frustration. "I'm not sure. I don't think she killed Jesse, but I think she decided to take over when he was taken out. It was an opportunity she couldn't resist. And she knows the operation inside out."

"So what you're really saying is someone actually did her a favor by killing Jesse and clearing the way for her to take over. Then that same person killed Barry?"

"I think she ordered Barry's assassination, probably by the same person who killed Jesse."

"She knows who it was?"

Toni nodded. "I think that's what fits. She knew and had the knife. She used it to force someone to do what she wanted. She and Mitch are pretty tight," she added with meaning.

"He's capable, but you say he's the one she called the night Jesse was murdered. If she was really at the murder scene and called him to come get her, he didn't do it. Just the same, I'll see if anyone has checked his prints against those on the knife."

"After Branson, Jesse was at Kickapoo," Toni said, picking up on the timeline. "There are probably several current students and past graduates from there who are involved, but the ones we know about for sure are the secretary and her son. The woman was besotted with Jesse, and I don't think she has what it would have taken to commit murder, at least not the physical method that was used."

"The son is a former student of Jesse's," Quint continued. "But what's his role in the gambling setup?"

"He seems to be just a runner. He's not a thug like Mitch. But what motive would he have for murdering his old coach?"

"Maybe he didn't like the man's relationship with his mother," Quint said, and then he paused. "He's the one who showed up with the bail money for Mitch."

"He's a college student, and his mother just gets by. He doesn't have much money, so that wasn't his cash. He's just a delivery boy," she said with certainty. "My bet is Sonya sent it. She was in that apartment with Mitch and Dean, and she has access to the gambling money. That means Corey is another of her personal flunkies."

"Okay, but I don't know where that leaves us. Jesse's next job was the construction company. Do you think he made any connections there?"

Toni chewed on her lower lip, shaking her head. "I doubt it. He took that job when he was without a school contract and probably broke. Up until that time I think he was playing around with the sports betting, but I doubt he was highly successful yet. In construction he was working with adults, and the gambling setup is centered on students and school sports. I think he worked that job during the day and built the gambling business during the evenings and weekends—except for time devoted to dallying with a married woman."

"That makes sense," Quint agreed. "By the time he was offered the job at Ozark he was ready to go big time."

"He found a computer nerd there and branched out into online gambling," Toni continued. "But then he got distracted by another woman and ended up married to her."

"The Harcourt and Patrick boys are pretty young," Quint said. "But murderers come in younger versions all the time. Would either of them have done it?"

"Like Sonya Finch, Vince Harcourt is ambitious," Toni said quietly. "Both of them may have decided to take over after Jesse was dead. Barry's death happened when one of them made a power play. Not only do I think Sonya is older and stronger, but I think Vince's inexperience and being questioned by the police combined to make him back off."

"He's such a kid that, if he was involved in silencing Barry, he's probably scared. If he wasn't, he was probably scared out of his mind when it happened," Quint theorized.

"Your logic is garbled, but I agree…I think," she said. "I'm certain there are a lot more kids involved from all the schools."

"I agree, but the only way we can stop them is by shutting down the whole operation. We're doing our best to accomplish that."

They both reached for another slice of pizza. For the next few minutes neither spoke.

"I think I'll take a shower and get rid of the chlorine," Quint said when he finished eating.

Chapter 24

Once she was alone, Toni continued to sit there, lost in her private thoughts and taking an occasional sip from her soda. In sudden decision she stretched over and fished her phone from her purse. She punched in Mickey Carringer's number.

"Mickey? This is Toni Donovan. Sorry to bother you again, but I was wondering if you've talked to your kids any more."

"Oh, hi, Toni," Mickey greeted her brightly. "I was just thinking about calling you. No, I don't have anything exciting to report," she said quickly. "But I did have another interesting conversation. The last time I saw you I had only talked to Mike, but today I managed to catch Julie long enough to question her a little. She's only a sophomore, but she hears the gossip and knows about pretty much everything that goes on in the school, even in the summer. She says her friends have talked about the murder a lot."

"Did she know about Jesse's affair with your secretary?" Toni wasn't sure why she was asking that question.

"Oh, yes. She was only in middle school when Jesse was our coach, but she remembers him and the talk about him. She and her classmates and friends have older siblings who have kept up with him and can provide the latest scoops. She told me all about how Jesse and Joyce had an affair back then, and how they started up again after he got back into coaching."

"What about her son? Did she say anything about him working for Jesse?"

"She did. According to the kids who have older siblings his age, he was quite a hot shot. He made no secret of the fact that he was going to be a pro basketball player. When he didn't even make a college team, it turned into kind of a joke around school. The kid thought, because his mom was the coach's mistress, that he would get some kind of special help and make it big. But he was only an average player and also average in academics. Everyone knew he didn't have the athletic talent for anything beyond high school."

"Sounds like maybe he decided that if he couldn't get rich playing the sport, then he would do it playing the odds."

A husky chuckle came from Mickey. "Could be. Julie says it's common knowledge that he was a gambler in high school. Oh, and she said the word is that he's on academic probation right now."

"What about his finances?"

"I asked Julie about that. She said she's heard he's a bad gambler, and he's been losing big money."

Toni couldn't think of anything else to ask.

"Like before, none of this probably helps," Mickey said, "but I like talking to you. Unfortunately, it seems Jesse got what he asked for. I don't feel happy about his death, but I'm glad he can't mess up the lives of any more students."

After thanking Mickey and ending the call, Toni sat motionless, the phone in her hand. She felt tired, but she also had a sense of relief and satisfaction. She was free of responsibility now and anticipating the arrival of Kyle and the boys. She was anxious to know if Kyle had made a decision about his job and their future. But there was still an itch inside her that was not related to his job uncertainty.

She recognized that it was lack of closure. She was disappointed at not seeing a murderer brought to justice. She hated having to leave with the case incomplete. She believed she knew who the killer was, but she couldn't prove it.

Lost in thought, she jumped when the phone jangled jarringly in her hand.

"Toni, do you still have the key to my classroom door?" Kara asked.

Toni clenched a fist and shook it at herself in aggravation. "Drat. It's in my pocket. I meant to turn it in at the office for you to pick up later, but I forgot. I left your textbooks and grade book in the top left drawer of your desk like you asked."

"I don't want you to make a special trip over here just to return it," Kara said. "You could just leave it with Quint. But I'd love for you to come over and spend a little of your last evening in town with me. There's no telling when we'll get another chance."

"I'll be right over." Toni disconnected and went to the closed bathroom door. "Quint," she called through it. "I forgot to leave Kara's key at the office. I'm going to run it over to her."

She heard like a sputter that told her he must be brushing his teeth.

"Wait," he called. "Don't go alone. Give me a few seconds and I'll go with you."

"That's not necessary," she called back, hitching her purse onto her shoulder and digging out her keys. "It's only a little before nine and not quite dark yet. I'll be careful."

As she headed to the door, she heard a commotion in the bathroom, but she kept going. "I won't stay out real late," she called over her shoulder as she went out the door.

The parking lot was still light enough to see that it was sparsely inhabited. Automatically Toni checked her surroundings, but didn't see anything unusual, no one sitting in any of the parked cars. She got in her van and backed out.

She didn't see a figure rise from a slumped position behind the wheel of a dark car parked about a block and a half up the street. She was rolling down Ingram Mill Road when it eased into the street in the distance behind her.

The drive across town was pleasant. The streets were quiet and peaceful, with light traffic at that time of evening. Toni relaxed in the calm scene. She had enjoyed her time in the town, grown familiar with it, and learned to love it. But it wasn't home.

She pulled to the edge of the street and turned onto Battlefield. When she glanced in the rear view mirror to check behind her before changing lanes, she noticed a pair of headlights in the distance make the same lane change. Another pair of lights did the same behind that one.

A ripple of unease threaded through her, making her muscles tense and her mouth go dry. She pushed the accelerator a little and watched behind her in the mirror. The lights sped up as well, keeping pace, but staying well behind her. She switched to the center lane. The lights switched too. That was when she called herself stupid for leaving the apartment alone.

Fully alarmed now, Toni sped up and veered back onto the right lane, seeing street lights in a blur. Suddenly the headlights bore down on her, moving up on her tail. Then she was rear ended with a jolt that hurled her head forward into the steering wheel. She jerked back and shook her head against the pain. It took her a moment to realize that the ringing she was hearing was not her head, but her cell phone.

Heart thudding, Toni wrested the van back under control, blinking repeatedly in an effort to clear her vision. She reached over and grabbed the phone, but before she could answer it there was another sickening sound of metal against metal. Her forehead hit the steering wheel again. In desperation she jerked her head back and held onto the wheel. She jammed her foot down on the accelerator, the phone still ringing in her hand.

She flipped it open, peering alongside her on each side of the street and charging forward. "Lo," she yelped.

"Toni! This is Quint. I'm behind you, and I see what's happening. There's a private school up the road two or three blocks. When you get there, pull into the parking lot. You hear me?" he demanded when she didn't respond.

"Yes!" She was struggling to hang onto the phone, keep the van in the road, and look for the school. Seconds later she spotted the parking lot.

Steeling herself, she dropped the phone and yanked the wheel hard, making a sharp turn that had her tires squealing and the van tilting. As the wheels left the highway, the dark car behind her swerved and caught the edge of her bumper as it flew past.

Fighting the wheel and riding the brakes, Toni tried to regain control, but the van spun in a half circle and slid across the asphalt. Dimly she saw her purse fly in the air and land in the floorboard. There was a sudden explosion of air bags around her, and then the van came to a jolting stop.

Stunned, she sat gasping for air and trying to comprehend what was happening. Looking up, she realized that the van had reversed direction and was sitting facing the highway. Up ahead, the car that had hit her had stopped, reversed, and was now coming back toward her. In a daze, she ran a hand over her eyes, trying to clear her vision, and fumbled beside her on the seat for the phone. Miraculously she found it and wrapped her hand around it. Clutching tightly, she stumbled from the van.

The black car backed up past the entrance, stopped, and shot forward. It came to a screeching halt just a few feet from her. Moments later her attacker emerged and came toward her with a tire iron raised in one hand. A baseball cap and the near darkness obscured an identity.

Backing away, Toni started to run. Just as she did, Quint's pickup squealed into the lot and screeched to a halt next to the black car. Looking back over her shoulder, Toni saw her brother leap from the truck before the sound of the motor had died away, and break into a run. He made a flying leap at her pursuer, taking him down in a bone jarring crash. The tire iron went clattering across the parking lot.

Her hands trembling, Toni dialed nine-one-one. She was giving the operator their location when a police car came flying down the street, lights flashing and siren screaming. It veered into the lot.

"Never mind. Help is here," she said, dimly comprehending that Quint had already summoned assistance.

Sprawled on the parking lot, her assailant was now face-down with his arms pulled behind him. The tire iron and baseball hat lay on the asphalt beyond him. Toni stepped forward and gazed down, recognizing the highlighted tips of hair that was no longer covered. As she suspected, it was Corey Franklin.

Quint looked up at Toni while snapping cuffs into place on Corey's wrists. "I've been following you all week. I'm glad I did."

Standing, Quint let the officer who had just arrived help him yank Corey to his feet.

Corey gave Toni a wild glare. "She forced me to do it," he yelled. "She blackmailed me."

"Do what?" Toni asked. "Are we talking about Sonya Finch?"

"Of course," he sneered derisively. "She's running things now. She made sure Barry couldn't shoot off his mouth or take over."

"The knife is yours, but she got her hands on it and used it to make you kill Barry. Is that what you're saying?"

"That's it," he yelled. "She was with Coach the night he came to meet me at the park. After our fight, she came looking for him and grabbed the knife. She threatened me with it when she wanted Barry shut up. Told me I had to do it. Said I could work off my debt and she wouldn't give the knife to the police."

Toni looked at Quint. "When your detectives take his prints, they'll find they match the unknowns on their murder weapon."

He grunted. "Yeah, yeah."

"I'll take him in," the officer, whose name badge read D. W. Rogers, said to Quint. "Soon as Chilton gets here to take care of that car, you can bring your sister down to make a statement."

Quint released Corey to officer Rogers, who marched the boy to his cruiser.

Toni's attention traveled from that scene back to the young man's car, noting its black color. Garrett's words, 'watch the black car,' came back to her. But something didn't feel right. The phrasing nagged at her. Her youngest son didn't *predict* things. He just *found* things.

Then it came to her. Maybe he had not said, 'watch the black car.' Maybe he had said 'watch *in* the black car.'

"Wait!"

The officer and Quint both jerked their heads around. "What's wrong?" Quint asked.

Toni stepped next to him so she could speak without being heard. "I think you should search that car right now." She repeated what had just occurred to her.

Quint gave her a long hard look. "That kid's spooky," he said at last. "And his track record is even spookier."

He knew details about the two previous murders Toni had helped solve had been kept confidential, so he understood why she didn't want to explain to another officer.

When he turned abruptly and headed to the car, Toni was right behind him.

He peeked inside. "The keys are in it."

Toni watched him lean inside the open door, look under the seats, and run a hand under them. Then he opened the glove compartment, being careful to touch as little as possible. He pulled a pen from his pocket and used it to probe the contents.

Finding nothing, he pulled the keys from the ignition and backed out of the car. "Nothing," he muttered.

Toni followed him to the rear of the vehicle and watched him pop the trunk and raise the lid. He peered inside. "It stinks back here," he said, waving a hand in front of his nose. "Smells like something dead."

"The knife was a hunting knife," she reminded him. "He probably hunts and puts dead game back here."

They surveyed the contents. A spare tire. A jack. A pile of camouflage hunting clothes and a pair of boots. A small gas can and some camping gear. "Nothing out of the ordinary that I can see," Quint said.

Moving to one side a bit, he peered down at the spare tire. Then he reached down and ran his hand between the tire and the cavity in which it was mounted. When he pulled it out, he held a small plastic bag.

Toni moved closer as he opened it and looked inside. When he looked up, he was grinning. "Why do you think Corey has a watch stashed back here?"

"Let's ask him," she suggested.

Together they walked over to the cruiser where Officer Rogers stood waiting by the driver's door. Corey glared at them through the glass of the back window.

"We need to ask your passenger something," Quint told the officer.

Rogers opened the door and pressed a button to lower the rear window.

"Care to tell us why you had this hidden in your trunk?" Quint asked Corey.

Corey glared and clenched his jaw. "I took it because I didn't want him to have it. It was an expensive gift Mom couldn't afford. It was bad enough when she got involved with him the first time because she thought he would get me a scholarship. Well, he didn't do it. Then he left the school. I thought their affair was over, but it wasn't." He was red faced and rigid, his fists clenched in his lap.

"What happened?" Toni asked.

"It was so stupid," Corey said, his mouth starting to tremble. "She started up with him again and let him keep stringing her along, even while he was hitting on his buddy's wife. She loved the jerk and robbed her savings to give him that special gift for his birthday." His emphasis on the last phrase was harsh and sarcastic.

"But was that enough reason to kill him?" Toni asked, stunned.

He shook his head sharply. "He didn't get me the

scholarship. He was treating my mother like dirt. And he wouldn't cut me an inch of slack."

She got it. "You mean he was pressing you for payment of your gambling debts."

"Yeah. Now leave me alone."

Another cruiser with flashing lights veered into the lot. "Let's go," officer Rogers said, sending the rear window glass up and getting into the vehicle.

Epilogue

"Hey, Mom."

Toni looked up. Gabe stood in front of the caves on the far side of the bridge, aiming a pair of binoculars at her. She waved.

Satisfied, Gabe turned and trotted over to join Garrett at the entrance to the biggest cave.

The plan had been to barbecue at the Donovan home, but the boys had wanted to come back to Sequiota Park. It was so hot that they had the place practically to themselves. Only a handful of people were out in the sweltering hundred degree weather.

Following the meal, Kyle's parents and Toni and Kyle sat in lawn chairs near the picnic table to visit. The food had been cleared away except for a cooler of drinks and a covered cake pan still sitting on the table.

Quint, who had eaten with them, strode across the lawn, returning from a trip to his pickup on the parking lot. "I picked up a paper this morning," he said, tossing it to Toni.

She caught it.

"I thought you might like to see it." He dug a soda from the cooler.

Toni unfolded the newspaper and saw the front page headline, TEENAGE GAMBLING RING

BROKEN UP BY POLICE.
She began to read.

While investigating the death of Jesse Campbell, the coach from Ozark who was murdered at Sequiota Park, the Springfield Police Department uncovered a local gambling operation. Headed by Mr. Campbell, the setup was sophisticated and dealt in huge amounts of money. Students from several junior high schools, high schools, and colleges in the area were involved. Police have arrested eighteen people and issued warrants for twenty others. An unspecified number of students have been released under restraining orders. A significant blow has been dealt to local sports gambling operations.

Law enforcement officials say they believe Barry Kuzman, the young man who was murdered last Sunday, was a bookie for the organization. The motive appears to have been to prevent him from giving details of the gambling operation to police.

Corey Franklin, a student at Ozark Technical Community College, has confessed to murdering both Mr. Campbell and Mr. Kuzman. He has implicated Sonya Finch as the person behind the attempt to take over the operation after the death of Mr. Campbell. According to Corey, she knew he was the person who killed Mr. Campbell and blackmailed him into killing Mr. Kuzman to silence him.

Police are still identifying students involved in the running of the operation, as well as those placing bets. Names of juveniles are not being released. The students placing bets are not expected to face charges, although they may be subject to disciplinary measures by their schools. Further details are being withheld due to the continuation of the investigation.

When Toni finished reading, she looked up at Quint.

"Satisfied?" he asked. "They kept your name out of it like you wanted."

"Relieved," she said. "I don't want any publicity."

"Or Garrett's name involved. I understand."

"May I see that?" Barb Donovan dragged her lawn chair over next to Toni. "What's wrong with giving Garrett credit for finding that body?"

Toni and Quint exchanged a quick glance of regret at having said anything in her hearing.

"He found things in the other two cases I was involved in," Toni explained to her mother-in-law. She gave her a brief overview of those cases.

"That's amazing," Barb said when Toni finished. "I had no idea he did such things."

"We prefer to keep it private," Kyle told his mother.

"We respect that," Dan Donovan said, having been a silent listener. "And I agree with you."

Barb didn't say anything, but it was easy to see that she was not convinced. She dropped her eyes to the newspaper and began to read.

"I need to go get ready for work," Quint said, finishing his soda and rising from his chair. "I guess the next time I'll see you guys will probably be Thanksgiving."

Lost in thought, Toni watched him walk away. Kyle's touch on her hand startled her.

"Let's go for a walk," he said, his tone and look conveying that he wanted to talk privately. Her inner muscles tensed. He hadn't said anything about his job decision yet, so she guessed that was what was coming.

She stood, her hand still in his.

"We'll be back in a few minutes," he said to his parents.

As they strolled alongside the lagoon, Kyle was quiet. Toni wasn't sure what to expect. Her stomach clenched at the thought of hearing that they must start packing to move. She shoved her free hand in the pocket of her shorts to steady it.

When they reached the end of the lagoon near the woods, Kyle steered her onto a small nature trail. They progressed a few yards to a small clearing next to the stream fed by the water from the spillway.

"Let's stop here," he said quietly. He turned her to face him, his expression so grave it scared her. She braced to hear that she needed to put the house on the market.

Kyle swallowed and cleared his throat. "I've decided what I want to do about my job. But I need to know your feelings about it."

Toni pulled her hand from her pocket and gripped both his hands with hers, but she didn't speak. She just waited.

"The transfer is still available," he began. "But I don't really want to uproot us. It's not that I think we can't adjust. It's that we're happy in Clearmount."

Toni's heart lurched with hope, but her throat was so tight she could hardly speak. "But what kind of job would you find in Clearmount? I don't want you to give up the work you love."

"I wouldn't," he said. "I would work for myself. I've been contacting people this week. There's some acreage I could buy, and I've located a plane that's for sale in a doable price range. I've talked to Gary at the bank, and he says I can get the financing."

Toni's heartbeat quickened as his words began to slowly penetrate. "You want to start your own business," she breathed, hardly able to believe it.

"Only if you agree with the idea," he cautioned. "It would take everything we can scrape together, plus financing, to get started. It would be an unbelievable amount of work, and it could take years to become profitable."

"What are you doing, trying to get me to talk you out of it?" Toni fought to keep her voice steady.

"No, I just want you to understand that there are risks involved."

Toni gave him a steady look, and then she smiled. "You're a hard worker and dependable. You have a strong sense of commitment and a fair amount of business sense. I know you wouldn't have made such a decision without having prayed about it. I believe in you."

As for her, she knew that struggles and trials would not disappear, but she could trust God to give her peace in the midst of them.

The somber look on his face was replaced by a wide grin, and he pulled her to him. "Thank you for the support."

"I can't wait to tell the boys. They're getting old enough to help out some, and I'm sure they will love having you around more. We'll make it a family challenge," she said with fervor. Then she buried her face in his chest to hide the dampness in her eyes.

His arms tightened around her, and his head bent to hers. Just as he kissed her, they heard a shout nearby.

"Mom! Dad!" It was Gabe, searching for them.

Within seconds there was the sound of rustling in the woods near them, and then Garrett shouting, "Here they are. I found 'em."

The End

BOOKS by Helen

Ozark Sweetheart
Ozark Reunion
Ozark Wedding

Bandit Bride
Prairie Bride

Bootheel Bride
Bootheel Bachelor
Bootheel Betrothal

Show Me Love
Heartland Illusions
Mozark Vision
Missouri Catch

Paige's Proposal
Brooke's Bargain
Haley's Hero
Kelsey's Keeper
NOVELLAS by Helen

Hawthorn Hope
Tree of Hope
River Town Romance
(2 in 1: Hawthorn Hope & Tree of Hope)

Pasque Plight
Black-Eyed Susan's Secret
Love Blooms (2 in 1: Pasque Plight & Black-Eyed Susan's Secret)

Shamrock Ruby
Dream Team
Mother Road Matches
(2 in 1: Shamrock Ruby & Dream Team)

Secrets in the park

Made in the USA
Monee, IL
23 November 2020